# SON-IN-LAW

A totally addictive psychological thriller
with a shocking twist

JANE E. JAMES

JOFFE BOOKS

Joffe Books, London
www.joffebooks.com

First published in Great Britain in 2023





Cover art by Nick Castle

ISBN: 978-1-83526-234-4

*For Mam*

# THEN

Wind circles the building, howling like an injured wolf, while the old wooden barn braces itself against the winter storm. Lashings of silvery, ice-cold rain explode through its cracks like clawing fingers trying to find their way in. There is no moon tonight to light up this blackest of mountains. No lights twinkle in the adjoining farmhouse to shine down on the valley below. Everywhere is shrouded in a terrifying blanket of darkness.

Inside the barn, an upturned mobile phone casts an eerie white light over the damp, dusty interior, revealing an ancient tractor cloaked in what appears to be white powder, empty animal stalls with doors hanging off their hinges, a broken ladder leading to nowhere except more blackness, a strewn pile of cut logs, and a heavy axe left on its side, that looks like it could kill a man with one swing.

A glimpse of scarred flesh catches the light . . . the gleam of metal. There's a cough. Then another. A ragged intake of breath that sounds like it's somebody's last. A dark silhouette. The collapsed shape of a man slouching against a stack of hay. He has something glossy and dangerous in his hands. It looks like a gun. The man's head, dusted with hay, is slumped on his chest. His eyes, black as coal, are someplace else. Anywhere but here. He knows what he has to do . . .

'Do it.' A voice instructs.

The man's head bounces, jarring his tense body. He twists around to face whoever is lurking unseen in the shadows. His eyes flood with regret as he gulps anxiously. Then, there's the fear.

'I can't . . .' His brow furrows, his chest heaves, and tears stream down his grazed cheeks. 'Please,' he implores.

'Do it.' The voice returns, this time sharper, followed by a scrape of movement he doesn't want to hear. He recoils when a handful of photographs land at his feet — a young girl of about nine or ten years old with straw-coloured hair and delicate blue eyes smiles up at him. One picture shows her astride a white pony. Another of her cuddling a baby lamb. One more of her in a swimming costume. The man doesn't attempt to pick any of them up, but a low groan escapes from within him.

'Now.' The final command.

His ears are filled with the sound of the relentless rain beating on the slate roof. Will this be the last thing he hears? He's chilled to the bone and damp around the shoulders, and his stomach, not understanding the gravity of his situation, cramps with hunger. As he lifts the firearm that has been handed down from generation to generation, and cocks it, he inhales the dusty fragrance of last year's hay. He had cut that grass with his own hands, with fingers that had once long ago accidentally gone into a baler and emerged crushed and bloodied, needing extensive surgery.

When he slides the barrel of the rifle into his mouth and wraps his lips around it, the metal tastes of sweat, salt, and fear. The gun also seems unusually heavy in his hands but he remains calm. He knows that when he pulls the trigger everything will stop. One squeeze is all it takes . . . and then there will be silence. No more rain. No more guilt . . .

# CHAPTER 1: BETH

*Now*

They're here. I watched them arrive from the kitchen window, which has a prickly collection of cacti and a flyer advertising a sheep auction on its sill. The dogs are agitated because they know we have guests. When Cerys's pink Fiat pulled into the farmyard, they immediately recognised its princess livery. Anything other than green Land Rover Defenders is worth another look around here. Now, they're getting under my feet and trying to second-guess when I might open the stable-style back door, their thick tails whacking my legs. They go insane when they hear Cerys's new puppy yapping outside. With all of this commotion, I can't hear myself think.

'Toad. Gypsy. Be quiet,' I reprimand them firmly, but even though they calm down they remain on heightened alert. Ears pricked, they track Cerys's and her new husband's progress as they get out of the vehicle. Although it's her car he seems to drive it all the time these days. *To protect the bump*, he says, even though Cerys is only four months gone.

Through the glass, I watch my lovely daughter plant kisses on her puppy's nose. She insists on dressing him in glittery costumes, and keeping him on her lap, which she knows

I don't approve of. Dogs should be allowed to be dogs in my opinion. Elvis the dachshund is adorable, but he'll look out of place on a farm with his scurrying, too-small legs. Luckily my two took to him straight away. They'll need to get along if we're all going to live together.

I still can't get my head around the fact that they're moving in today. My friend Bryn, from one farm down, thinks I'm mad to have them come and live with me, but I have my reasons. At least I'll be able to keep an eye on Luke while he's under my roof. Besides, with Luke out of work, *no surprise there*, and Cerys pregnant, what else could I say but yes?

I try not to remember that Luke bought Elvis for Cerys as an engagement present only five short months ago, in place of a more traditional diamond ring. Two months later they were married and pregnant, not necessarily in that order. They've barely known each other for six months. I, on the other hand, have known Luke Griffin a lot longer than my daughter.

When Cerys gestures to the boot, Luke dutifully goes to retrieve something out of it but his gaze is drawn to the house and the window. He knows I'll be watching him but he has no idea how much of that I plan on doing. I turn away from the window as they stroll towards the house, for the first time not holding hands. Is it because he's carrying a box, careful not to drop it, or might they have argued? One can always hope.

The exterior of Pen-y-Bryn farmhouse, which means "top of the hill," in English, is a mishmash of old stone and newer brasher yellow brick sections that have been stitched together over time to accommodate generations of growing families, but it's warm and welcoming on the inside. My own mam, and her mam before her, had once stood cooking hearty family dishes on the antique stove, which delivers warm hugs from dawn to sunset. Because of this, I could never get rid of it. The rooms are large, the ceilings are low, and the windows are smaller than they should be, as is typical of Welsh farmhouses. This gives the rooms a gloomy appearance. Everywhere except the kitchen, that is, which gets direct sunlight all day. This is the heart of the house. It's where both my daughter and I grew into women.

Wet paw prints, extra-large and enormous, and flipped-over dog bowls cover the flagstone floor. There are cosy dog beds in every nook. Leads hang from hooks, though they're rarely needed on our ten acres of black mountain. The dogs are mostly let loose. They are my protection as a woman living alone in the middle of nowhere. Toad, the Rottweiler, is large and has an impressive foamy bark, but he's old, soft, and doesn't have many teeth left. It's the young collie you've got to look out for. She's an obsessive stalker, is always working, and can sometimes be snappy with strangers. She doesn't like Luke, I can tell. Clever girl.

Mam's enormous Welsh dresser heaves with oversized farmhouse style serving dishes that never get used anymore and the scarred, faded-to-white pine table, which sits eight, and had to accommodate many more back in the good old days, is already set for tea. We do things the old-fashioned way around here when we have guests. A proper teapot. With tea leaves. Milk in a jug. Hand-crocheted — *not by me* — placemats. Sugar cubes in a bowl.

Don't get me wrong, my life is anything but a whirlwind of afternoon tea and fancy cakes. Life on the mountain is hard. There are logs to be chopped, essential if you want to stay warm. Dykes to clear. Fences to be repaired. Sheep to be sheared. And guests to look after. Owen, my late husband, built Cuddfan, meaning "hiding place," a rustic wooden cabin nestled on the lake behind the farmhouse, so that we could let it out to holidaymakers as a way of supplementing our income. Back then, there wasn't much money in sheep and tractor repairs. There still isn't.

This is where my daughter and son-in-law will be staying. Not in the main house with me. That way, each of us will have some privacy. The cabin is small and simple, yet it's a perfect retreat for those wanting to escape from it all. It's described as a quirky, romantic getaway on the Brecon

Beacons surrounded by nature and wildlife. I worry about the loss of income though. It's not as if I can charge Cerys and Luke any rent.

There's chaos for a full five minutes when the door opens, and Cerys and Luke step inside. Whining. Sniffing. Shuffling. Jumping up. Play bowing. It's only when my two calm down that Cerys places Elvis on the floor. He's feisty and can look after himself, regardless of his size. Toad is all over him, gentle as a giant, but Gypsy sulks in the corner, her jealous blue eyes never leaving Cerys. She was always more my daughter's dog than mine. She was a homecoming surprise for Cerys when she returned home after travelling around Australia with her friends.

'Beth.' Luke's eyes are downcast as he acknowledges me but I notice how he leans proprietorially against the butler's sink, as if he were already the man of the house. His hands are in his jeans pockets now that he's put the box on the table. I realise it's a shop-bought cake, no doubt intended as a nice gesture, but he must have known I would've gone to the trouble of baking a homemade one. At six feet two, he's too big for this house. *And his boots!* Yet he's small in so many other ways.

'Luke.' I greet him with a tight smile that he recognises as fake.

'Mam, it's lovely to see you.' Cerys, as emotional as ever, doesn't hold back. She throws her skinny arms and skinny legs into my arms and clings to me as if I hadn't seen her two days ago. She fits into my body as if she'd never left it.

'And you,' I say, eyes filling with unexpected tears, suddenly reminded of when she was still mine, and not Luke's.

# CHAPTER 2: CERYS

The shop-bought cake is far superior to anything Mam could have baked, but I'm careful not to point this out. Her burnt, heavy-looking contribution sits untouched on the kitchen table next to the remains of the lighter, creamier one Luke picked out in the Angel bakery in Abergavenny. I've had two slices already, and whilst this seemed to please Mam, who's keen for me to put on some baby weight, Luke had pulled a face. He snorted at me as if I were a pig when Mam wasn't looking, and I giggled. He's hilarious. Elvis sits on my lap and I sneak him bits of cake when no one's watching. Mam would have the poor thing outside in a kennel, in all weathers, if she had her way, to toughen the little guy up. But he's still a baby. I don't know what's got into Gypsy though because she growls at Luke every time he moves and Mam, for once, doesn't threaten to box her ears.

The puppy is even more precious to me because he was a present from Luke. A much more meaningful engagement gift than a glittering stone. This shows just how well Luke knows me. Besides, I then went on to receive the one ring I truly wanted, a gold wedding band. Imagine that. Twenty-three years old, married and expecting a child. Some of my university friends were surprised when I pulled out of my equine and veterinary science BSc degree course at Aberystwyth University to marry and have a baby. But as soon as I found out I was pregnant, all I wanted to do was go home. To Pen-y-Bryn. Mam. And my black mountain.

My best and worst memories are here. In the farmhouse kitchen, sitting on Grandad's lap. Out on the farm, baling hay with Dad and herding sheep. Grandad taking me to working sheepdog trials in Pontypool in his beat-up old truck. Out on the mountain, riding my horse. Driving the jeep under supervision from Grandad. Helping Dad fix tractors in the barn.

The barn . . .

Nothing has been the same since Dad died eleven years ago but I'm hoping I can provide my child with the same wonderful childhood I'd known up until that day. The first time the baby stirred inside me, I felt a strong desire to return home. Pubs, clubs, parties in halls and celebrating good grades didn't come close anymore. I had Luke. And he'd pledged to love me forever, to keep me safe in his arms and to never hurt me. What more could a girl ask for? Knowing that mine and the baby's future were safe in his hands, it was easy to walk away from the undergraduate lifestyle I'd once thrived on. I knew I was incredibly lucky to have Luke, no matter what Mam thought, since he was drop-dead gorgeous, a ringer for Brad Pitt, and kind and intelligent too. So, when he chose me, Cerys Williams, over everyone else to go out with, all of my friends were envious.

I was on a night out with the girls when we first met. We were all so studious and serious back then so we weren't on the lookout for men. Until Luke came along to liven up my world. We'd all noticed him at the bar, of course, I mean who wouldn't? But it was me that his brilliant blue gaze lingered on, sending chills up my spine. The next thing I knew I had abandoned my girlfriends and was engaged in deep conversation with him, and it turned out he shared my views on a wide range of topics. It was as if we were made for each other. Of course, I didn't know at the time he was Mam's Luke, and it would take us weeks to realise it. By then it was too late. We were in love. And I wasn't going to give him up for anything.

'Do you have to feed that dog at the table?' Mam complains, her affronted gaze returning to the uneaten home-baked cake.

'He isn't a dog. He's the king.' I chuckle heartily, secure in the knowledge that my mam loves dogs. All animals in fact. As does Luke.

Luke grimaces and gets to his feet, scraping back a chair. 'Yeah, well, maybe it's time Elvis left the building.'

'You should have been a stand-up comedian,' I snigger, impressed all over again by my new husband's wit. Unlike boys my age, who are mostly tongue-tied around girls, he has a lot to say. I love and admire that about him. Emotional intelligence is one of the qualities I look for in the opposite sex and Luke has it in spades. He can strike up a conversation on any subject. When we first started dating, we'd often sit up all night talking. We haven't done that in a while though.

I hand Elvis over to Luke, who, now that he's on his feet, is being stalked by Gypsy, with a rounded spine and a curled-back lip. 'Go pee-pee with Daddy,' I say, kissing the little fella on the nose. Luke seems less impressed than Elvis, but I know he's conscious of not overdoing things in front of Mam. He's considerate like that, which is why he's escaping out the door now, leaving us womenfolk alone to talk.

Once the door is closed, Gypsy pounces on it, scratching at the handle and softly whining.

'See. Gypsy does like him,' I point out, too eagerly, I realise as soon as the words are out of my mouth. 'She's missing him already.'

'Who, Elvis?' Mam's eyebrows crisscrossing, says it all.

'You know perfectly well I meant Luke.' Her frown slides onto mine, as I say this. But she already has her back to me, her shoulders going up and down as she attacks the washing up.

'Why don't you use the dishwasher, Mam?' I groan, glancing at the never-used domestic appliance that Granddad installed, as a birthday present for her, four years ago.

'The suds wash the dirt out of my fingernails.'

'Gross,' I remark, admiring my pearly-pink gel-painted fingernails.

Mam and I couldn't be more different. I am tall and slim, with waist-length blonde hair and larger than average, sky-blue eyes, and she is solid, like a tree trunk, and has mousy brown hair cut into short, easy-to-manage choppy waves. 'Lesbian hair,' my LGBTQ university friends would have labelled it. Her eyes, which often squint with disapproval, are darker than mine, and are not so wide-set. Her go-to daywear consists of a checked flannel shirt, rolled to the elbow, jeans and muddy boots or wellies, whereas I prefer to dress in whites and beiges and go barefoot. In contrast to my more self-reflective, free-spirited, ever-so-slightly Bohemian nature, she is gruff, down-to-earth, and sees things in black and white. Mam may not be soft and feminine, but she is someone you would always want on your side.

Since marrying Luke, I've been on the other side of that coin.

# CHAPTER 3: BETH

'You can dry if you like,' I tell Cerys, unceremoniously throwing a tea towel at her. As I hear her climb to her feet, a sigh escaping from her cupid's bow mouth, which looks as if it had been drawn on with a pink crayon, I feel a giant exhale of my own coming on. Watching Luke playing with Elvis outside through the window, now that the dog has been *pee-pee*, is like a sharp claw down my back.

'I never had him down as a dog lover,' I snip, in a meant-to-be-casual way, only for it to end up sounding like a complaint anyway. Because it is.

There I said it. Now, I must wait for the reaction!

'He adores them just as much as I do.' Cerys comes to stand beside me, looking concerned, as she picks up a soapy bone china cup, twirling it in her fingers as if she doesn't know what to do with it. As if she hadn't been brought up in this kitchen. On this farm.

'I'm not sure why you would think that,' she adds, clearly irritated.

*Because I once caught him kicking one*, I bite back the retort and instead say, 'I seem to remember him mentioning he wasn't a fan, that's all.'

'You must have him confused with someone else,' Cerys replies innocently enough but darts me a wary look anyway.

I wish that were the case because I'd give anything for my son-in-law to be anybody other than Luke, but of course, I don't say so. Telling the truth has become impossible since my daughter decided it was a good idea to marry my ex-husband. A man I couldn't wait to be shot of. If he wasn't good enough for a practical, hard-working, strong woman like me, how could he hope to be worthy of my young, beautiful, some-would-say naive and fragile daughter whose main flaw was being overly trusting?

The words she'd used to announce her engagement to this pretender — *I won't call him a man* — haunt me still. 'Mam, I have something to tell you and you're not going to like it . . .'

When I received that incriminating testimony in a text, my confused mind scrambled from one word to the next. I initially had trouble understanding what she was writing, and it even occurred to me that Cerys must have been drunk to send such a text: *I swear to you, I had no idea who Luke was* and *Imagine our shock when we found out.*

Filled with dread, I was trembling all over when I rang her, but she didn't pick up until the fourth attempt. 'What's going on, Cerys?' I demanded. But all I could hear down the line was my daughter's sobs. Eventually, when she could bring herself to talk, she admitted to being heartbroken and went on to tell me that she had met this wonderful man and that they had been dating for a couple of months. This in itself was a red flag because she'd never mentioned any one boy's name in particular to me, so I had no idea she was seeing anyone. I just assumed she was having a good time in halls with her girlfriends.

'Even when he told me his surname, I foolishly failed to see the connection. I mean, Griffin is a common enough name in Wales.' I heard the fear in her voice. It crawled inside me like a demonic possession that hasn't left since. Luke Griffin was not a name I expected to hear from my precious daughter's mouth. She'd then gone on to explain that when Luke admitted to having been married before to a woman named Beth who lived on a farm, there was no hiding from the fact any longer . . . Cerys had unknowingly been dating her mother's ex. When I accused her new boyfriend of purposefully orchestrating their meeting, she had for the first time in her life hung up on me.

Naturally, I rang her straight back, only to find myself speaking to the man himself. And Luke had another surprise for me. My daughter was pregnant, hence why she now felt compelled to tell me about their relationship. 'But I want you to know, Beth, that I'm going to do the decent thing and marry her,' he had said. It felt like a threat. Because it was a threat.

Looking back, it was no wonder she'd gone dark and silent on me during those first couple of months, claiming she was extra busy with her studies. Once she found out who Luke was, it was obvious she wouldn't want to tell me about him. She'd have been too scared. They'd been very sly and secretive about their relationship and for good reason. Luke must've known I'd do anything to break things up once I found out Cerys was seeing him. But by the time I did get to hear about it, it was too late. My daughter was already expecting his child. Oh, and *surprise, surprise*, they had nowhere to live and wanted to come home.

I was labelled a would-be murderer for even suggesting termination as a possibility, after all, Cerys was so young, with her whole future ahead of her but she was appalled by my suggestion and made it clear to me in no uncertain terms that she was keeping her baby no matter what. I never told her how much I admired her for this and I'm not sure I've been completely forgiven, but the matter has long since been dropped. It bothers me that Cerys might think poorly of me when all I've ever tried to do is support her in anything she does. *Apart from marrying him.*

'How about fish pie for dinner?' I change the subject. 'I know you're vegetarian but you still eat fish, don't you?'

'Sorry.' Cerys shakes her head, preoccupied with drying the same cup. 'We went vegan a month ago.'

'We?' I ask, puzzled.

'Me and Luke.'

'What? Are you telling me he's a vegetarian too?'

'Yes, Mam. He is.' Cerys grins as if to show her acceptance of old people's ways, forgetting for the moment that her husband is my age.

'That's new,' I state, not knowing what else to say. Not only do I have to walk on eggshells around my daughter, but I also have to walk barefoot on cut glass.

When I was married to Luke, which was only two years ago, now I come to think of it, he was a meat-and-two-veg guy all the way. The type who made fun of vegetarians and environmentalists like my daughter. I recall him remarking once that if 'cows weren't meant to be eaten they wouldn't be made of meat.' He believed he was being amusing at the time even though no one else had laughed.

'What about your pregnancy? Don't you need iron and vitamin D for the baby, which you can only get from fish and meat?' I ask, alarmed.

'Mam, it's okay. I take dietary supplements,' Cerys reassures me.

'Well, I'm not sure what I'm going to feed you now. I wished you'd told me this before I went shopping yesterday.'

'We don't expect you to feed us, or look after us, while we're here.'

'Why else would you come home if not to be looked after?' I insist.

'Luke thinks we should be self-sufficient and not rely on others.'

'Others being me? Your mother?' I huff.

'He's only thinking of you, Mam. He doesn't want you wearing yourself out. You're not getting any younger, you know.'

There's no way I'm going to let that go without retaliation, daughter or not. 'You are aware that Luke and I are the same age? I'm actually two months younger than him.'

'That's absurd,' Cerys begins to giggle, then quickly stops as she realises what I'm saying is a fact. 'Oh, my God. I hadn't considered that.'

She can blush all she likes. I'm not done with her yet. I'm about to point out that Luke will never be self-sufficient as long as he's living rent-free in my holiday cabin, but I know if I do that, Cerys will end up in tears and that's the last thing I want.

So I say instead, 'That's what you get for marrying someone twenty-seven years your senior.' I bang saucepans as I say this, anything I can get my hands on, while Cerys, looking suitably chastised, celebrates finishing drying one cup.

# CHAPTER 4: CERYS

The cabin on the lake is a ten-minute walk from the farmhouse, down a muddy track which isn't accessible by car. The dogs accompany us, Gypsy circling Luke all the way. The sheep in the field to the right of us are so used to holidaymakers they barely look up even when Elvis tries to wiggle out of my arms to yap at them. I can't wait for spring and the lambing season. By then I'll be heavy with child myself. I wonder if he or she, once they're born, will enjoy bottle-feeding the lambs as much as I did.

Built with reclaimed wood, by my dad's own hands, the cabin is accessed by a long wooden bridge over the water and is tucked away, out of sight. The bridge sighs and creaks with each step we take, as if unsure whether to welcome us or not. I pause to lean over the water, which is dirty brown at this time of year. Bubbles rush to the surface and a grey squirrel, on the prowl for food, watches us from the bare branch of a tree.

When I was younger, around fourteen or fifteen, I'd help my mam prepare the cabin for guests. Hoovering. Dusting. Sweeping. Filling the outdoor basket with logs for the fire and putting together the welcome gift box, which contained freshly baked bloomer bread, eggs, homemade jams, and fruit. They were happy days.

As we get closer to the cabin, I notice grey smoke trickling from the chimney, indicating that Mam had thoughtfully lit the log burner for us prior to our arrival. It can get very cold in the cabin at this time of year.

Luke marches ahead, unusually quiet for him, as though eager to relieve himself of the two heavy cases he's carrying. He'll go back for the rest of our things once we've settled in. The cabin door isn't locked. It never is. There's no need out here as it's very secluded. Luke throws open the double glass doors and turns on the lights. It's only 3 p.m. but the overhead trees make it seem later, and darker.

I know the cabin well, obviously, and used to stay over with friends on occasion but I've never lived in it for an extended amount of time. Outside, the covered wooden terrace overlooks the lake and is furnished with a hanging chair and a love seat. And inside, I'd forgotten how small it was. But it's beautifully decorated in a vintage style and the confined space is cleverly optimised with a pull-out table and miniature furniture. It's as if I'm walking into a doll's house. If it feels that way to me, what must it be like for my six foot two husband?

'I would have carried you over the threshold but those two slices of cake you ate might have put my back out of joint.' Luke cracks a joke.

'Ha ha.' I poke out my tongue at him and look around the living space as he enters the adjoining bedroom and places the cases on the bed. This time when Elvis squirms in my arms, I put him down on the floor and he scampers off to explore, his long nose to the ground sniffing. The other two dogs remain outside. They know they're not allowed in.

The interior is just as I remembered it. Very rustic. One wall is taken up by the blood-red, well-equipped kitchen, cleverly designed by Dad to include a hidden microwave and smaller-than-average fridge freezer. He also built the matching miniature Welsh dresser which houses a selection of crockery. A vintage leather two-seater sofa with fat tweedy cushions at each end is shoved up against another wall. A coffee table, cleared of holiday guides for once, warms itself by the log burner.

Although we're not strictly guests, I'm touched that Mam has left bread, butter, eggs, and jams in the welcome box for us, even though we can't consume dairy or eggs. Lots of warm snuggly blankets have been carefully folded and left out for us too. We'll need them, especially on the cold, damp mornings. The smell of burning wood is another reminder of my childhood — Dad chopping logs on the coldest of days to keep our family warm. The log burner gives off a comforting heat. The kind that warms my cheeks and makes me want to curl up on the sofa with a good book.

But now that I'm a wife, with a husband to consider and a baby on the way, my time is no longer my own.

'Need any help?' I call out to Luke, who I can hear peeing in the tinny sounding ensuite bathroom which overlooks dark woodland at the back of the cabin.

'Nah. I'm going straight back for the cases,' he answers. 'You can stick the kettle on though for when I'm back if you like. I'm parched.'

'Okay,' I respond, opening the fridge. I'm on the hunt for soya milk but can only find cow's, so when I see some beers rolling around at the bottom, I pull one out. 'How about a cold beer instead?' I twist the lid off and set the bottle to the side, ready for him. I'm looking around at the bird prints on the walls and the fairy lights that bring the room to life when he comes back in.

'Hey, you.' He grins at me in a way that has my stomach doing cartwheels.

'Hey, you.' I grin back, wishing Mam could see how happy he makes me.

He approaches me then and takes my left hand in his, bringing it to his lips, and kissing the gold band on my finger.

'I'm somebody's wife,' I murmur, leaning into him so that my head is resting on his strong, dependable shoulder.

'You sound surprised.'

'I am.'

'You'll get used to it.' He chuckles, lifting my chin with his finger, to kiss me on the lips. It's not enough. I want more.

'I'm not sure I want to.'

'No?' Luke's eyes light up when he sees the beer and I realise I've lost his attention. I don't take it personally. He has a short attention span.

'No. I want us to stay just as we are. Like this. Forever.'

'I don't know about forever.' He pulls a face before gulping his beer. I'm not sure how he escaped my grasp but he's already halfway across the room.

'Hey,' I object, playfully pouting my lips.

'I meant here.' He gestures with his hands to the room. 'Not you. Obviously.'

'Obviously,' I mimic, playing with my long hair in the way I know he likes. It's not long before his gaze is following my hands. He's so attractive, with his shoulder-length, wavy, golden-boy hair, glowing skin, and toothpaste-white teeth, I could stare at him all day. As for that hot body! I've never lusted after a man so much before. Despite being pregnant my nipples harden if he so much as glances my way. But it's not just about sex. I love him to bits. And he feels the same about me.

I like how he's tilting his head to one side as if he's genuinely interested in what I'm going to say or do next. As my dad used to. The blue of his eyes seems to reach inside me as if he gets me in the way I want to be got. I've never felt this way about a man before. The feeling is new to me.

'Take it off,' he instructs, motioning to my dress with his chin. I know then that he won't be fetching those cases anytime soon.

His lowered lustful eyes make me tremble with desire.

As I obediently slip off my beige woollen dress, pulling it over my head and making my hair go all static with electricity, his gaze never leaves my body. I don't want it to. He knows what effect he has on me. I can't do anything about it. I'm his. And I won't give him up.

But as he comes towards me, eyes smouldering, I suddenly can't shake off the thought that this might have been how Mam once felt about him.

# CHAPTER 5: BETH

The dogs came running back from the cabin as soon as I whistled them and are now in the back of my Defender as we set off along the narrow lane to Forest Farm, which is half a mile further down the mountain. This is where Bryn Morgan, a former friend of Owen's, rears free-range pigs on his thirty acres of pasture and woodland, but, like us, he has also built holiday homes on his property — two shepherds' huts, each with a hot tub, which he refers to as the Bolthole and the Lookout. As neighbours, we help each other out on occasion.

Although we're both single and live alone, we're strictly friends, although I sometimes suspect Bryn would like us to be more. I certainly have no intention of changing my circumstances. Twice married is more than enough for me. But it is nice to have someone to talk to from time to time. Sometimes we have a meal together at the Crown in Pantygelli, but not too frequently as we don't want the locals to gossip. Even if our friendship is no one else's business. Everybody knows Bryn's wife left him six years ago for another woman and that he doesn't like talking about it, which is understandable in my opinion. Everyone has something they'd rather keep to themselves. I'm no different.

He's not in the yard when I arrive at the farm, so after telling the dogs to stay, I walk around the back of a massive steel building to where the pig paddocks are. There's no point in looking for him at the farmhouse. If it's daylight he'll be out of doors. I'm not wrong. I spot him straightaway and as usual, he's knee-deep in mud, a bucket swinging from one hand.

'Bryn,' I yell from the other side of the electric fence.

'Two seconds,' he announces, looking pleased to see me.

When I notice a half-dozen bear-sized sows trailing behind him, their snouts and eyes fixed on the bucket in his hand, my face relaxes into a smile. It's my first of the day and it's almost four o'clock, which means it'll soon be dark. Sighing, because everything is so depressing at the moment, what with Cerys and Luke, I watch Bryn make his way over to me and feel ridiculously grateful to have him as a friend.

'Mrs Williams, what can I do for you?' Bryn asks playfully, stepping over the electric fence. Everyone on this mountain pretends my marriage to 'Griffin,' as they call Luke, never happened and insist on addressing me by my old marital name. *I'm one of them.* Cerys, if no one else, should be pleased that I'm destined to remain Owen's wife for the rest of my life as she was opposed to me marrying Luke in the first place. *How I wish I hadn't.*

When Bryn flashes his forest green eyes at me, I can tell he's thinking of me in a non-platonic way again. There's only one way I know of dealing with a man's expectations and that is by crushing them.

'I can't stay long,' I tell him bluntly, but then soften the news with a smile, 'I wish I could though.'

'Shame.'

He's a man of few words, which is a relief after Luke, who never shut up in the three years we were together. Bryn isn't a handsome man, not in the traditional sense, but he's strong, gentle, and kind. He's also not very tall, standing only five foot eight, but he has stunning green eyes that are as dark as the trees behind him. He also has a lot of wonderful black curly hair.

'Have you got time for a cup of tea?' He wants to know.

'Always,' I say, following him back to the farmyard.

His farmhouse is older and larger than mine. Much grander too, but in a faded sense, like the dusty old carpets. It has sash windows dating back to the 1700s, a cellar and a secret stairway that was originally used by servants. Every room I've ever entered has been painted regency red. I know my way around, so I make us a cup of tea while he takes his wellies off in the hall, which has a winding oak staircase going off it.

'How's it going with Cerys and Luke?' I hear him shout.

'As you might expect,' I grumble back.

When I turn around, he's standing directly in front of me, so I hand him his tea and we drink it standing up.

'Would you like to talk about it?'

'Says the man who refuses to discuss anything personal,' I mutter, but one glance at his hurt expression and I'm apologising. 'I'm sorry, Bryn, that was inappropriate of me. Please put it down to my lousy mood. I suppose the answer to your question though, is yes *and* no.'

'Which one wins?' He smiles, never one to hold a grudge. One of his mottos is "Let bygones be bygones," but I can't apply that logic to Luke.

'Why did he have to go and meet her?' I sigh into my cup.

'I think we both know the answer to that.'

'Oh, what?' My curiosity is aroused.

'He wants you back.'

I'm startled. 'What? No way.'

'You haven't forgotten that he stalked you for months, no years, after you divorced him?'

'No, but that was only because I refused to take him back when he came crawling home after the girl that he left me for miscarried.'

'Some men can't handle rejection, Beth. I should know.'

'Yes, but you're not like him,' I say, ignoring that jibe. 'You're different.'

'Different in the sense that I would never have cheated on you in the first place.'

This conversation isn't going in the direction I want it to and is becoming more about Bryn and me — *we're not an item* — so I change the subject.

'Do you really believe he'd do that, use Cerys to get back at me?'

'Ask yourself this . . . when did he finally leave you alone?'

I rack my brain. 'About five months ago.'

'The same time he conveniently started dating your daughter.'

'Oh my God, yes. But then again, no. It's crazy to think he'd go to the trouble of getting Cerys to fall in love with him just to get my attention.'

'You know him better than anyone else.' Bryn shrugs, taking a noisy slurp of his tea.

'I'm not sure I ever knew him,' I say with clenched teeth.

'And you think Cerys does?'

'Not a chance. He pretends to have changed but he doesn't fool me. He's the same Luke deep down. A liar.'

When I hear the dogs' muffled barking from the back of the Defender, I bang my cup down on the side, spilling it, suddenly anxious to return home. To my daughter, who needs me, even though she doesn't realise it yet.

'But he'd never do that to Cerys, would he?' I ask, feeling suddenly cold. 'I mean you'd have to be the worst kind of person to break a young girl's heart like that. And for no good reason, since he must know I'd never take him back in a million years, regardless of whether he hurt my daughter or not.'

'Do you think he's capable of it?'

'They're married, Bryn, and she's having his baby.'

He pauses. 'That's not what I asked.'

My gaze, which has been avoiding his up until this point, comes to rest on his green, insistent eyes and I gulp before answering. 'Yes.'

# CHAPTER 6: CERYS

We're naked in bed, under the covers, listening to the birdsong outside as coots, spoonbills, cormorants, ducks, and waders settle in for the night. The walls in the living area have framed images and descriptions of each species, but in the snug bedroom, Mam has mounted humorous Welsh-themed takes on film titles to keep the tourists entertained. *Cwtch me if you can, Dial M for Merthyr, Cwtch 22* and *Last Tango in Powys.* Luke hadn't noticed them until I pointed them out, and he, like Mam, finds them hilarious. This is something I attribute to their age rather than their compatibility.

It's almost as pleasant to be intimate with Luke after sex as it is to be intimate with him during sex. I enjoy the feel of our naked bodies resting next to each other, as well as the casual way his hand supports my bump. When all three of us are together, like this, I feel as if we are already a family. The sight of Luke's hand circling and stroking my baby mound makes me want him all over again. I'm curious to know if Mam was this horny when she was expecting me. Of course, I can't ask her that. I mean, I would if Luke weren't my husband, but as it is . . .

I'd only ever orgasmed through masturbation before Luke. He's less selfish and more patient. Maybe it's because he's older, unlike the boys I'd slept with. My body count, including Luke, is now up to four. I don't ask him what his tally is. High, I expect. Mam is one of them, which I increasingly dislike thinking about. When I originally told her that Luke and I were in love, I was terrified of her reaction, but Luke quite rightly encouraged me to take a firm stance from the very beginning. 'Otherwise, your mam will fight us tooth and nail,' he'd warned. So, once I'd stopped crying, I pretended to be matter of fact about it. 'You'll just have to accept it, Mam,' I'd said. 'And Luke too, if you want to be part of my life. I love him, and he loves me. We just want to be together.' Knowing how she must have felt, especially when Luke took the phone out of my hand to tell her "we" were pregnant . . . I'm starting to wonder if it was cold and unfeeling of me to announce it in that manner.

It must have killed her to learn that I'd secretly been dating her ex behind her back and I hated lying to her, but by the time I found out he was *that* Luke, I was in too deep. I had fallen for him within days, not weeks. This was nothing unusual for me where love was concerned, except that I felt Luke really was the one this time. That's why I couldn't give him up. Even for Mam. Had I met Luke and known who he was from the start (i.e., Mam's ex) then our chance meeting would have gone very differently. I would have brushed him off and walked away from him that night in the bar without giving him another thought. But Mam had only ever shared one blurry photo of him, so there was no way I would ever have recognised him.

Luke doesn't like me questioning him about his exes or his past so I've learnt to respect his feelings. I think it's healthier that way. Less chance of jealousy rearing its ugly head. And yet, Luke is rarely jealous, or possessive, even when boys my age come onto me, which they frequently do. A wedding ring appears to make no difference. I don't understand Luke's behaviour since I don't see how you can have passion without jealousy, and we have an abundance of passion. Anyone would think he doesn't care, but I know that's not the case. He adores me. Isn't he always telling me so? I put it down to his being much more experienced in relationships than I am. He's certainly learned the hard way after a failed marriage, and countless prior relationships.

When Mam was divorcing Luke, she told me she regarded their three years together as the longest years of her life, and a complete waste of time, but Luke seems to believe they flew by in three minutes. Having heard both sides of the story, Mam comes across as the harsher and more bitter of the two and this leads me to suspect that she never loved him the way I do. And now that Luke is my husband, I have no choice but to take his side. I know how difficult Mam can be, even though I wasn't around at the time because I was travelling for the majority of those years.

I've always had the impression that Mam was unhappy about this, despite never once saying so or voicing any complaint about the fact that I never came home during the three years I was abroad, which meant I never got to meet her new lover and even missed the wedding. It must have hurt her even more when I flew back as soon as Grandad died. During our phone conversations she would drop hints about how lovely it would be to see me and how lonely she was while going through her divorce, but I never fell for the trap. She had no idea that I was still mad at her for replacing my dad with another man. There could never be another to take his place in my view, even though he had been dead for six years by that point.

I was unable to return home because of this as I couldn't have stood to see my mother married to someone else. Couldn't bear to think about her new husband using my father's equipment, walking his land, and sleeping in his bed. Not to mention hugging and kissing the woman he once loved so much. It would have felt like a betrayal. We were really close, Dad and I, and I idolised him almost as much as he did me. When I learned that Mam and Luke had broken up, all I experienced was selfish relief. Finally, I was able to go home. Sam, my then boyfriend, was unable to join me due to work, although we had discussed returning together a few months later. We weren't getting along as well anymore by the time I learned Grandad had passed away, so I decided to fly back to England alone. If I hadn't, I would never have met my lovely Luke.

'We'd better get ready soon, sleepy head,' I tell Luke, glancing at the clock. It's six thirty p.m. already.

'Do we have to go?' he complains, opening one piercing blue eye.

'Yes, I'm afraid we do. She's been planning this homecoming dinner all day and was going to go shopping again this afternoon, specifically for tofu.'

'What the fuck is tofu?'

'I can't believe you've been a vegetarian all these years and don't know what tofu is,' I tease, but stop quickly when I see his stricken face.

'It's not nice to laugh at people just because they don't know something,' he grumbles sitting up in bed and pulling on a T-shirt. 'I thought your mam had brought you up to be better than that.'

'You're right. I'm sorry. I shouldn't have assumed you knew what it was.' I try to prevent him from getting out of bed but fail. Even Elvis turns his back on me as if I'm not worth knowing. For the second time today, I listen to the tinny sound of Luke peeing in the ensuite bathroom.

'When you assume you make an ass out of you and me,' he calls out, flushing the chain soon after. 'Get it?'

'Yes, I get it,' I reply, wanting to say that I got it the first time, and the second and the fourth, and that it's a cringeworthy saying but I bite my lip because that would make me as patronising as . . . well, him. Except he doesn't mean it. It's just his way. I could kick myself for sometimes forgetting that he never went to university or even to college and has spent most of his working life pulling pints in pubs and serving cocktails in wine bars. As Mam would say, 'he's never held down a proper job' and it occurs to me for the first time that I have no idea how we're going to manage financially. As head over heels as we are, we can't survive on love alone.

'Besides,' he says confidently, strutting back in like a prize cockerel, his hair adorably ruffled from where he'd lain on the pillow. 'I never said I'd been a vegetarian for years, more like months.'

I don't say anything because I distinctly remember him telling me that he'd been a vegetarian since he was forty-eight and he's now fifty. I'm able to recall this in exact detail because I have an excellent memory, but in the big scheme of things, does it really matter? What's one little white lie anyway? He probably only said it to impress me in the first place. The important thing is he *is* a vegan now, because like me, he loves animals and doesn't want to see them suffer. Therefore, it shouldn't matter how long he had previously been a vegetarian. Or even if he ever was one prior to meeting me.

# CHAPTER 7: BETH

As I serve up Welsh Eve's dessert, Cerys's favourite apple pudding, I can't stop thinking about what Bryn had said about Luke. Is my ex capable of being that manipulative? Would he maliciously exploit my daughter, even marrying her and getting her pregnant, just to get his own back on me? And for what? For not taking his lying, cheating arse back after he dumped me for another woman? Is he even intelligent enough to come up with such a plan? He might be a pretty boy, even at fifty, but he isn't the sharpest knife in the drawer. And yet, sometimes, like now, I catch his gaze lingering on me, and I think I see a flicker of regret in their blueness.

'Didn't you like the tofu, Luke?' I ask as I clear his plate from the table. Most of it has been scraped into a small mountain at the side.

'I think that cake we had earlier gave me a dodgy stomach,' he complains, resting a palm on his ribcage. 'I should have stuck to your mam's,' he adds, with a glance at his wife, who is studying him intently, a slight crease on her pale forehead.

'You can't eat the tofu but you *can* eat the apple pie?' Cerys's voice is unusually sharp, and I turn to face her. But she's glaring at Luke as he shovels a spoonful of apple and custard inside him.

'Beth's homemade apple pie—' Luke pauses to swallow — 'is a must.' Then he throws us both a wink that only increases my daughter's irritation.

'How was the cabin? Do you have everything you need?' I interrupt, trying to diffuse the situation. Luke might be unaware of Cerys's growing frustration with him but I am not. I don't know the exact cause of it but it feels like a tiny victory. I still know my daughter better than he does. Pathetic of me, I know.

'Yes thanks, Mam, and it was sweet of you to light the fire and leave us blankets.'

When Cerys is considerate and caring like this, I'm overcome with maternal pride. It doesn't take much for my underappreciated heart to overflow with affection for her. *How did someone like me nurture such a beautiful on the inside as well as on the outside person?*

'I could always teach you how to make the pudding if you like,' I say quietly so that only she can hear me, but my gaze returns to Luke, who is now leaning back on his chair, looking stuffed. His spoon has been licked clean and returned to the bowl.

'This isn't the dark ages, Mam,' Cerys objects, sounding disappointed. 'Today's women don't have to cook to keep our men happy.'

I'm offended now, and ready to ask her what women of today do have to do to keep their men happy but realise I don't want to know as she could be referring to something of a sexual nature. It doesn't stop her from showing me, though, because the next thing I know, she's up on her feet, sliding her palms down Luke's chest and mumbling what I imagine to be racy words in his ear.

Luke, to his credit, appears as uneasy as I am. Why would Cerys rub my nose in it like that? Is she really that upset because I asked her if she wanted to learn to bake? It's not that I meant any harm by it, but I can see how it doesn't mesh with her modern approach to marriage. I'll have to practice biting my tongue more. I don't want to be accused of meddling after all.

It stings though, to be put in my place by my own daughter, and I have to turn away from them and appear to be really interested in washing up all of a sudden. In my haste to get to the sink I have to step over the dogs who are all lingering around the table begging for food.

'Let me give you a hand with that.' Luke is on his feet, bowl in one hand. He comes over to stand beside me and grabs a tea towel. This is horrible, because I'm reminded of when we were still together and he would always dry rather than wash up, because he didn't want his hands to get all wrinkly in the water and dry out. It didn't matter about mine.

'It's fine, Luke, honestly.' I don't look up from the soapy water because I don't want him to see my tears, caused by Cerys not him. 'You and Cerys go watch some TV and relax.'

'Are you sure?'

I nod. 'Absolutely.'

'Are you certain you don't want any help?' This tentative offer comes from Cerys, who is obviously feeling guilty now that she knows she's upset me.

'You know me, love. I've never needed any help in my life.'

That last phrase isn't entirely correct, but I wouldn't want them to know that. While I was all alone going through a traumatic divorce, I could have used some *help*, as Cerys calls it, but where was my daughter then? Throughout her trip around Australia and Bali, and God knows where else, she was nowhere to be seen. Not that I blame her for it. I knew she was heartbroken for me when Luke left me for someone else, but she still made up reasons why she couldn't come home sooner. I thought we were closer than that so I was shocked when her grandfather died and she caught the next flight home.

As I listen to them herding each other into the living room, the clatter of claws on the flagstone scrabbling after them, followed by the sound of something loud and boisterous on the TV, I take my hands out of the water and assess how wrinkly and dried out they are. I suddenly feel old and unattractive. I know Bryn desires me, but that doesn't say much about me when I'm the only single woman on this mountain. No, strike that. I'm the *only* woman on this mountain if you don't count my daughter.

After Owen died, I resolved that there would be no more men, or husbands, but once Cerys had gone travelling with her gang of stick-thin, wavy-haired pals, I became lonely. I've never been outside of the United Kingdom as sheep require care 365 days a year but, while on a rare night out, I met Luke in a pub and we hit it off. He was attractive, easy to get along with, and made me laugh. Back then, it was enough. He lacked Cerys's father's intensity and intellectual mindset, which suited me because I didn't want complicated, but that's exactly what Luke turned out to be. Fortunately, I fell out of love with him long before his womanising became public knowledge. I was actually relieved when he left me for the other woman and considered she'd done me a favour. Lynn, I think her name was. Poor lass, I can find it in my heart to feel sorry for her now, after being left high and dry having just lost a baby.

My main fear right now is how many more hearts Luke is capable of shattering. Is he in love with my daughter as he claims to be, or is he just acting? It's easy to see why he's drawn to Cerys. She's young, gorgeous, and wonderful to be around, albeit a little emotional and overly sensitive, but what does she see in Luke beyond his looks? After all, he's a bit of a buffoon, and she could have had anybody she wanted. But she chose him. And I know I have to accept that for the sake of my daughter. But if Bryn is right about Luke, and he intends to harm my child, he'd better be careful.

Luke has no idea what this Welsh farmer's daughter is capable of, or what I've done in the past to protect myself and my daughter from men like him. I'd do it all over again in a heartbeat. He thinks he's the one calling all the shots but I'm prepared to play the waiting game. I have the patience of a wronged woman and all the fury of a protective mother on my side. It's my farm. My mountain. My daughter. And my rules.

# CHAPTER 8: CERYS

Luke had gone to bed in a strop, having thrown up earlier, complaining that Mam had slipped something into the Welsh Eve dessert to poison him 'on purpose,' to get her own back on him. He refused to listen to my more logical argument that, since I'd eaten the pudding too, and I was fine, it was unlikely that Mam had put anything other than apples and cream in it. I'd even suggested that it was the four glasses of red wine that had upset him, after very little supper, but he scoffed at that as well. He acts like a spoilt child at times, which I find amusing, and I can empathise with him to a point because I was also spoiled rotten growing up. Not by my mother though, who was the only authoritative figure in my life. Both Dad and Granddad spoiled me and couldn't bring themselves to tell me off.

The atmosphere around the table had been strained tonight. It never was a good idea, Luke and I coming back to the farm, but at the end of the day, I'm still her daughter. Where else would we go? We don't have the money to put down a deposit on our first home. But Mam is a widow with her own financial concerns and I'm aware that by living rent-free in the cabin, her income will be reduced even further.

I don't share my concerns with Luke because he seems to believe that Mam owes him something. He's always hated the fact that he was made to sign a prenuptial agreement before they married, which meant he couldn't make any claims on the farmhouse or land. While I sympathise, I'm inclined to agree with Mam on this one, I'd hate to see my family home sold just so the proceeds could be split two ways.

Luke has no family to whom we can turn. His mother emigrated to Spain five years ago and they've lost contact since. His dad, like mine, is dead. That's another thing we have in common, as well as not having any money. I suppose I could sell the car bought with the money left to me by my grandad but it wouldn't go far. Or perhaps I could get a job as a veterinary nurse once I've had the baby. My ambition was to become an equine vet, and still is, even though that has been placed on hold for now, but I may be just as happy in a role with less responsibility once I become a mother. Luke could work nights in a bar in Abergavenny and I could do days, meaning we'd share the responsibility of looking after our child, only it would mean we'd hardly get to see each other. I suppose it would be too much to ask Mam to look after the baby during the day when she has a farm to run. I can imagine what she'd say to that — *no fucking way.*

Everyone was taken aback by my decision to become a vet even though I've always loved animals. Mam most of all. She expected me to pursue something more dramatic, 'to suit my personality,' she said, such as acting or fashion design, which proves how little she knows me. Mam looks down on me because she thinks I'm weak and overly soft. She never could cope with my tears and emotional outbursts. All she sees is how feeble I appear, but I have an inner strength she is unaware of. She thinks she's got Luke all sussed out too, because of his bad boy persona, and that I'm being taken advantage of, but I know exactly what he's like and accept him for who he is. That's what you call unconditional love, which my mother has never experienced.

And I have inherited her toughness. She just doesn't know it yet. I'm sure she's mad at me for siding with Luke when he denies ever cheating on her. She'd be surprised to learn that I continue to suspect him of lying. An example of this was his attempt to cover his tracks after being caught out lying over how long he'd been a vegetarian, which I've decided to forgive, because the past is irrelevant. It shouldn't matter to me what he said when he was trying to woo me, as most men tell lies to get girls to sleep with them. I have a harder time convincing myself that it doesn't matter whether or not he cheated on other women when he was with Mam, so I tell myself all that matters is how he treats me. Now. In the present moment. I see nothing wrong with giving others the benefit of the doubt, which is a result of being raised by a mother who had a fierce black-and-white approach to life, with zero tolerance for those who didn't share her belief system.

She should hear herself when she refers to people my age as "snowflakes," a disparaging slang term for someone who has an overblown sense of entitlement or believes they are unique in some way. It's embarrassing to hear her go on like that. Personally, I believe that we are all unique individuals who deserve to be treated with love and respect. Mam, on the other hand, believes that trust has to be earned. I strongly disagree.

Mam treats me as if my bones could easily be broken, whereas she considers herself strong and muscular from chopping wood and fixing fences. Whatever a man can do, Beth can do. That's her motto. She likes to tell me that she learnt the hard way, through Luke's treatment of her, and that men can't be trusted. However, once more, I disagree. Nothing makes men happier than protecting the women they love. It's second nature to them. That is, at least, how it has been in my case. My grandfather and father both adored me.

Mam and me were once quite close too, but not anymore, for obvious reasons. She swears she was over Luke long before divorcing him, but I suspect she still has a soft spot for him. I noticed how her gaze lingered on him during dinner, and how she became upset when he went to help her with the dishes. Poor Mam. I do feel bad for her. But I can't feel guilty forever, and she needs to move on for her own sake. Luke and I have agreed to do whatever we can to help her do that. He's good like that.

# CHAPTER 9: BETH

My daughter acts as if I'm at war with her, but it's her husband I want to put a bullet in. I can't get images of them having sex out of my head. It sickens me to imagine his hands on her innocent young body. It isn't so long ago that Luke shared my bed and I can still remember the things we used to get up to between the sheets . . . It's not natural. This situation. It's not what mothers and daughters should be made to endure but I'm powerless to stop it. I've got to accept their relationship and move on. Isn't that what everyone keeps telling me? Cerys included. Everyone but Bryn. He's the only one who understands how I feel, which I think stems from him going through the public embarrassment of his wife carrying on with another woman. Poor Bryn. According to mountain gossip, she was there one day and gone the next. But life has taught me that people are complicated, and things are never as simple as that.

Thank God I have the farm, that's all I can say. I prefer to be kept busy and there's plenty to do here. I'm up at 5 a.m. most days and don't fall into bed until 10 p.m. I got up an hour earlier today since I couldn't sleep last night. My brain hurts from all the stress and worry. People assume I can cope with anything, but they are mistaken. They think they know me because I've lived on this mountain all my life. 'Beth is as strong as an ox,' they claim. 'That Beth Williams is a survivor. She'll be farming that mountain when the rest of us are gone from it.' I've heard it all before, but the truth is that my daughter's predicament is killing me.

Being in the same place as Luke, even though they're at the cabin and I'm in the big house, is driving me insane, and it's only been one day. When my daughter fixes her Nordic blue eyes on me, as if to say, 'Be nice to him,' I want to snarl like an angry dog. This is the man I never wanted anything more to do with. 'If I never see you again, Luke Griffin, it'll be too soon,' I'd told him that last time he came around, with flowers and a villain's smile, attempting to win me over. And yet, here he is, like a bad penny, back on my doorstep, which is exactly where he wanted to be five months ago. You couldn't make this stuff up. Luke has made a laughing stock out of me on my own mountain and I'll never forgive him for that.

With a rifle slung over one shoulder, I've stomped my bad-tempered self all through my ten acres of farmland. While I watered and fed the sheep, the dogs ran around chasing squirrels. I'd then gone on a hunt of my own and was fortunate enough to nab an old rabbit that was still good for the pot. Not for me, but for a neighbour at the mountain's base. Even though the old boy has no teeth left, he can still munch his way through flesh and bone. Rightly or wrongly, killing something has lessened my anger somehow. I've never had a problem with hunting animals for food because I grew up on a farm. I'll say it's better than the abattoir. Yet, there are many people, usually men, who dislike seeing a woman with a gun. Fuck them, is what I say. It's not my problem; it's theirs. Cerys is the only person whose opinion I care about, which means I'll have to keep the rabbit and the rifle hidden from her. She'll be in tears for the rest of the day if she finds out I killed it. How she survived a childhood on the farm, I'll never know.

It's a beautiful day. The sky is a clear winter blue. The air fresh. The cloud that had hung over the mountain like a cloak of mistrust has since lifted. Sugar Loaf Mountain's nippily shaped peak can be seen in the distance, which gives me a spring in my step. We can start thinking about springtime once Christmas is over. December is always difficult for us as a family since it reminds us of Owen's death, but it's something my mind refuses to let me linger on. My feelings about him are someplace in my head, but they're as securely locked away as the rifles in the gun cabinet. Overall, I'm feeling much more upbeat than when I started my hike, so I whistle the dogs to heel and return to the farmhouse.

As its three brick chimneys come into view, smoke from the range pouring out of only one of them, I'm surprised to see movement in the yard. My heart stalls when I see Cerys and Luke spill out of one of the stables.

'Down,' I command the dogs as I notice Cerys leading out a fully tacked-up Zorro. I don't want them to bolt in their excitement to greet Cerys and spook the horse. I can't bear the thought of my daughter or her unborn baby being harmed, even if it is Luke's child. Cerys would be devastated if the baby were to die. She's going to be an excellent mother. Warmer and softer than me, which isn't a bad thing. I could never be that way with her because the men in our house ruined her. Someone had to show her what was right and what was wrong, and that she wasn't always going to get exactly what she wanted in life. Because, for most of us, life isn't like that and I didn't want her to grow up with unrealistic expectations and get hurt.

I can see now that Cerys is dressed in jodhpurs and a riding hat. What can she be thinking? She can't possibly intend to mount him, can she? Not while she's expecting. I haven't ridden Zorro in weeks, not since I took him for a canter over the Beacons. He'll be frisky as anything.

After stashing the rabbit and the rifle in the mosses and ferns on the hillside — *I'll come back for them later* — I snap leads onto the dogs' collars and let them pull me the rest of the way home, husky-style. *Just wait until I catch up with them.* They're going to hear what I have to say about this and I don't care if they think I'm interfering.

I blame Luke. What was he thinking by allowing her to do this? Doesn't he care? Can't he see the danger she's in? One slight fall is all it will take for her to miscarry. Cerys is a great rider, and she may not realise it yet, but where she was once confident on a horse, now that she's pregnant and has an unborn child to protect, she'll realise she's no longer the same brave rider she once was. Only a mother and fellow equestrian would understand this. As a result, she will no longer be able to manage Zorro as she previously did. He may be ancient, but he's a thoroughbred and full of life.

'Cerys. Cerys,' I shout, knowing my calls won't reach her. I'm too far away. They don't even look up.

As I puff and pant down the grassy slope, rope leads burning into my palms, another more disturbing thought enters my mind.

Is that what Luke wants? For Cerys to lose the baby? Is it part of his plan to exact vengeance on me?

# CHAPTER 10: CERYS

Zorro's hooves collide with the concrete yard as he prances around, excited at the prospect of going for a gallop across the black mountains. I lead him in an ever-tightening circle to keep him under control while he paws the ground. His black coat gleams and breath steams in the frigid morning air. He's a handsome beast even at twenty. I've had him since I was fourteen, so we have a long history together. His warm, musty odour makes me want to bury my face in his coat and daydream about the good old days but I don't do that in case he bites me. He may not be the most affectionate horse but I've missed him more than I realised.

Although he's a gelding, he's a mean horse. Most of his days are spent terrorising the sheep in the paddock. He once trod one of the tiny lambs to death, and Mam threatened to get rid of him, saying he was simply an extra expense now that I'd left home. But I kept assuring her I hadn't left home for good, just gone to university, as I'd always planned on doing once I had finished travelling, which she couldn't understand because Aberystwyth was close enough for me to come home on weekends but I didn't want to. That was the whole point. It had been just me and Mam for six whole months when I eventually returned to the UK and, whilst we grew close again — bonding over Granddad's death — I needed more than just her. Besides, they couldn't keep my university place open forever. I couldn't have imagined back then that I would drop out six months later due to a man, as I loved my time in halls.

A group of us would spend our weekends at the coast, swimming in the freezing water and barbecuing on the sand and shingle beach at night. They were great times. More recently, I'd tried to include Luke in our impromptu undergraduate parties, but he stood out like a sore thumb. My friends praised his looks, agreeing that he was a Brad Pitt lookalike, whose picture I used to have on my bedroom wall when I was younger, but they didn't know what to say to him. His age intimidated them.

Zorro stands sixteen hands tall and is also very intimidating. When I'm in the saddle, he becomes even more highly strung because he knows I'll give him a loose rein and encourage him to gallop as fast as he can and jump as high as he can, whereas Mam rides him in a more controlled manner, keeping his head down on a tight rein so there are no surprises. She isn't afraid of riding him, but she doesn't think she can afford to break any bones at her age and we both know I'm the better rider. I'm a lot more daring. Mam used to turn away and hold her breath while I competed in cross-country competitions, taking on increasingly larger and scarier jumps.

I'm in my element in the saddle which is why I was looking forward to being out on the mountain on my own for a while, just me and Zorro, like in the old days. I haven't ridden in over six months, and Mam has had to exercise him for me, adding another chore to her day, so he doesn't become overly excited and difficult to manage when I return home from campus.

And now Luke is yelling at me. Telling me I can't go riding. Accusing me of not caring about the baby. Elvis, who has never seen a horse this close up before, is yapping for England in his arms. This makes Zorro even more anxious.

He's never been tolerant of dogs and will bite and kick given half a chance. Toad and Gypsy have learnt to avoid him. Unlike some horses, Zorro does not enjoy human contact and if you are unfamiliar with horses, he will take advantage, requiring a firm hand.

And I'm taking that attitude with Luke now because, even though we're married and I love him, I'm not going to be told what to do or have my independence curtailed.

'You're not listening to me, Cerys,' he complains.

'No, you're the one not listening. I'm perfectly safe on Zorro, I've been riding him most of my life.'

'You weren't pregnant with my child then.'

'It's my baby too in case you've forgotten,' I retaliate childishly.

I watch him giving me that odd enquiring look again. The one that is only just now cottoning on to the fact I'm not as malleable and people-pleasing as he thinks I am. I'm sure he was hoping for the opposite of Mam's temperament when he married me but he's gradually beginning to work out that we're not as dissimilar as we seem when it comes to stubbornness and getting our way. It's just that our MO is different.

'Please, Cerys, I'm begging you.' He changes tack. 'You can do all the riding you want once you've had the baby, I promise. What're a few more months?'

I take a moment to look around at the lovely and diversified landscape of rolling hills, pastures, and the sweeping red sandstone ridges of the mountains. That view is one of the main reasons I wanted to return home. Its size protects me and hugs me from all sides. Mam may refer to it as her mountain, but it is equally mine. I was born here just as she was. I know it like the back of my hand. As I do Zorro. If I backtrack and change my mind now, I'll have lost some ground. I can't have Luke showing me that he's won. I'm a woman, not a girl, and I'm capable of making the right choices when it comes to *my* pregnancy and *my* baby. I've given up everything to be with him, but sacrificing my freedom is a step too far.

'I'll be fine. You don't have to worry about me,' I tell him.

'How do you know that?' he groans, agitatedly running his hand through his floppy blond hair, nearly dropping a wiggling Elvis in the process.

'I've not taken this decision lightly, Luke, I can assure you. I've sought medical advice from the doctor.'

'You have? You never mentioned it.'

My heart flutters in my chest because he sounds lost and bewildered, but I'm not going to change my mind.

'I'll be OK as long as I'm careful. Besides, exercise is good for pregnant women, and it's not like I'm inhaling deadly cigarette smoke or knocking back vodka shots. I've researched my pregnancy every step of the way because I want it to be a joyful experience rather than a burden. Life must continue.'

'Maybe for you,' he rasps, in attacking mode. 'But what about the baby?'

'You have no right to criticise me or accuse me of selfishness! Of course, I would never put my baby in danger, but just because I'm pregnant doesn't mean I have to be babied. I'm the parent, not the child, and it's my choice.'

More barking ensues, alerting Zorro, who stands taller, gaze locked on the mountain, nostrils flared. Luke and I both turn to see Mam running towards us with the dogs, or, more accurately, being dragged along by them. This is all I need.

'Cerys, what are you thinking? You're not taking that blasted horse out by yourself, are you?' she yells, pulling to a halt and yanking the dogs away from Zorro in case he strikes out.

Disputes with Luke are one thing; facing Mam is quite another. I yearn for independence all the more; even an hour away from the pair of them will lift me. Being back on the farm is already making me feel claustrophobic. It's not so much the house, the cabin, or the mountains, which I adore, as it is the tension between Mam and Luke. Then there's the barn . . . With Dad's eleven-year death anniversary coming up in three days, his suicide is obviously on my mind a lot.

I sigh heavily and don't waste another second. Throwing myself into the saddle, I pick up the reins, and we're cantering out of the yard with one squeeze against Zorro's flanks and the smallest of bucks. All I can hear behind me are the dogs barking and Mam and Luke teaming up to shout after me. When I look back over my shoulder, they're standing side by side in the yard, open-mouthed. If my act of rebellion doesn't bring them together, I'm not sure anything will. Joining forces against me is the perfect solution to our issues; I don't know why I didn't think of it sooner, and perhaps they'll have become friends by the time I return.

What could possibly go wrong?

# CHAPTER 11: BETH

'I can't believe she'd do something like that,' I gasp, still unable to believe my eyes as I watch Cerys and Zorro galloping up the hill. Tearing my eyes away, I turn on Luke. 'Or that you'd let her. You must realise she's putting herself and the baby in danger.'

'Hey! You've got everything wrong, Beth.' He looks at me, wide-eyed, with those Caribbean blue eyes I remember so well.

'Have I?' I snap. 'One tumble is all it takes. She could miscarry just like that.' I snap my fingers and watch his eyes cloud over with either terror or pain. Suddenly I recall that he's already lost one child.

'I begged her not to go riding, telling her it was unsafe. But she wouldn't listen,' he grumbles, obviously still shocked that Cerys would defy him.

'Selfish girl,' I mutter as I examine my hands, rubbed raw from the dog leads.

'She needed some alone time, I think.' He says this while gazing after Cerys. 'She's got a lot on her mind.'

'You mean with the baby?'

'No. She's taking that in her stride. I meant Owen.'

'What about him?' I squint to look at him since the fierce morning sun is on my face.

'Cerys said it would be eleven years this Saturday since he died.'

'Oh yes. Of course.' I nod in a suitably grief-stricken way, pretending that he's always in my thoughts, but the truth is I push my late husband from my mind whenever possible.

'Do you think she'll be all right, Beth?' he asks in that boyish, feel-sorry-for-me tone that I've come to expect from him. 'I couldn't stand the thought of anything happening to her or the baby.'

I pause, a little taken aback by what could be sincerity in his voice.

'You'd think she'd be more considerate knowing you've previously lost a child,' I say kindly but I don't look him in the eyes because I don't want him to think I've softened in the two years he's been gone.

'I'm amazed you care or remember.'

I have to turn away when his gaze meets mine and I detect a whisper of the old Luke behind his eyes. If it means not looking at him for the rest of my life, so be it. Anything is preferable to remembering we were once a couple and that he is now doing to my daughter what he used to do to me.

I'm not jealous at all; in fact, my body rejects the idea of him touching me in any capacity. But as I've said before, the situation we're in is not healthy for any of us.

'I don't,' I finally retort. 'That's Cerys's job. Not mine.'

As I say this, his head falls on his shoulders and his body slumps. He looks tired. Worn out, to be precise. Cerys must be keeping him up all night. On that thought, I kick myself once again. I need to retrain my brain. Forget that I ever knew Luke and treat him like the stranger he is, and always was. So, I give in and feel sorry for him when I promised myself I wouldn't.

'Cup of tea?' I offer without so much as a smile.

'Thanks.' He beams at me with a grin that's meant to dazzle as bright as the sun in the sky. It's a competition he can't hope to win.

* * *

'Don't be so hard on her,' Luke says a few minutes later, peering into his mug of steaming builder's tea, made without milk as requested, but not seeming to enjoy it.

'My God. She doesn't know what that means and never has.' I'm standing by the window, waiting for Cerys to return. My shoulders will not relax until I know she's home safe. I've never wanted shot of that horse as much as I do right now. I should never have caved into her pleas to buy him for her fourteenth birthday. He's been trouble from day one.

'Has anyone ever told you that you can be incredibly blunt?' Luke inquires quietly.

I glance over at him, ready to feel insulted, but when I catch him grinning, I shrug one shoulder in a "who gives a flying fuck" fashion, before joining him at the table.

'Are you saying that I'm not going to win a prize for being the best mam? Like that would come as any surprise.'

'That's not what I was saying at all,' he chuckles, trying to avoid a face wash from Elvis who is sitting in his lap.

'Does that dog even have legs?' I grumble, pulling a disapproving face.

Luke sighs and places the dog down on the floor, with Toad and Gypsy. Like the suspicious female she is, Gypsy growls softly whenever Luke makes a sudden movement.

'I actually think you're a good mother,' he acknowledges as he wipes dog hair from his jumper.

'You don't say.' A smirk tugs at the corner of my mouth, but I keep it hidden. Even so, it's the nicest thing anyone has said to me in a while. Then, I remember that the last time Luke was genuinely nice to me, was when he said 'I do' at the registrar's office in Abergavenny, and I replace the almost-there smile with a scowl.

'I know I'm not all that either, but I'm trying to be,' he admits as if he honestly believes it.

On impulse, I offer him my hand. 'I may regret this later—' I heave a sigh — 'but do you want to be friends?'

'Nope.' A flash of the famous Luke Griffin grin again.

'Nor me,' I agree, but I spit into my hand and extend it once more. 'Truce.'

'Truce.' He nods, grasping my hand.

I can't tell you how relieved I am that I feel nothing when his skin comes into contact with mine. The influence this man had on me sexually was one of the reasons, if not the main one, our marriage lasted as long as it did. That's why I excused his infidelity. Not because I loved Luke, but because I lusted after him. I catch myself wondering if my daughter feels the same way, and my cheeks flush from the intrusive thought.

We both jump to our feet when we hear a diesel engine plough into the yard. I suspect we are thinking the same thing. Is Cerys all right?

But it's only Bryn, and as soon as he gets out of the front seat of his jeep, he's waving and smiling and he wouldn't be doing that if there was something wrong. Luke and I both exhale slowly at the same time, united, for once, in our mutual relief.

I'm walking to the door to greet my friend, ignoring the trio of whining, barking dogs, when I hear the violent smash of a door opening behind me, so I turn around to see what's making the commotion.

'I might've known he'd still be sniffing around after you,' Luke scolds in a darkly jealous tone, before storming off into the hallway and slamming the kitchen door behind him.

# CHAPTER 12: CERYS

All it took for us to part company was a pheasant flying out in front of us and a loose pair of not-paying-attention reins. After a good hour's hack, during which I'd given Zorro his head and we'd galloped for over a mile uphill until he tired, we were coming back at a leisurely walk through a grassland trail that in the summer is shaded by an attractive archway of tall green trees. However, in the winter this archway is brown, bare, and ugly. The ball of colourful plumage had come at us out of nowhere, and teamed with the hysterical squawking from the bird, Zorro had reared up in panic when he saw it and then gave one mighty buck, at which point I slid off his glossy back onto the springy moss floor, quickly rolling to the side in case his hooves accidentally crashed down on my body.

I was unharmed, I think, but I put a protective hand to my tummy anyway, as I hurried after Zorro. I'm scared he'll run onto a road and be killed by an oncoming vehicle or return to the farm riderless. That would frighten Luke and Mam to death.

I'm out of breath after five minutes of jogging and Zorro has galloped off, but I can't stop. I must find him before anyone else. So, I continue. My breathing becomes laboured, and my throat quite dry. I see him two minutes later, just as I'm about to give up, unable to run another step. He's grazing with his head down, reins dangling carelessly around his neck. I want to hug him because I'm relieved, but as soon as he notices me behind him, he flattens his ears and turns his back on me in a threatening move.

Adjusting my hat and wiping sweat from my brow, I circle him carefully and approach him head-on, just as I've been trained. The biggest mistake any rider can make is to demonstrate fear in front of a horse, but it would be foolish to sneak up on one from behind. As he tries to bite me, I hit him across the chest and take a hard grip on the reins.

'Any more of that,' I warn as I tug him along behind me, 'and I'll let Mam send you to the slaughterhouse like she's always threatening.'

His ears perk up, and he nibbles tenderly on my hand as if begging for forgiveness. It's not the first time he's thrown me and it certainly won't be the last. I've never been afraid of getting straight back in the saddle after a fall though, until now, but when I think of my child going through the same thing, a shudder runs down my spine. I'm not sure I even want it to learn to ride. Maybe it's better if they don't. On that point, I'm wondering if Mam is right about selling Zorro, obviously not for dog meat, as I wouldn't consent to that. But I'm not sure I'd want to put baby Griffin on his back. Imagine if I had to wait at home like Mam is no doubt doing, for my child to arrive home safe after hacking out on an untrustworthy horse.

Earlier, I'd condescendingly informed Luke that I was a woman, no longer a girl, but at twenty-three, I realise I still have a lot of growing up to do. I should have listened to the two people who care about me the most. Why didn't I? I'll never forgive myself if anything happens to my unborn child as a result of my stubbornness. I may have gotten away with it today, thankfully, but only by chance. A tumble like that could have been far more dangerous on another day.

As I consider this, my eyes flood with tears. None of these concerns had occurred to me until today. It must be because I'm pregnant. Now that my body is not just my own but the home of another human being, I realise that my wants and needs no longer take precedence. Mam could have taught me this lesson at any time of the day or night if I had cared to listen to her. I wish she were here now to wipe away my tears. Not to say, 'I told you so,' but to reassure me that everything is fine and that there will be no complications or consequences arising from my fall. My tummy feels knotty, as if from period cramps, *or worse*, but it might also be the reassuring kick of my baby urging me to take better care of it, or else we might never get to meet. I'm crossing my fingers that it's the latter.

Even though the fall was easily avoidable and entirely my fault, days like today make me long for my childhood, when responsibility was a distant evil. When the only men I had to be concerned about were my nurturing family members and Mam smiled at everyone and wasn't as gruff and short-tempered as she is now. I suck in my breath as we clip-clop into the farmyard and spot Bryn Morgan's glossy new jeep in the yard. I've always thought he had a strange aura about him, even when he was Dad's friend rather than Mam's. I wish he didn't come over so frequently. I know she put a stop to it when I came home for those six months before leaving to go to university but it obviously started up again the second I left. What do men see in Mam, I wonder? Not in a harsh sense; it's simply that she's so . . . unfeminine. Besides, I'd quite like to have her all to myself for a change. Isn't that why I came home, to be cared for? And also, because I had quit university and we have no other home let alone any money.

Mam was right when she guessed as much. Except Luke wants us to be as self-sufficient as possible while living on the farm. Impossible when we don't have jobs or any savings. I wish he'd make up his mind because he says one thing one minute and then switches tactics the next. He'd just grumbled last night that the cabin wasn't big enough or good enough for us and that it would be better if we switched and Mam moved into the cabin while we took over the house.

I'd chuckled, saying hell would freeze over before she'd let that happen, but then I'd been concerned at how much Luke seemed to covet the farmhouse.

When Mam emerges from one of the darkened farm buildings, Bryn close behind her, I look around for Luke, but he's nowhere to be seen. She rushes towards me when she sees me on foot, and I'm tempted to run into her arms, but I don't. Just don't ask me why. And I'm annoyed because she has a man by her side who appears to be concerned about her since she is concerned about me when my husband might as well be invisible.

'Are you all right, love? What happened?' Mam removes the reins from me and hands them to Bryn, who accepts them albeit unwillingly.

When she wraps her arm around my shoulders, I have to fight back tears. I've never had to hide my emotions in front of anyone before. I was raised to be myself, so it's difficult for me to hide that part of me, but I have to, since I can't tell anyone the truth about my fall out on the mountain or my fears that the baby might not survive it.

'It's okay, Mam.' I shrug her off. 'Zorro's got a loose shoe that's all,' I lie, 'so I had to walk him back.'

# CHAPTER 13: BETH

'I'm no blacksmith, but I'm buggered if I can find a loose shoe anywhere on this horse,' I announce, baffled, as I set the last of Zorro's hooves back on the ground, ignoring his fake attempts to bite me, because he knows better than that.

Bryn, who knows nothing about horses, leans back against the side of the stable and shrugs. 'Maybe she got it wrong.'

'Not my daughter–' I shake my head – 'she'd know a loose shoe by the animal's gait.'

'Perhaps she got spooked and decided it was safer to walk.'

'You could be right,' I assert, secretly hoping that this is exactly what happened and that Cerys came to her senses, deciding a ride out on Zorro wasn't worth the risk after all. I don't go down the road of suspecting Luke of tampering with the horse's shoe in an attempt to kill off his wife, and making it look like a tragic riding accident, so that he can reunite with me, because that's several crazy steps too far. Besides, there's no way Zorro would let him get within an inch of him. And no way I'd ever get back with Luke either. As my daughter would say, *Gross*.

Bryn's gaze follows me, almost as if he can read my disturbing thoughts, as I slip off Zorro's headcollar and walk backwards out of the stable. Turning your back on a horse like him is never a good idea. But, instead of flattening his ears and chasing me out, as he sometimes does, he goes over to his net of hay and nibbles innocently on it.

'Why don't you put him out to grass, retire him? That way you wouldn't have to ride him.'

'I can handle him,' I reply, my back stiffening.

'I know you can. All I'm saying is you shouldn't have to.'

'If I stopped doing everything I shouldn't have to, nothing would get done around here.' I roll my eyes at him, before taking the saddle and bridle into the tack room at the other end of the stable block. There are three stables in total, with just one in use, but we occasionally have sick sheep stay for a night or two until they get back on their feet, and lambs in spring if they are unfortunate enough to be abandoned by their mother. I once had a ewe that rejected every single one of her lambs and I remember telling Owen I didn't want her on the farm, because it was unnatural for any mother to do that. Owen obliged me by sending her to slaughter, but not because he wanted to please me, rather the sheep wasn't making him any money.

'You're not getting any younger, Beth,' he points out.

I turn to glare at him then. 'That's the second time someone's said that to me in as many days.'

He chuckles. 'It's true.'

'I'm only fifty,' I object, hanging up the bridle and dragging the heavy saddle onto a wooden stand. *I notice he doesn't offer to help even though I'm not getting any younger.*

'Young enough to remarry if you wanted.'

'Is that a proposal?' I giggle, expecting him to join in, but I stop when I notice his cheeks reddening as if he's kicking himself for coming out with something like that.

'I think there's been quite enough talk of weddings around here,' I scold, wanting to put a stop to any talk of that kind. Sheer nonsense. That's what it is.

'How are things with the newlyweds?' he asks, changing tack.

'Well, they're still married. Doesn't seem to be a lot I can do about that.'

While I prepare Zorro's feed skip of horse pellets and moist molasses to go with his hay, Bryn's grassy-green stare follows me around like a sheepdog's.

'Do you know how long they'll be staying?'

'Why?' I ask curtly, sensing where this is leading.

'I won't get to see you as much, now that Cerys is back.'

I roll my eyes at his selfishness. 'The answer is . . . as long as she needs to. She is my daughter,' I grunt, and feeling like this conversation needs to come to an end, I take the skip of horse food into Zorro's stable, leaving Bryn in the tack room. Or so I thought, because when I turn around, he's right there in front of me, making me jump.

'What's up with you today?' I pull a face at him.

'Nothing.' He flashes me a weak smile that doesn't quite reach his eyes.

'Hmm, if I didn't know better, I'd think you were sweet on me.' I tease him without thinking, forgetting for the moment that he probably is sweet on me. I mean, I don't know that for sure, but if I were a betting person.

He scowls. 'Like Griffin you mean.'

We're standing quite close together because the covered walkway that goes the length of the stable block is narrow and I catch a whiff of Bryn's smell — he showers every day and is clean-shaven, a rarity in these parts, but it doesn't disguise the diesel and pig fragrance that clings to his clothes. *Eau de pig*, I call it. It's not the most pleasant of smells, it has to be said.

'I'm not going there today,' I tell him, even though the same thought had raced through my brain, faster than Zorro at a flat-out gallop when I witnessed Luke's reaction to Bryn earlier. 'I'm trying to reset my mind where he's concerned and give him the benefit of the doubt.'

'That doesn't sound like you,' he blurts out without thinking.

'Thanks,' I say, frowning. I get the impression that there are things going on in his head that he either doesn't want me to know or doesn't know how to say.

'I know this is none of my business, but wouldn't it be easier if they just bought their own house?'

'She's pregnant and has just dropped out of uni and he's unemployed,' I retaliate, thinking, *He's right, it isn't any of his business.*

'I could give you the money, so they could put down a deposit on a house,' he urges.

'No,' I say, stunned, adding as an afterthought, 'I mean, that's incredibly generous of you, but, God, no, Bryn, I couldn't borrow money from you.'

I'm beginning to believe that I've had enough surprises for one day when he slaps me across the face with another.

'I said *give*, not loan,' he confirms.

'Now why would you do that?' I quip, immediately suspicious. No man gets to own me by throwing his money around.

'Okay,' he exhales, 'it was just a thought. I find it hard, that's all, and only because I care about you, as to why Cerys came back here at all, knowing what a difficult position she'd be placing you in.'

'That's my daughter you're talking about,' I warn, narrowing my eyes to let him know he's on a hiding to nothing if he continues in this vein.

'Shame she didn't think about that when she married Luke,' he vents, narrowing his eyes right back at me.

I'm not sure if I should be impressed by his standing up to me, which is unusual for Bryn, who is typically docile and easy-going, or if I should poke him in the eye. I do neither. Instead, I issue him with a second warning. My motto is "three strikes and you're out," and he's getting close.

'Be careful, Bryn. It's my daughter, my house, my rules. And you don't have kids so you don't know what it's like.'

'Bullshit.' He turns on me, with eyes that fluctuate between hot and cold, like the red and green signals of a traffic light. 'And you're forgetting that I *do* have a child. It's hardly my fault I never got to see her grow up.'

'Oh, God, I'm so sorry.' *I deserve a good kicking for being so insensitive and for saying what I did.* 'You're right, I completely forgot. It's just that you never talk about her . . .'

'Besides,' he talks over me and the subject of his daughter. 'You don't have to have had kids,' he goes on, clearly not finished with me yet, 'to know the difference between right and wrong.'

I bite my lower lip in response and keep shtum, knowing he's right. Why did she choose Luke from among all the millions of men in Wales? And what happens if I give in to those feelings of hatred towards Luke? Do I banish my daughter? Make her choose between him and me. No good would come of that. I'd lose her forever. It would take a hundred Lukes to make me give up on my daughter, and even then, I'd fight them off one by one, like a Roman slave pitted against an arena full of gladiators. After going off on a tangent, my mind running away from me, I realise Bryn is saying something.

'What I said earlier. That makes two of us,' he says apologetically as if he knows he's gone too far.

'Make sense, man, I have no idea what you're talking about,' I mutter. Since when did Bryn talk in riddles? I thought he was as straightforward as one of his boars. Food. Sleep. Repeat. Turns out I was wrong.

'If Griffin is jealous, as I believe he is, then that makes two of us,' he frets.

Then he's gone, striding towards his vehicle with a nonchalant wave to signal there are no hard feelings. As I watch him leave, I get the impression that none of the men on this mountain are telling the truth and that they are all as secretive as each other.

# CHAPTER 14: CERYS

'What do you mean you're getting cabin fever?' I inquire of my husband, who is dramatically pacing up and down the living area, which in a room of this size, amounts to four strides up and four strides back for a man his height. 'It sounds a bit extreme to me,' I point out reasonably.

'It's a good job I'm not asking you then, isn't it?' Luke sneers.

'We'll continue this conversation when you're in a better mood,' I tell him as I head towards the bedroom, but as I steal a furtive glance at his profile, to see if he's about to come running after me, he pulls me back in with huge apologetic eyes as if realising he has gone too far.

'I'm sorry for snapping, Cerys, but being trapped in here makes me feel claustrophobic,' Luke grumbles, jerking his head about the room as though everything is its fault.

'How can you say that when we have the mountains right outside our door? You could always go for a walk,' I propose.

'In this?' He motions to the rain falling on the wooden terrace beyond the misted-up glass doors.

'It always rains in Wales. You know that. You'd have to stay indoors all the time if you never ventured out in it.'

'Cerys, I'm not like you. I've never been one for the countryside or the mountains. I miss the town.'

'It's only been two days!' I'm about to try to coax him out of his bad mood, but another thought occurs to me and I become suspicious. 'Are you sure it's the cabin and not me that's getting on your nerves?' I demand.

'Don't be silly. Of course not.'

He appears sincere, but he makes no move to come over and comfort me, which is not what I'm used to. Is he going off me already? We're approaching the six-month mark, which I've heard is when couples start to see each other's true colours. Not that I've ever been anything other than myself around him.

'You lived in the countryside with Mam for two-and-a-half years, Luke, yet you can't tolerate two days with me.' As I say this, my voice breaks, and my eyes well up with tears.

'That was different,' he admits.

'How?' I jut out my chin and raise my shoulders in defiance.

'Because we lived in a farmhouse where there was plenty of space.'

'We're not back on that subject again, are we?' I groan.

'I don't think it would be too much to ask Beth to move in here for a little while, just until we find our feet. There is only one of her and there will soon be three of us. It would be better for the baby and—'

'You,' I interrupt, thinking how selfish he can be at times. He doesn't appear to be remotely aware of how difficult things are already. His presence is enough, on its own, to drive Mam up the wall. Something I hadn't given much thought to before I married him. Because I had been thoughtless and selfish. Thinking only of myself and my desire to have Luke.

'It's not just me, sweetheart. I'm thinking of all of us. You know I have your mam's best interests at heart.'

'How is asking her to move out of her home, where she's lived her entire life, to accommodate you, in her best interests?' I fume.

I expect him to be angry, to retaliate even, so when he breaks into a grin, the kind that gives me a dreamy feeling, he throws me off my stride.

'When you put it like that,' he concedes.

'I have a better idea,' I announce, sitting on the tiny sofa that isn't quite big enough for both of us, but I'm suddenly exhausted from squabbling and want this debate over. This is our second argument of the day and it's not over yet. There's still the rest of the afternoon to go.

'Go on,' he says cautiously, 'I'm open to suggestions.'

'Instead of asking Mam to move out, we could ask to move in.'

'What do you mean? Live together in the same house? All of us?' He looks at me incredulously.

'Yes. What do you think?' I sigh, thinking he's right and that it's a terrible idea. I don't even know why I suggested it. There's no way it would work.

'I think it's a great idea,' he replies, surprising the hell out of me.

* * *

I told Luke I was going to take a shower and then lay down on the bed to rest. He said he'd go out and chop some logs now that it's stopped raining. And I'm grateful for it because I haven't had a moment to myself since I went out riding this morning. Mam gave me a hard time at first, once she'd recovered from her relief that I was okay, and then Luke, once he was located, behaved like I was the worst mother in the world, until I burst into tears, and it was only then that everyone apologised for picking on me.

I blame Mam for getting him so wound up in the first place. She'd have told him horror stories of women miscarrying from riding accidents, no doubt. And why not? Isn't that what I was worrying about following my tumble? Whatever happens, Mam always turns out to be right about things. She just has this knack of knowing. All I can hope for is that she's wrong about Luke. That he's not trouble and that we *are* destined to be together.

My emotions are all over the place and I don't think it's all because of the pregnancy and my changing hormones. One minute I feel capable and together, like just now when I was about to walk away from an unpleasant conversation with Luke. At other times, I'm blaming Mam for all my problems, when all she's done since learning about me and Luke is support us both. Even though it must anger her to do so. Why, why, why did I fall in love with my mother's ex-husband?

So far, none of the cramps I experienced immediately after the fall have reappeared, for which I am thankful, and there is no sign of bleeding. All of these are encouraging signs. Can I assume from this that my baby is fine and I'm out of the woods? I sincerely hope so. Mam and Luke would both kill me if they discovered I'd lied about Zorro having a loose shoe and had actually fallen off and harmed myself. The bruises on my upper thigh and the inside of my arm are already visible. Luke is bound to notice them when we're in bed together, but I'll make something up. He'll believe what I say. He always does. Unlike Mam.

My hair is damp from the shower and fanned out on the bed around me, like an undeserving halo. The mattress is comfortable and I'm starting to feel drowsy with sleep. I'm struggling to keep my eyes open, when . . .

Another alarming thought occurs to me that has the power to propel me forwards until I'm sitting bolt upright in bed. When I suggested us moving in with Mam, Luke appeared pleased . . . really pleased.

Almost as if that's what he'd wanted all along.

# CHAPTER 15: BETH

'You want to move in here, with me?' I gulp down a mouthful of too-hot tea as I say this, hoping to mask my surprise, but judging by Cerys's disappointed expression, I don't succeed.

It's eight o'clock in the evening. The living room fireplace is lit. The whiskey decanter is out. Every night before bed, I have a tipple or two. Cerys told me earlier that they were going out to dine at the Crown in Pantygelli tonight — *I wonder how they can afford it* — so I hadn't cooked dinner. I wasn't invited so I made myself some Welsh rarebit instead.

Cerys has caught me out in a drab old dressing gown, with a tray on my lap and slippers on my feet, because I wasn't expecting company tonight. I'm glad she came alone. I wouldn't want Luke to see me like this. I never thought to lock the door, and Cerys, being my daughter, doesn't knock. Nor do I expect her to. I want her to feel that this is still her home, and I would gladly welcome her back, but Luke living here . . . that's a whole different story. On the other hand, it might not be such a bad idea after all. At the very least I'd be able to keep a closer eye on him.

'You think it's a bad idea, don't you?' Cerys appeals, her cheeks flushed.

Poor Cerys. She looks so uncomfortable sitting there that I want to put her out of her misery and say yes immediately. It's obvious that Luke has put her up to this. He seems as determined as ever to get his feet back under the table.

'I can see where you're coming from, Cerys, about the cabin being on the small side.'

'Small!' She chuckles. 'It's like living in a doll's house.'

It makes me happy to hear my daughter laugh. There hasn't been enough of that lately, so I don't ruin it by mentioning that her modest flat in university halls wasn't much bigger, and she had to share it with three other girls.

'I agree that you couldn't have the baby there, but what are your long-term plans? You haven't really said . . .'

'We don't have any.' She shrugs despondently. 'When Luke gets a job, we can rethink things, but until then we're pretty much homeless.'

'You'll never be homeless while I'm alive,' I reprimand sharply.

'Thanks, Mam.' She throws me a grateful smile, which is meant to soften my hard heart. It works.

'Is he actually looking? For a job I mean.'

'Mam—' her body tenses as her eyes narrow — 'don't start.'

'Okay. Okay.' I hold up my hands in surrender. After getting to my feet, I stroll over to the coffee table by the window where I keep the decanter and pour myself a glass, just as I was about to do when Cerys first came in but had to settle for tea for two instead. 'Well, if you're going to have the baby here, I suppose it's better if you move into the farmhouse because emergency services wouldn't be able to access the cabin.'

'Emergency services?' Cerys screws up her face in alarm.

Cerys has dreaded the wail of sirens ever since she awoke the night her father committed suicide and glanced out of the window to see the night sky lit up by the flashing lights of police cars in our farmyard.

'In case you went into labour and needed assistance.' While I'm explaining this calmly, so as not to panic her, I can't help but recall the amount of times it had happened to me, right here in this farmhouse. How many babies had I miscarried before Cerys came along? Six, that's how many. She doesn't need to know. Not now. Not ever. I'm ashamed that I've never told her about her missing brothers and sisters but I still think it's for the best.

'How about you move in on Saturday? That way, we can spend the entire weekend settling you both in.'

'That's fantastic. Thank you very much.' Cerys wiggles on her seat with delight, and she reminds me of her dog at that moment. Normally, he is never far from his mistress.

'Where is Elvis by the way?'

'Luke took him for a walk.'

'On the mountain?' I ask, unable to contain my surprise.

'Yes, Mam. On the mountain,' Cerys grumbles, then opens her mouth nervously, as if to say something important, but stalls.

'What is it, Cerys? You know you can tell me anything.'

'It's just that, well, Luke is different with me. He's not the same person you used to know. And if I tell him to like the mountain, he'll at least try.'

'Oh, we're doing this, are we? Talking about Luke and me,' I ask irritably.

Cerys squirms. 'Mam,' she says. 'There is no you and Luke; there is only Luke and me.'

'I'm aware of that, love. That's not how I intended it to sound.'

When I think about what I just said, my cheeks burn with embarrassment. Earlier in the day, I thought I was mistaken about Luke and that he actually loved my daughter because he was so worried about her going out riding and what would happen to the baby if she fell off, but then he revealed his true colours in the kitchen by displaying his jealousy towards Bryn. I'm still on the fence regarding my son-in-law. I mean, the jealousy could have nothing to do with me, and be more about him acting like he's the alpha male around here, feeling threatened by Bryn's presence, and wanting to protect his home and his women. Except he's not an alpha male, and as Cerys pointed out just now, I'm no longer one of his many women. There had always been at least five of us in our marriage, *the cheating dog*. On that score, I had easily beaten Princess Diana.

'But can we not do it on Saturday?' Cerys continues as though she wants to forget her last remark.

'Do what?' I ask absently, immersed in my own thoughts once more.

'Move in,' she says, exasperated.

'Why not? I thought that was what you wanted.' I almost said, 'what Luke wanted,' and I'm so glad I didn't.

'It's Dad's eleventh anniversary,' she reminds me, bluntly.

'Oh yes, of course.' It's my standard response for anything Owen related.

'I was hoping we might go to his grave together. Just me and you.'

'That would be lovely. I'd like that,' I lie splendidly, I think.

Cerys's willingness to spend time with me alone, away from Luke, is a good start, and I'm grateful for it. I just wish it didn't have to be so focused on Owen.

'Let's not put the move off then. How about we do it tomorrow?'

'Do you really mean that, Mam?' Cerys rises to her feet and approaches me for a hug. She smells like a meadow of wildflowers.

'I do. I'll get Grandad's room ready for you first thing.'

'Oh.' She frowns, leaning back to scrutinise my face. 'Not my old room then?'

'Heavens no.' I take a breather as I search for the right words that won't offend my sensitive daughter. 'It's much smaller than Grandad's room, and after all, space is what you wanted.' I smile to soften the blow, knowing she can't argue with that.

On the inside, though, I'm groaning. Luke three doors down the landing from me is bad enough, but Luke making love to my daughter in her old bedroom, which is next to mine! That is not going to happen.

'I can't wait to tell Luke.' Cerys hops up and down on the spot, and I see the young girl in her then, when she was around ten and full of energy and mischief. That's when I notice the bluish bruises on her upper arm.

'My, God, Cerys, what happened to you?' I gasp, clutching at her arm, lower down so as not to hurt her.

'Oh, I bumped into something in the dark.' As she says this, she tugs at her sleeve to conceal the bruising. 'That's how small that cabin is.'

I know she's lying because her gaze is avoiding mine and she has turned away from me to stare out of the window, even though the curtains are closed and there's nothing to see. Whenever I caught her telling fibs as a child, she used to do exactly the same thing.

'You don't fool me, madam.' I bristle. 'Did Luke do this to you?'

'Mam! What a horrid thing to say. I can't believe you'd think something like that.' Cerys goes to sit straight-backed on the sofa, out of reach of my arms, and clutches her head in her hands.

We don't say anything else because, right on cue, the man himself has just walked in. I don't mind my daughter not knocking, but I object to the fact that he has just done the same thing.

'Evening all.' He slurs, making his way across the room to kiss Cerys on the cheek, but she snatches her face away from him, making him grimace. At a guess, I'd say it's because he reeks of alcohol. Instead of arguing in front of me, he collapses onto the sofa next to Cerys and picks up her hand in a calming gesture. That appears to work because she visibly softens and her shoulders drop an inch or two.

I wouldn't put it past Luke to hurt Cerys, despite what she says. He'd never tried anything like that on me, but I'm not like my daughter. She's as delicate as a flower, with her raised cheekbones, light complexion, and long lemon-scented hair, whereas I'm as robust as an ox.

'Mam has invited us to move in with her so that we'll have more space for the baby when it arrives,' Cerys informs Luke, but she lacks the zest she'd shown earlier. And I understand why. It's clear to both of us that he's been drinking again. That he probably had no intention of walking the dog on the mountain at all, and that he just said that so he could go back to the pub, alone this time.

'Fantastic,' he replies as he leans back in his seat, revealing a glimpse of his lean stomach beneath his T-shirt. 'I can't wait to move back into my old room.'

There is silence as Cerys and I exchange shocked glances. I wouldn't be at all surprised if we weren't wondering the same thing, *what planet is he from?*

'I'm kidding,' he roars with laughter. 'Talk about tumbleweed. You women take yourself far too seriously.'

'Why should a woman not take herself as seriously as a man?' I bite, even though I told myself I shouldn't, but he'd immediately put my back up by saying that. Luke always knew exactly which buttons to press.

'Mam,' Cerys warns, shaking her head at me as if to say pick your battles, but as I sigh and back down, I'm buggered if she doesn't leap in herself.

'What you said was completely inappropriate, Luke, and as you can see, no one is laughing.'

'No one ever does in this house,' Luke mumbles and looks around the room, as if bored.

I'm familiar with the look. It used to signal to me that Luke was craving excitement elsewhere. For Cerys's sake, I pray I'm mistaken this time. She claims he's changed and is different with her, but I don't see any proof of this.

'I know, let's play some Tom Jones to celebrate you both moving in,' I get to my feet, eager to dispel the dark mood that invaded the room when Luke did. As I hunt for my favourite CD album by The Tiger, as Tom is known, I smile as if I'm over the moon at the prospect of sharing a house with my ex-husband, now son-in-law.

'Gross.' Cerys pulls her *if I have to hear that old dinosaur sing one more time, I'll die* face.

'I'm a big fan of Tom Jones.' Luke, on the other hand, seemed to spring to life, leaning forward in his chair and clapping his hands together with excitement. 'You can't beat a "Sexbomb", can you Beth?'

# CHAPTER 16: CERYS

When Mam gets up early in the morning and lets the dogs out, they race over to the cabin, anxious to greet us, and then pad around on the terrace outside, whining and pawing at the glass doors, annoying Luke, and causing Elvis to yap from his end of the bed.

'Your mother does it on purpose,' Luke protests, his mouth sticky with toothpaste as he comes into the bedroom, bare-chested. He continues to brush his teeth while stomping around the room, yanking on a sock with one hand. I can't take my eyes off him. He's so beautiful.

'You think it's funny, don't you?' he growls.

'I think you are.' I giggle, but as he tries to kiss me with a toothpaste-smeared mouth, I raise both hands in surrender. 'Okay, you're not. Why are you up so early anyway?'

'Hard not to be with the collie-who-hates-me dawn chorus every day. Every time I go out there, she tries to bite me.'

When I hear Gypsy aggressively barking outside the door, Toad's booming whoof, and Elvis's less significant yap, I giggle again. 'Gypsy's a young dog and isn't used to strangers, but she's a big softie really and will come around in the end, once she gets to know you. You wait and see.'

'Like your mam?' He lifts a brow.

‘It’s our last morning here,’ I reassure him, ignoring his attack on Mam, which I feel is undeserved, considering all she has done, and is still doing for us. ‘Tomorrow you can have a peaceful, bark-free lay-in.’

‘And today is moving-in day, so I figured I’d get started early.’

‘Luke, it doesn’t take two of us to pack. That’s something I *am* capable of doing, even when pregnant. It’s not as if we have any furniture or other items to take with us, just clothes.’

‘I suppose that’s my fault as well, for losing the flat and all my furniture,’ he niggles, as if spoiling for a fight.

‘I never said that and you never really told me what happened to your flat anyway,’ I object. Because in reality, I’d never been permitted to sleep over or even visit. He claims it was because he was embarrassed by how squalid it was, so he used to sleep over in halls, which was totally against the regulations. It didn’t go down well with my flatmates either because he was a noisy lover and they were embarrassed by it. Luke was perplexed since he imagined they were all screwing boy after boy. He couldn’t get his head around the concept that we were different from him and that our studies were more important than boys, at least they had been until he came along.

‘I got evicted. I told you that,’ he responds tetchily.

‘You may have done. I can’t remember.’ I’m equally irritated with him because I suspect he may have been living with someone when he first met me, and that’s the real reason I wasn’t allowed to visit his flat in Aberystwyth. I wish I’d been brave enough to show up out of the blue one day and knock on the door.

‘The bastard landlord changed the locks on me and wouldn’t let me take a single thing, claiming I owed him two months’ rent.’

‘But you lived alone. Not with a woman?’ I insist.

‘Of course not. What do you take me for?’ He collapses on the bed, acting deeply wounded.

'Luke,' I sigh, anticipating his reaction to what I'm going to say, 'leave me to sort out our stuff and take the car and drive into Abergavenny.'

'What for?'

'To look for a job. We don't have any money.'

'I'm sorry I've let you down by failing to provide for you,' he mopes.

'We're both young. We've got all the time in the world to make our fortune.'

'You might have. I'm just a down-and-out who can't even take care of my wife. I don't know why you bother with me.'

I know he wants me to feel sorry for him and that he's trying to manipulate me into saying he doesn't have to get a job just yet, but I need him to show Mam that he's doing his best. So, I take a more playful approach, saying, 'You know why I bother with you, sexbomb.'

That does the trick. He's smiling now and strutting around the room in a sexy manner as he puts on a T-shirt, followed by a faded denim shirt over the top. When he pulls on a pair of tight jeans, I want to tell him how gorgeous he looks, but if I do that, he'll come back to bed and make me forget all about his finding a job. It's not that he's lazy or unambitious. He just hasn't found the right position for him yet.

'I look ridiculous driving around in your pink girly car, a man of my sexier-than-Tom-Jones status,' he jests. 'Do you think Beth would let me take the Defender if you asked nicely?'

'No,' I answer curtly, flashing him a warning glance. 'It's too soon to ask for any more favours.'

'Yes, ma'am.' He gives a playful salute and clicks his heels together.

I fall back onto the pillows, laughing. Despite everything, being in love is the most wonderful sensation in the world. It's addictive. As is Luke.

He dazzles me with his trademark bad boy grin and throws me a kiss, which I pretend to catch, before exclaiming, 'I love you to the moon and back.'

Then he's gone, with a cheeky wink. I can't help but smile as I hear Gypsy snarling and Luke groaning outside as they clash.

* * *

It takes less than an hour to pack and the suitcases are neatly zipped and ready on the bed for Luke to take over to the house later. I learned my lesson with Zorro and am not about to tackle heavy cases. Unlike Luke, I was able to return to sleep after he left without being awakened by a single bark. That has made me feel so much better. Now I'm certain all is well with the baby, he or she has been vigorously kicking this morning and I've had no more cramps, a weight has been lifted from my shoulders, which coincides with the sun coming out. As I stare out of the open glass doors, where I can see tiny green and yellow finches flitting from tree to tree and ducks paddling in the water, which is less brown than before, I decide to go for a walk.

'Come on, Elvis,' I say, grabbing my raincoat and pulling on a pair of wellies, which I'd left out for our trip back to the farm later today.

I know if I stay at the cabin all morning, I'll simply stress about Luke finding employment and worry that he'll spend too much time in bars chatting and watching sports on the big screen instead of asking about work. He's an experienced bartender, so he shouldn't have too much trouble finding a job, however temporary. Even if it's only minimum wage, it will be better than nothing. Nothing is precisely what we have. And let's not forget how appealing he is to the female clientele. Bar owners are wise to that. Hiring attractive members of staff is good for business. He's also well-known in Abergavenny because he worked the bars there when he was married to Mam. So, all in all, I have high hopes for him.

I decide to walk through the woods behind the cabin and out that way, which will lead me across fields, past Bryn's house and back to the farm. While I'm out, I'll call in on

Mam for a cup of tea and check how she's getting on with Grandad's bedroom. If she lets me, I might even be able to help her. It will be like old times when I used to help her make the beds.

As soon as my boots crunch on the woodland trail, a murder of crows raise the alarm, leaving their nests and cawing frantically in the wintry-blue sky. My ears are filled with a cacophony of woodland sounds. Insects buzz, trees groan, leaves rustle, squirrels chatter and rabbits dart out of nowhere to scuttle to their underground burrows. These are the sights and sounds of my childhood. The damp, earthy fragrance of the woods with its mossy undertones is one of my favourite scents. It makes me feel alive. Like the mountains do.

'It's okay, Elvis,' I soothe, because, unlike me, he appears unsettled in the woods, surrounded by tall black trees that block out the light. Because he's trembling from head to paw, I pick him up and carry him the rest of the way. I set him down again when we exchange woodland for green pastures and rolling hills, and he wags his tail as soon as we leave the trees.

Once we're on the narrow mountain road, we're surrounded on both sides by pastures that climb upwards to higher peaks. There are sheep everywhere. One black face for every hundred white ones. Crumbling dry stone walls prevent them from escaping. I pick Elvis up whenever we come to a farm gate, so we can climb the stiles together. When I breathe in the stench of pigs and hear their foraging snorts, I know we've reached Forest Farm. Yet I can't see them because of the dense hedgerow that surrounds the piggery. Bryn's jeep is in the farmyard and one door is open, but I don't see him in person, which I'm grateful for. I always feel tongue-tied around him. He exudes a melancholy, depressing vibe, like a character in one of the Bronte sisters' books, that I find off-putting. Don't ask me why.

I pass by the two shepherd's huts and notice they're both in use. I experience an attack of guilt when I realise Mam could be charging a premium holiday rental for December, as I'm sure Bryn must be. I'm hoping she might be able to secure a late booking for Christmas week once we move out. It's not too late to decorate and make it all festive.

As we turn off the road and head for the farmhouse, Elvis runs off in the wrong direction, yapping his little heart out with his ears flipping inside out.

'Elvis,' I call after him, wondering what he's seen. If it's anything bigger than a baby rabbit, he wants to hope he doesn't catch up with it because it will have him for dinner. Mam was right about him not being a suitable breed for farm life. But I love him anyway, so I hurry after his wiggly, chocolate-brown body when he vanishes over an incline, wondering at the same time why I can't hear Mam's dogs barking from the house. Perhaps she's taken them into town in the Defender. When I reach the top of the small hill I come to an abrupt halt as fear steals the breath from my lungs.

The barn . . .

The big tarred-black door is slightly ajar as if inviting me in. How did I end up here when I usually go out of my way to avoid it? It's situated where the original farmhouse had once stood. Built over four hundred years ago, it burned down in the early 1900s, which is when Pen-y-Bryn was built. Some of its stone foundations are visible to this very day. It's a shame the barn escaped the same fate but at least it's isolated and a good distance away from the farmhouse so I don't have to see it every day. I wish Mam would have it demolished and its rotting wooden bones burned on a large bonfire, but I'm sure it would cost money she doesn't have. Nobody goes in it anymore, which is understandable. Except for my dog, who can be heard yapping joyfully from inside. The sound is like a knife scraping on glass, and it stresses me out to the point that I wish Luke had bought me a border collie puppy instead.

'Elvis. Come out, there's a good boy. Elvis.' I approach the gap in the door and try to peer inside, but I can't see anything through the dark cloud of blackness. Suddenly the yapping stops and I hear Elvis's whimper. I freeze. This means I have no choice but to go inside and rescue my dog who may or may not have hurt himself.

I have my phone in my pocket, even though it's incapable of picking up a signal out here, so I switch on the flashlight and push open the creaky door. Inside, it smells of musty old hay. 'Elvis,' I hiss childishly, not wanting to alert the barn to the fact that I've returned after an eleven-year absence.

Because the torch's white beam only picks out what is directly in front of me, I swing it around in a full circle. My breathing is too loud, yet not loud enough to mask the sound of little mammals scurrying away into corners, and I scream when something comes close enough to brush my leg. Too late, I realise that it's Elvis, who has rushed past me, and is out of the door without even a backward glance in my direction. The traitor!

I'm about to creep out after him when the door bangs back on its hinges, and I can't move because all I can think of is how much like gunfire it sounds. Nothing can keep me from hearing rain pelting the slate roof and wind squeezing the structure like a giant hand after that. I imagine the smell of blood. See the blood spatters on the wall. Hear the blast of the gun as it came into contact with Dad's mouth. I'm twelve again, waking up to the sight of flashing police cars in the farmyard, not knowing that I'd never see my dad again.

Renewed yapping outside breaks the spell I'm under and I'm propelled forward, shuddering as I walk through one cobweb after another to reach the door. As soon as I'm outside in the fresh air, I lean over and retch. Elvis, sensing he is in trouble, rolls on his back in a submissive gesture. I reluctantly rub his tummy.

'You're going on a lead next time,' I grumble.

Yet as we walk away, I can't resist another glance over my shoulder at the building that I used to think took my dad away from me. I recall that day as if it were yesterday. I wasn't allowed in the barn as I was a child, but I saw through the window as they carried him away in a body bag. Naturally,

Mam had wanted to shield me from the horrific circumstances surrounding his death, but I didn't realise he'd committed suicide until someone at school mentioned it. After that, I decided to read the newspaper articles for myself. Mam couldn't stop me doing that.

Accepting the suicide was the easy part. Every day, people take their own lives. The difficulty was understanding why. Dad loved us. Mam and me. But me most of all. He would never have voluntarily left us. There wasn't even a note. No explanation or gesture of affection for the family he was leaving behind, knowing how devastated we'd be. It made no sense.

All these years later I'm still no closer to the truth. And Mam refuses to discuss that night. I know it distresses her to relive it, as it does me, but she uses her grief as a weapon so nobody presses her on it. Tomorrow, when we go to Dad's grave, I'm going to demand some answers. I have a right to know what drove him to kill himself. It might help me come to terms with his passing because, for me, his ghost is still very much alive in the barn.

# CHAPTER 17: BETH

Cerys came by earlier, appearing pale and out of sorts, but when I pressed her on how she and the baby were doing, she shrugged off my concerns and said she was just tired. She seemed pleased with the bedroom though. I'd rearranged the furniture, put fresh linen on the bed, and hung new curtains at the dual-aspect windows that I'd rushed into Abergavenny to buy this morning. She seemed quietly appreciative of the potted Christmas poinsettia on the windowsill and the just-out-of-its-box kettle and pretty bone china mugs I'd placed on a tray on the chest of drawers so that they could enjoy a private cup of tea in the morning before going downstairs. I wanted her to know that I was trying.

But when Luke returned with a massive cellophane-wrapped over-the-top bouquet for Cerys — *how he could afford such expensive flowers is beyond me* — it made my potted-plant contribution seem insignificant in comparison, even though I knew my daughter preferred less obvious displays of affection. She isn't into being wined and dined, expensive cars and luxury holidays. She'd rather travel on a budget, staying at a hostel, and given the choice, she would opt for wild mountain flowers, environmentally friendly cars and vegan street food eaten on the go. My daughter may look classy and expensive, but she's a sweet girl who loves her family and her home life, appreciates her surroundings, and adores animals.

After that, they'd vanished, returning a few hours later with their cases, immediately going upstairs to settle into their new room. As I was preparing the evening meal, I could hear them giggling. I didn't intend to cook all of their meals, but because it was moving-in day, I figured I'd go the extra mile and try and make them feel welcome. I'd also dressed more elegantly than usual this evening, swapping jeans for a plum-coloured jersey dress, and adding gold earrings.

When they came crashing down the stairs an hour later, I felt ridiculous in the dress because Luke kept staring at me. As if I were mutton dressed as lamb. His favourite meat, before he became a vegetarian.

'You look lovely tonight, Mam,' Cerys marvelled, brushing her mouth against my cheek. 'Doesn't she?' she'd said, turning to glance at Luke.

'Always.' He had grinned.

I'm never sure if he's laughing at me or not, but I decide it doesn't matter. I can't let anything ruin tonight's dinner. While I was in town, I grabbed one of those boxes of cheap red wine for Luke which should keep him happy and out of my hair. It might not be the expensive Merlot and Bordeaux he prefers, but beggars can't be choosers.

'Guess what? Luke has found a job already,' Cerys enthuses, unable to contain her excitement. As I watch Luke come to stand behind her, sliding one arm around her waist in a possessive gesture, his unwavering gaze fixed on my face the whole time, I feel pleased for her, not him.

'Isn't he clever?' Cerys gushes, staring at Luke with pride, instead of seeing him as the down-and-out he really is.

'Very,' I respond, sighing inwardly and focusing on the steaming pans of food on the stove. I'd never heard of jackfruit before, but it appears to be highly popular among vegetarians, vegans, and people who follow plant-based diets. I chose to create a curry out of it, but it looks terrible to me, and I expect I'll be constructing a mountain on the side of my plate with it as Luke did the tofu. I'm still certain he's only pretending to be a vegetarian, sorry vegan, to impress her. In an attempt to win her over, he appears to mimic her in a variety of ways, but how long can he keep that pretence up? It won't be long before he lets his mask slip and what then? He never bothered to hide his true self from me though, so Cerys may be right when she says he is different with her. I sincerely hope so for her sake.

'Dinner's ready,' I announce over my shoulder, and I hear the scraping of chairs as they take their seats at the table and wine glugging into Luke's glass.

'I'm starving,' Cerys declares, ripping apart a sizeable chunk of flatbread while I dish up the foul-looking curry.

'Steady on, Cerys,' Luke admonishes, knocking back a large gulp of wine that stains his lips blood-red. 'You know bread isn't good for you.'

'Since when?' I ask, perplexed.

'He actually means my weight.' Cerys pulls a face while munching on a mouthful of food.

'She's stick thin as it is,' I grumble loudly, not looking at Luke.

'All I'm saying is that you'll end up with stretch marks and a floppy tummy if you're not careful about weight gain.' He directs this to Cerys.

I'm supposed to be on my best behaviour this evening but I can't help but respond. 'And what's wrong with that?'

'Just ignore him, Mam.' Cerys shrugs as if she's not remotely bothered by Luke's comments. 'I do,' she adds, tossing her hair playfully at him.

'She knows I'm only joking. Don't you, sweetheart?'

Cerys shrugs again, pulling off another piece of bread and stuffing it in her mouth. 'My body is a place I inhabit. Where I exist. It doesn't have to be perfect. Just functional.'

Now, Luke and I do exchange glances and lift our brows as if to say, *Only the young believe their bodies are going to last forever, and only the perfect don't worry about what they look like.*

'You obviously kept yourself in great shape during your pregnancy, Beth,' Luke remarks, knocking back more wine but leaving his plate of food untouched. 'No one would believe you'd had a child just by looking at you.'

He has no idea how many babies I've carried in my stomach because I never told him about the miscarriages.

I'm about to grudgingly thank him for the unwanted compliment when: 'You're just as fit as your daughter, Beth, even at fifty.'

Cerys and I both flush as red as his cheap Shiraz when he says this but for different reasons. I'm uncomfortable because it feels like he's referring to how I appear naked, whilst Cerys must be mortified by the harsh comparison of an older former lover being just as fit as her, even if he is speaking to her mother. Luke appears to be utterly oblivious to how improperly he's behaving, so we ignore him as if he were a misbehaving child and continue with our supper.

When I've sat long enough, making stilted conversation with my daughter, while Luke stares into his wineglass, his nose turning redder by the minute, I eventually make my excuses, yawn, and say I'm going to bed. When Cerys offers to clear the table and put the dishwasher on, I don't argue. I'm exhausted. Wishing them good night, I take myself off to bed.

* * *

I'm still awake hours later when I hear them coming upstairs whispering and giggling. I hear Luke crashing into furniture in his drunken state followed by a hushed, 'Fuck.' Sounds cascade down the landing and underneath my door. Water running. The spitting out of toothpaste. Toilet roll spinning on its holder. The flush of the loo. And then, the dreaded creaking of the mattress that my Tad (dad) passed away on. God rest his soul. The cantankerous old bugger, meant affectionately, had outlived Owen, and he even saw Luke out, which was his main goal, before passing away a year ago. He was eighty-five when he died of heart disease. The secrets he and Owen took with them to the Church of St Martin's graveyard in Cwmyoy will have livened the place up.

My crafty old ears detect the patter of Elvis's claws clacking on the wooden floor and I realise that Cerys has already broken one house rule. I told her he'd have to sleep downstairs with the other dogs, half knowing she would disobey me. A sigh escapes me as I look out of the window. The curtains are open and my bed is positioned so that I have a view of the valley below where lights twinkle in the distance. I often think about the town folks in their beds, staring up at the mountain, gazing at the lights of the farmhouse as I look down on them. It helps me feel less alone.

When I hear the inevitable moaning coming from three doors down, I cover my ears with my hands. I never thought I'd have to suffer the sound of Luke's lovemaking ever again, and yet, there it is. That, teamed with the rhythmic squeaking of the bed transports me back to two years ago when he shared a room with me rather than my daughter — when Luke's hands were on *me*. His voice in *my* ear, whispering words no church-going woman should want to hear. The taste of him was on my lips. My body had writhed as he pleased me with his mouth. Oh my God, it's so embarrassing and shameful to recall. I can't bear to remember but there's sod all I can do about it. Anyway, I don't know why I should feel humiliated. I've done nothing wrong except marry a pretty boy, have great sex while it lasted, get cheated on multiple times, and then get divorced. Should have been end of, but he had to bounce back like a slapped arse.

Part of me wishes I were downstairs in the kitchen with Bryn having one of our cosy chats over a pot of tea. Although reserved, and as emotionally unavailable as Crug Hywell or Table Top Mountain in English, he gives friendly *cwtches* when needed and actually listens to my ramblings. Instinctively, I know that he would like something more than what we have but I have no desire to commit to him or any other man. Once bitten and all that . . . besides, I have a particularly good reason for keeping him at a distance.

Good Lord, I'd forgotten how loud Luke could be and how sound travels in old houses like ours, with their paper-thin walls. I might as well have put them in Cerys's old bedroom next to me as she'd wanted. When I'm able to pick out the exact words he's saying to my daughter, I feel my cheeks flame. He's repeating word for word the dirty things he used to say to me, which makes me feel sick. Can't he change his MO for the woman he's with or at least try? Cerys would be devastated to know that he's still the same old Luke under the sheets. His repertoire hasn't changed one bit.

One more squeak, one last moan, and then . . . silence. Finally, it's over. He's done. Thank God. And my whole body unwinds. Luke's presence is never far away and it's getting to me. One minute I think we can be friends and the next I want to kill him. Cerys is keen to convince me that he has changed and I go along with it for her sake and because I'd like to think that this might be true, but deep down I know he hasn't altered. He's the same old Luke. The only change he's made is the woman he's with.

Even now I suspect him of being deliberately noisy in order for me to hear him. Knowing how egotistical Luke can be, he'll imagine I'm lying in my bed alone pining for him. Nothing could be further from the truth. He actually makes me cringe. And I know my daughter will feel the same about him one day. It's a shame she had to get pregnant with someone like him. I can't imagine anything worse than being tied down with a child to a man who cheats and lies, which he's bound to do at some point. Cerys will have to learn the hard way just like I did, but at least she'll have me there to pick her up off the floor in the end, which is more than I had.

She's different around him I've noticed. More tense. And I put this down to the fact that he is constantly nagging her about her weight. I didn't enjoy the conversation, company, or food tonight and I get a sinking feeling in my chest when I consider how many more evenings like that I'll have to put up with before Luke's mask slips and he screws up. It seems to me that if it weren't for Luke, myself, Cerys, and the baby could be quite happy living together on the farm. If it weren't for Luke . . .

I stiffen when I hear the click of a door opening and closing. And then, bare feet softly padding along the landing. I hold my breath, afraid to make a sound. I don't want them to know I'm awake because they'll assume I heard them making love which would be really embarrassing for Cerys and me. *Whoever thought it was a good idea for them to move in?* There is movement outside my door. A pair of shuffling, shadowy feet beneath it. I shrivel down in bed, about to hiss, 'Is that you, Cerys?' when the doorknob turns . . .

A head of floppy golden-blond hair appears. Then, a pair of deep blue seductive eyes.

'Luke!' I shriek, tightening the covers around me.

He hovers, seemingly unconcerned, as if he's thinking of coming in. His hand rests lazily on the doorknob like he owns it.

'Sorry, wrong room. I must have got lost.' He smirks, then looks about the room to see whether everything is still the same as he remembers before returning his possessive gaze to the bed, and me. '*Nos da fy*, angel.'

I'm out of bed and storming over to the door as soon as he's gone, locking it with a savage twist of the key. Once I'm alone, and feeling safe, a deep ragged breath shudders all the way down to my toes. *Lost, my eye.* He spoke in Welsh on purpose in case Cerys overheard him. She doesn't understand the language. Only us old-timers do, and even then, we rarely use it. You have to travel into north-west Wales for that.

How dare he call me *his angel*?

# CHAPTER 18: CERYS

As we climb the green hill up to the church where Mam attends morning service every Sunday and has done for years, I'm convinced that the leaning tower, originally caused by a landslide, has worsened since I saw it a year ago when we buried Grandad. St Martin's is a thirteenth-century Gothic structure recognised as Britain's most crooked church. When I was a kid, I thought I was being dropped off at a wicked witch's home whenever I went to Sunday school.

Old stone gravestones gravitate towards the paved pathway, as if drawn to the living who pass by them but we make our way to the newer section, where Dad and Grandad, as well as other generations of the Williams family I've never met, are buried. Mam has been silent all morning, which is understandable. Getting through today while honouring Dad is difficult for both of us. That doesn't mean I'm going to be gentle with her. I'm determined to obtain some answers, and she won't be able to make excuses and vanish out here, where there are no sheep to feed, chickens, and ducks to let out of the henhouse, stables to muck out, or logs to chop.

I've brought the ridiculously expensive bouquet that Luke purchased for me yesterday, and I'm going to divide the flowers between both graves. Luke won't even notice they're missing. I thought he knew how I felt about crude displays like this, but evidently, he wasn't thinking straight. The excitement of starting a new job had made him act out of character. Mam hasn't brought anything except for herself and a gloomy mood.

The sky is dark and cloudy as if it is about to rain, and there is a nip in the air that slips in through the open cuffs and neck of my coat to chill my bones. Mam wears a dingy grey knitted hat covered in dog hair, and her nose and cheeks are as ruddy as a farmer's are supposed to be. I feel like a white-faced, white-haired ghost standing beside her in the hollow of the silent valley. Dad's grave is speckled with bird droppings, as usual, and Mam takes out a damp cloth and a spray cleaner from her bag and proceeds to clean it as I sort the flowers. One rose for Dad, one for Grandad, and so on. They have no scent, unlike the strongly fragrant wildflowers found on the Brecon Beacons.

I cast a worried glance around the graveyard to make sure we are alone. Mam can be tough to approach at times, and I'm beginning to worry that my bravery has faded, like her smile has in recent months . . .

'Thanks for asking me to come today,' Mam says over her shoulder, her back turned on me. 'It means a lot.'

'Me too,' I admit, relieved that she's finally broached the subject. Snapping off a few dead leaves from the bunch of flowers in my grasp, I watch them flutter away on the breeze and vanish in an instant, before venturing to say, 'I know how difficult it is for you to be here.'

Her head shoots up when I say this, as if in denial. That's how fresh Dad's death is for her. It's obvious she doesn't want to discuss it, and now that I'm in love I can understand why. I'd be the same if something happened to Luke. I'm convinced I'd never marry again if I were a widow. I remember feeling astonished and disappointed when Mam chose to do so. Mam and Dad had loved each other so deeply and they are the source of my romantic views about love. I also suspect that having lost my father at such a young age makes me more attracted to older men, like my husband, but not in a fatherly figure sense. Luke hardly fits that bill but he'll have to when our baby is born.

'You know, Mam, I'm going to be a mother myself soon and I want to be able to tell him or her the truth about what happened to their grandfather.'

'What are you talking about? You know what happened,' Mam snaps, her jaw dropping in an irritated scowl.

'I know he committed suicide, but I never knew why. There has to be a reason. And now that I'm a married woman I'm more than old enough to be told the truth . . .' I trail off, intimidated by Mam's outrage.

'If you wanted the truth, why marry a liar like Luke Griffin?' she barks, blinking away a few chilly raindrops. It's so cold up here that my hands have turned blue. One finger is dotted with blood from snagging on the rose thorns. I suck it clean while staring at Mam's fierce expression. She's trying to evade the matter once more, this time by feigning fury. But it won't work this time.

'I'm going to pretend you never said that,' I chastise, refusing to be the first to look away. No, not today.

'You wouldn't ask for the truth if you knew what Owen had done.'

I wasn't anticipating her bitter reaction, rather more excuses. But her dark tone carries a menace that I want to back away from, as I would a dangerous animal. The clouds darken and encircle us until everything around us appears to be shrouded in a grey cloak of ashes, reminding me of the bodies in the ground. My lip quivers as I inquire, 'Mam? What did he do?'

'There's no easy way of saying it so I'll just come out with it. He was a member of a paedophile ring. He killed himself before anyone found out.' Mam says this without any emotion, but her head falls to her breast.

'What? No.' I almost laugh at the absurdity of her statement but I stop myself when I notice she appears deadly serious. 'That's not true. You're making it up.' I match her severity with my own.

'Ask yourself why I would do such a thing given the disgrace and suffering it caused me?'

Despite the dreadful topic we're discussing, I notice she's still cleaning the gravestone with the cloth, circling the words: *died on December 22, 2012, leaving behind a devoted wife and daughter.* I want to yell at her to stop, but I'm too stunned.

'When your dad didn't leave a suicide note at the scene, which seemed out of character for him,' she continues, 'the police searched the house and his PC to see if they could find one elsewhere.'

'Where was I?' I ask, gulping.

'Your grandad drove you somewhere out of the way.'

'He knew?' I gasp, more hurt than I care to admit by this betrayal when I should be focusing on this earth-shattering, life-changing discovery.

'They found pictures of young girls in a secret folder on his computer,' Mam murmurs, narrowing her eyes at Dad's grave. Her anger at him, which I'd confused with grief, is still very evident.

'How old were they?' I demand, allowing the flowers to fall to the ground, petals fluttering across my father's grave. They were staining my palms red with their awful stickiness. Their vivid unnatural colours look ugly in this environment anyway. Like the sickening things Mam is saying — they don't belong on my mountain. Or in my thoughts, where I keep all of my fond memories of my father and grandfather.

# CHAPTER 19: BETH

Her face is a picture of horror and loathing. Too late, I realise that coming here with Cerys today was a mistake. I should have made her go alone so as not to spoil her treasured childhood memories of her father, which have incensed me for years. I'm not angry at her for duping me into accompanying her simply so she could elicit information from me. I'd have done the same if it were me. But I wish I didn't have to tell her about her father. I'm not sure what I should tell my daughter next, or how much information I should divulge. She's pregnant, and her hormones are out of control. Can she handle this on top of Luke and everything else?

'How old, Mam?' she repeats in an insistent voice, her pale blue eyes a shade darker than they were a moment ago.

I close my eyes against the disturbing images that come to mind of her father, say a silent prayer and hope for the best . . .

'The same age you were, Cerys, when he died.' I try to break the news gently this time.

'I don't believe any of this.' She turns her head in the direction of the rolling green-and-brown patchwork hills, as if contemplating climbing them. My biggest nightmare has come true. She's in denial and is holding me responsible for this. A sign that she isn't as mature as she claims to be.

We both stand there saying nothing and getting soaked as the drizzling rain evolves into a downpour. Her hair is limp and loose about her shoulders, and her delicate face is drenched with raindrops. She's shivering from the cold, and I want to reach out and draw her into my arms, stroke away the anguish, but I know she won't let me near her just now.

'Cerys, I—'

'No. Don't talk to me.' She stomps away, hands over her ears, to a stranger's grave, pretending to read the headstone.

'Don't walk away from me,' I find myself yelling, a righteous rage rising within me. At Owen. At Luke. The men who have hurt me. The daughter who betrayed me. Who never loved me the way she should have done. As I wanted her to. It was always Dad this or Grandad that with her, no time for the mother who raised her. Who taught her right from wrong, only to have all my lessons thrown back in my face when she met Luke.

'You asked for the truth about your father, demanded it with the same entitlement you've always shown and I'm giving it to you. Because, as you pointed out, you're married now, with a baby on the way, so you're old enough to hear it.' Resentfulness infiltrates my voice, making it harsher than I intended. I'm completely screwing this up. She'll probably never forgive me for the way I'm handling this traumatic eye-opener. 'He also uploaded pictures of you, Cerys, for others to see.'

There, I said it. It can't be unsaid now.

She slowly turns to face me. A shadow of her former self. Pale face. Skinny foal-like legs. Looking at her now, she could be thirteen again. I wish she was with all my heart. She is devastated. Her life has been irreversibly altered. She will never be the same again. It hurts me to witness her transform into the kind of woman I never wanted her to be, right there in front of me.

'I'm sorry,' I murmur, as her frigid stare sweeps over me as if she were examining a stranger, someone she's only met a few times. 'But I'm not the monster here.'

'You do a good impression,' she sneers.

'I really shouldn't have said anything. I've gone too far.' I want to take everything back, so I can protect her as I've always done. My bloody mouth and temper. I've never been able to control it.

'Did anyone know about this before he took his life? You? Bryn?' She inquires conversationally but hatred shadows her every move.

I'm taken aback. 'No. Of course not.'

'Bryn was Dad's oldest friend. They talked about everything. He must have suspected . . .'

'Nobody had a clue until Owen was gone.'

'That must have been hard for you,' Cerys concedes grudgingly.

We're both soaked to the skin now, and I'm tempted to propose that we leave this horrible, dismal place and finish our conversation in the car, but I don't want to take the past with us. I want us to leave it here, where it belongs, with the dead and the damned. I also need her to hear my story. Finally. For my sake, this time, rather than hers.

'I've never been able to grieve for him knowing this. He wiped out fourteen years of marriage when he pulled that trigger and left me to deal with the fallout and the shame.'

'What about the pictures of me though?' she cuts in desperately. 'What happened to them? Who . . . saw them?'

I catch the panic in her gaze as her mind inevitably returns to what must be truly traumatic for her to process. Impossible even. Never mind her father's betrayal. It's natural for her to worry about what those images contained.

'We still have them, Cerys, don't worry.'

'Don't worry?' Her eyes stretch with indignation.

'They were all innocent enough. There was one of you riding your pony. Another of you bottle feeding a lamb. One of you . . .' I pause to gulp, before guiltily admitting, 'In a swimming costume playing in a paddling pool.'

She turns away from me then, visibly disgusted, so I reach out an arm and reel her back in, as if she were a fish squirming on a hook at the end of a fishing line. 'You were fully clothed in all of them.' I point out firmly, adding, 'Do you understand what I'm getting at?'

She blinks frantically while nodding repeatedly to show that she understands exactly what I'm getting at. Knowing my daughter as I do, I can tell that her thoughts are now wandering off onto another more palatable tangent.

I know I'm right when she says, 'Do you think Bryn was involved?' Cerys's eyes spark with a flash of intrigue. 'Part of the same ring? Is that why they were friends, do you think?'

I realise at this point that she isn't interested in my side of things. This is all about finding someone else to blame. It can't possibly be Owen's fault.

'Why would you think that?' I ask, puzzled, shaking my head, and peering up at the shifting clouds in the sky. A wintry wedge of blue has appeared as if trying to persuade me that better times are on their way. I don't believe it. The sky can stay dark forever all I care.

'There's something creepy about Bryn. I've always felt it. The way he used to look at me when I was growing up.' She pulls a thoughtful, faraway face as if reliving the experience. 'What if they were in it together, Mam?'

As I watch her face crease up with possibilities, I imagine alarm bells going off in her head. I've had years to process all this, but it's all terrifyingly new to my daughter. It's natural for her to want to question what happened but I can't allow her to pursue this route, so I stammer by way of an explanation, 'They weren't. The police would have uncovered that in their investigation if that were the case.'

'I don't want him coming to the house anymore,' she protests, crisscrossing her barely-there eyebrows.

'You don't get to make that decision.' I thrust out my chin and fold my arms, my hackles up. I've never shied away from a challenge to my authority, and today is no exception. When I notice her stunned expression, I try to cushion the shock. 'I'm sorry, but it needed to be said. I realise you're upset and looking for others to blame, but I can assure you nobody but your dad is responsible for the wreckage he left behind. If it makes you feel any better, as far as I know, he never interfered with any children.'

'As far as you know?' Scepticism drips off Cerys's tongue.

'He wasn't on the police sex offenders register,' I argue, 'and he rarely left the farm. He just liked to look on the web, that's all.'

'That's all!' she exclaims, horrified. 'Oh, my God. I wish I'd never asked.' Cerys sobs into her hands, her fragility finally getting to me. My beautiful daughter. Who I love with all my heart. If only I could take her pain away.

'You think I should have gone on protecting you from the truth forever?' I mumble at last, cursing myself yet again for unleashing this on her.

'Yes. That's what mothers do,' she yells angrily and storms off, back towards the road. But instead of getting into the Defender, she continues walking. There's no point running after her, so I plod back to the vehicle and climb inside, allowing tears to stream down my already wet cheeks. It was raining the night Owen died, I remember. The thought unsettles me, but unlike Cerys, I don't believe in ghosts. Only devils.

Something much bigger than Luke has sprung up between me and my daughter and I have no idea how to repair it. I don't know why I had to go and pull a stunt like that just as I felt she was starting to see a few cracks in Luke's character and siding with me more. Of course, she'll cling to him now more than ever, blaming me for her father's crime and rubbing her new husband in my face to punish me.

And I'll take it because that's what mothers do.

# CHAPTER 20: CERYS

'No, Cerys, that's not true; you've got this all wrong. Your mam loved Owen,' Luke protests, preoccupied with his driving, as he casts a sidelong glance to the right, checking for traffic. The tiny, lightweight vehicle groans from the strain of the potholed country lane and the pelting rain. Luke was right when he complained that he looked ridiculous in my car. Because he's so tall his head comically whacks the ceiling whenever the car hits a bump.

'You're mistaken. She might have done once. But she now despises him and who can blame her?' My teeth chatter from the cold as I say this. I'm soaked to the skin from being in the graveyard, and then the long tramp home in tears afterwards. When Luke eventually answered his phone, after many failed attempts, he came to pick me up in the pink car, but instead of being sympathetic and taking my side, he's defending Mam, which is only making things worse.

'Sweetheart, she never got over him. It's the main reason we got divorced. His ghost was there between us all along.'

'Nothing to do with the multiple affairs you had then. Not to mention the woman you got pregnant?' I lash out, not wanting to hear this.

Luke slams on the brakes, savagely kills the engine, and swings around to glare at me. 'I didn't do any of the things I was accused of and you swore that you believed me.'

'I know what I said, Luke, but I would have said anything to be with you at the time, so I pretended not to care.'

'And now?' he challenges.

'I'm not sure what to think any more. Why would Mam make up any of that? It was before I met you, so what did she have to gain by lying?'

'What did she have to gain?' he asks, enraged. 'A simple way out of our marriage, that's what. And a tool to poison you against me.'

'This is not about you and Mam, Luke, it's about Mam and me and Dad.'

'You're right.' He softens. 'Look, try not to get so upset, it's not good for the baby.'

'I feel like my family has lied to me my entire life. What else don't I know, Luke?'

'Hey, come here, you.' Luke pulls me into his warm arms, and I bury my snivelling, wet face in his damp Elvis-scented jumper. This causes me to cry even more, till my body heaves from the trauma.

'Shush . . . it's okay. I've got you,' Luke murmurs in my ear, helping me forget about the cheating allegations I'd just levelled at him. I'm not interested in what happened when he was with Mam. She probably didn't deserve his loyalty anyway. He's now mine. I mustn't push him away.

'Are you done?' he asks, his eyes twinkling in that manner that gives me goosebumps.

'I think so.' I chuckle, wiping my runny nose with the back of my palm.

'You know I love you, right?' he whispers, his eyes full of concern.

'I know. I love you too.'

We bump noses and stay there, enjoying each other's warmth, while the car fogs up with mist, rendering us invisible to the rest of the world. His breath smells strongly of something I can't pinpoint but it's unpleasant.

'I still can't believe it about Owen.' Luke is the first to break away. I notice his eyes have gone all hazy, but I can't tell if this is due to anger on my behalf or a desire to protect me. Both, most likely.

I scowl. 'No matter what Mam says, I think there's something suspicious about Bryn Morgan. I've never liked him.'

He grimaces. 'That makes two of us.'

Mam always said that Luke was envious of her friendship with Bryn when they were married. But I know Luke would disagree if I pushed him on it, so I don't. I can't change his and Mam's past, so I leave it alone.

'How could I have been so blind? Even at school, no one mentioned what Dad was,' I marvel.

'You were only a child. It's natural that everyone would want to shield you from the truth.'

'You think Mam was right to keep it from me?' I raise one eyebrow.

'Most adults screw up, Cerys.' Luke's face creases into a frown. 'We're all just trying to do our best and your mam's no different.'

'You're forgetting I'm an adult too.' I bristle.

Luke sighs, as if bored. 'She probably should have told you when you were eighteen.'

'I wasn't around then. I was travelling.'

'I guess you've got your answer then. It's not something she'd have wanted to tell you in a text, is it?' he says irritably.

'I suppose not,' I grumble. 'But she could have told me when I came back, and before I went to university.'

'I imagine it's been very difficult.' Luke shrugs casually before wiping away the condensation on his side window, allowing him to gaze out at the mountains that fence us in on both sides. His attention is clearly elsewhere. *Away with the fairies*, as Mam would say.

'For me or her?' I say tetchily, my shoulders going up a notch.

'What would you like to happen next?'

'I'm not certain. I'll have to think about it.' I fret, secretly wanting to be at home, snuggled up in a warm bed. With him making love to me. I can picture myself afterwards, basking in his adoration, my hands wrapped around a hot cup of soothing herbal tea.

'Let's get you home.' Luke vocalises my thoughts as he restarts the engine. 'And in the warm. I'll make you one of those strange-tasting teas you like to help you relax.'

When he says this, I smile through fresh tears because he has reaffirmed once again that I have nothing to fear where he's concerned. He can read me like no one else. And that's real love. Whatever he had with Mam is no longer there. It belongs in the past. I need to focus on the future and our child. This news about Dad, while devastating, and I feel so much shame about it, is something I need to put to the back of my mind for the time being. Mam seems intent on driving a gulf between us at a time when I need her most. Talk about self-sabotage.

But then Luke has to go and spoil everything by saying, 'You look just like your mam when you cry. All red-nosed and cute.'

# CHAPTER 21: BETH

When I hear Luke's footsteps coming down the stairs, I'm stoking the log burner in the snug, making it all cosy. Rather than descend the stairs like any normal person, he creeps, pauses, and then creeps some more. The rain has not stopped all day. The mist has settled on the mountain like an impenetrable fog so that even the sheep are invisible. Cerys and Luke were in their bedroom upstairs when I returned to the farm and for once, I was thrilled that they were curled up in bed together having an afternoon nap. Anything was preferable to confronting my daughter and witnessing the sadness and hurt on her face that I knew I'd inflicted on her.

Once I'd finished all of my farm chores, like lumbering wood into the house, luring the chickens and ducks back into their houses so Charlie (the fox) wouldn't eat them, exercising the dogs, and bringing in Zorro from the field, who was so pissed off at being left out in the rain he aimed a killer kick at Toad, narrowly missing him, I'd made a pile of sandwiches, cellophaned them and left them on the kitchen table with a sticker saying, *supper for two. Now*, I'm holed up, hiding from Cerys and Luke. I reasoned that if I stayed out of her way, she could be persuaded to come down and eat. She and Luke can spend the evening alone in the living room, while I remain stuck in here with only the dogs for company.

When the dogs hear Luke's socked feet sliding on the flagstones, their ears perk up. Toad is thinking only of the sandwiches on the table, and drooling, while Gypsy, whose mouth has instinctively curled back into a snarl, has Luke on her mind. 'You and me both,' I say quietly in her ear. Various sounds follow Luke around: the opening of the fridge, the clunk of a kettle starting to boil, the metallic stirring of a spoon, the rustle of cellophane. He's humming softly along to 'Sexbomb,' of all things. I bow my head in frustration, wanting to tell him *to give it up*.

I don't come into the snug very often, except to tidy, since it was Owen's domain, where he would come to read a book, pour himself a glass of port, smoke the occasional cigar, reflect, contemplate, and muse. Whereas I spent all of my time in the kitchen or outside because I was born a farmer's daughter, it didn't come naturally to Owen, who, like Luke, didn't come from an agricultural background. He struggled to adapt at times. Especially since Tad ruled the roost and had every right to do so because it was his farm. I believe Owen would have been better suited to an academic career. His head was always immersed in a book and Cerys took after him. They were as thick as thieves and I often felt excluded. Then again, I did have a farm to run. Tad was afflicted with arthritis and couldn't get about as he used to and Owen had no real interest in sheep. He was more skilled with machinery and building things, like the cabin. That is until he mangled his hand while baling hay one summer.

We met in Cwmbran at a livestock and agricultural sale. He was looking for a vintage tractor in need of repair, while I was on the hunt for a replacement ram after our last one died of ovine brucellosis, an infectious condition common in male sheep. We married after an eighteen-month courtship, during which nothing extraordinary occurred, which felt like a good omen at the time. Owen and I were more content than most married couples we knew. We got along perfectly well as long as we respected each other's space. The only hiccup was that I couldn't seem to carry a baby full term. Owen hated seeing me go through the physical and emotional pain of losing all those babies, so when Cerys arrived, we were overjoyed and decided to stop trying for more. She was everything we had wished for.

I'm known for being hard as nails but our little girl developed into an emotional, sensitive being who was overly sentimental about our farm animals, wanting to name each and every one of them. I'd routinely discover a variety of creatures all over the house. Chicks hatching in the airing cupboard, a litter of flea-ridden, runny-eyed kittens in a basket by the fire. She'd rescue tiny rabbits from the dog's mouths and try to save them, even though we knew they wouldn't survive. We even discovered a sick rat in a box under her bed once. I'd put my foot down over that, ignoring her sobbing as I booted it outside, giving the dogs orders to kill.

Our barefooted, white-haired mountain girl softened us all over time, giving us a new perspective on the world. She was such a blessing that my nightly prayers centred on just her, nobody else. She had me, Tad, and Owen all spellbound. She was our entire world. At her request, we stopped sending the older unprofitable sheep to slaughter, instead letting them see their last days out on the farm. We neutered and vaccinated the farm cats and let them stay by the fire. Tad even hung up his gun to please her, but that was a step too far for me. Cerys believed that all life was precious, she was clearly destined to be a vegan even back then, and she wanted to protect all living things. But even she couldn't save her beloved father . . .

I'll never forgive Owen for what he did — for leaving me in the situation I'm in — or for the decisions we had to make that night, for which we're still paying the price years later. Cerys is right to be suspicious about Bryn Morgan, but not for the reason she thinks.

# CHAPTER 22: CERYS

I pounce on the plate of sandwiches as soon as Luke places them on the bed in front of me. There's beetroot and hummus on brown bread, my favourite, and avocado, tomato, and rocket in white. Sometimes, Mam is the best. Even when she's at her worst, if that makes sense.

'I'm starving,' I say, taking a large bite out of the soft, gooey beetroot, and hummus offering. 'You not eating?' I stare at Luke as he puts on a crisp black shirt that I haven't seen before. He looks incredibly sexy in it.

'I'll get something when I'm out,' Luke replies, pulling a less than enthusiastic face at the rapidly disappearing sandwich in my hands.

'Out?' I gape unattractively. 'Is that what the new shirt is for?' Indignation fills my voice. We don't have any money and are living off Mam, but he went out and bought new clothes.

'Cerys, it's uniform.' He lets out an exasperated breath. 'It's my first night at the Bear in Crickhowell. Please don't tell me you forgot.' He grumbles as he runs his hand over his newly washed and blow-dried, wavy blond hair, which is as neatly styled as any woman's.

'Sorry,' I grimace, patting the bed for him to sit down, but he ignores the gesture and continues getting dressed. 'I'm really pleased about the job, but can we afford for you to eat out when we're meant to be saving money?' I scold gently, not wanting him to blow up on me.

'It's free,' he protests. 'We get unlimited soft drinks and a meal up to the value of fifteen pounds per shift.'

'Wow. That's amazing. You always did manage to fall on your feet,' I respond innocently enough, but when he swings angry dark blue eyes my way, I know I've messed up, again . . .

'What do you mean by that?' he demands.

'Nothing. It was just an observation.' I cringe at how desperate to please I sound.

'Maybe you should keep your observations to yourself.'

'I didn't mean anything by it. Don't take everything so personally.'

'Everything *is* personal,' he insists. 'People who tell you otherwise are nothing but bullies.'

'Well, I hope you don't think I'm one of them?' I exclaim in horror.

Ignoring me, he examines his reflection in the full-length, swivel mirror, fiddling with the collar of his shirt and twiddling the ends of his hair, before lavishly spraying himself with aftershave. I have no idea where it came from as I haven't seen it before but it looks expensive.

'In case you forgot, I've already had one type of emotional trauma today, so please don't ignore me.' As I say this, I notice my voice trembling.

'I'm sorry, Cerys. It's not your fault. It's me.' He walks over to the bed, sits down next to me, and takes my hand in his, holding it to his cheek. 'I must be stressed and nervous about starting the new job.'

I don't buy it but I don't say anything because something is clearly playing on his mind. He's been preoccupied all afternoon since learning what happened with my father. He wouldn't even make love to me when we got home, despite how badly I wanted him to. This was a first. I hope he's not going off me. I couldn't bear it. Perhaps the baby belly is turning him off. Is he right about me being too fat?

On that thought, I put my half-eaten sandwich back on the plate and push it away.

'I'm thinking of paying Bryn Morgan a visit in the morning. To see whether he knows anything more than Mam. I'm sure he does. He and Dad were like that,' I tell him, crossing my fingers.

'Want me to come with you?'

'You and Bryn in the same room. I don't think so.' I chuckle. 'Besides, you're not going to be home until late and deserve a lie-in.'

'How do I look?' Luke is on his feet, strutting up and down in front of me like a model on a catwalk, as if his appearance is far more important than what I was saying.

'Gorgeous as ever,' I mutter, refraining from saying what's really on my mind, such as, *I'm sure you told me you weren't starting your new job until tomorrow.*

'Don't wait up.' He throws me a kiss, which I pretend to catch because it's our standard farewell. 'Love you to the moon and back.'

And then he's gone, and Elvis, next to me, whines precisely twice and then curls himself back into a ball, his nose twitching at the smell of food, but disregarding it because it's not meat. I listen to my husband's slow-moving feet descend the stairs, wondering why he has to creep around so much, like a thief in the night. But there's no crash of the front door closing, so I know he didn't leave right away. Instead, I hear the murmur of voices echoing up the stairs from somewhere below.

He must be talking to Mam. He seems to have plenty to say to her, whereas I could hardly get a word out of him all afternoon. Scrambling out of bed, I pad over to the door and gently open it a fraction, praying it won't creak on its rusty hinges and give me away. I strain my ears but can't understand what they're saying, so I return to bed and crawl under the covers. When my eyes are drawn to the plate of sandwiches, I viciously kick it off the bed and it lands with a soft thud on the rug.

'There is no moon tonight, Luke Griffin, in case you hadn't noticed,' I seethe, crossing my arms in a childish, sulky gesture.

# CHAPTER 23: BETH

My reminiscing about old times, not always pleasant ones, is cut short when Luke enters the snug. I assumed I was safe in here. Cerys and I need to talk about boundaries. I have a right to privacy, and I can't have him barging in on me whenever he feels like it, especially in my bedroom — like last night! Toad lifts his head and then lowers it in boredom, whereas Gypsy immediately drops to the floor in herding mode. She'd run Luke off a cliff if she could, and I for one, wouldn't do anything to stop her.

'Bethan.'

'I haven't been called that in a while,' I remark, gazing at him through my diamond-cut whiskey glass.

'May I?' He motions to the saddle-brown leather sofa across from me. I nod, keeping a wary eye on him as he collapses into it. The wood burner creates flickering orange shadows around the room, and the crackling of the wood masks the sound of the rain battering the side of the house, much as it did the night Owen died.

'Is Cerys all right?' I ask, sounding and feeling tired to my own ears.

He shrugs, before saying, 'I'm off to work, in a bit. You'll keep an eye on her for me?'

'Of course, she's my daughter, I think I know how to do that.' My foot twitches rapidly as my anxiety levels go up.

'Why didn't you tell me?' Luke then gets right to the point of his visit, his eyes blazing into mine with a frightening intensity that doesn't belong on any married man's face.

'Tell you what?' I stutter, biding my time and placing a cushion across my lap as if it will shield me from further interrogation.

'About the circumstances surrounding Owen's death.'

'It was a private matter.' I take another sip of my warm medicine, which has transformed into a sedative, nightcap, and mood-lifter all in one.

'Private? We were married. You should have told me.'

'There were plenty of things you didn't tell me,' I remind him harshly, before adding, 'namely, about the other women.'

He has the grace to appear chastened and uncomfortable, but only for a minute.

'She's taken it badly,' he says, sighing loudly and raising his eyes to the ceiling as if I don't know who he's referring to.

'I'm not at all surprised. How else are you supposed to react when you find out your dad was a kiddy fiddler?'

'Even for you, that's crude,' he observes.

'Aye, well, I stopped being a nice person when I clocked off duty at six o'clock,' I say tetchily, topping up my glass, two is my limit, and I'm already on three. I don't offer him a drink, because he must have guessed by now that I'm not in the mood for company.

'Don't say that.' He exhales, dropping his head onto his chest and closing his eyes as if in pain. 'I know you're blunt and to the point, Beth, but you're also the kindest person I've ever met.'

'I doubt Cerys would be impressed to hear you say that.'

'I won't tell her if you won't.' His head bounces up and I see that he is grinning now, his eyes bright with mischief.

'I don't keep secrets from my daughter,' I reply, offended.

'Except you do.'

'What's that supposed to mean?' I narrow my eyes at him, suddenly fearful that he knows something. Had I foolishly, drunkenly hinted at my dark secret when we were still together, and he now wants to remind me of it. That would certainly put him in a position of power. And danger. Because whatever happens, I will fight to the death to protect my family.

'It means you never told her about her dad until now,' he explains, seeming perplexed by my question.

Relief floods through my veins as I realise that he knows nothing. My secret is safe. For now.

'You know what hurts the most, Beth?' he continues. 'I always assumed you were still in love with Owen, which is why you never truly committed to me. I even tried to be sensitive to your feelings.'

'That's the most amusing thing I've heard all day.' I laugh. 'And excuse me, but since when did marrying someone not imply commitment?'

'Anyway, it is my business n*ow* . . .' Luke is plainly irritated by my reaction since it contradicts his untrustworthy narrative.

'What? How?' I mutter.

'Because it affects my wife. And what hurts her hurts me.'

'Ha.' I let out a long overdue sarcastic laugh. 'Don't even get me started on that. You don't fool me, Luke Griffin. You never have. You're no more in love with my daughter than you were with me. And do you know how I know that, huh?' I snarl.

He grimaces. 'Be my guest.'

'Because you never think about anyone other than yourself unless it benefits you. You can pretend all you like to Cerys that you've changed and are a different man, but it's all a lie.'

He lurches to his feet, clearly upset.

'Have my words hit home at last, Luke?' I demand.

'You're wrong about one thing.'

'Oh aye, and what's that?'

'I did, and still do, love you. You were always the one. You must know that.'

'More like the one that got away.' I huff, acting as if what he has just said hasn't affected me. But I would be lying if I said it hadn't. Even if I were to believe him, which I don't, I can't get over the fact he has dared to voice his thoughts out loud while my daughter, his wife, is upstairs right now . . . probably crying buckets over him. That tells me all I need to know about him. Luke the lover, my eye.

'You don't fool me, Luke. This is all about revenge. When you crawled back to me after your girlfriend, the "alleged" love of your life, lost the baby, you couldn't tolerate being rejected. Is that why you went after Cerys, to get even with me? Is that what this is all about?'

'You threw me out onto the street. Left me homeless and broke.'

'When have you not been either of those things?' I say this quietly, not wanting Cerys to overhear, even though I long to get in his face screaming. 'I won't let you hurt my daughter, which is why you must never, ever say any of those things again in this house.' I spring angrily to my feet and use my glass to poke him in the chest. 'Do you hear me?'

Sensing I am under threat from Luke, even though it's actually the other way around as I'm aching to punch his lights out, Gypsy makes a beeline for him, snarling and growling; causing him to freeze where he stands.

'Call your dog off, Beth,' Luke warns, his eyes wide and cowardly avoiding eye contact with the dog. 'Before she gets hurt.'

'She'd have your guts for garters before you got a chance,' I taunt, enjoying watching his terrified expression.

'You remember Wolf, your old German Shepherd . . .'

'What about him?' I enquire, curious as to where he's heading with this.

'He didn't take to me kicking him that one time, did he?'

'And I warned you what would happen if you ever lifted your boot to him again.'

'But I didn't have to, did I? Because he got run over on the road a few days later, didn't he? A coincidence, don't you think?'

'Oh my God, what are you saying? That you—'

'Like I said, call your dog off,' Luke threatens even while breaking into a sweat. I watch it trickle down his forehead, onto his nose, and his curled lip. 'If you don't want anything bad to happen to her . . .'

'You wouldn't *dare*. And don't think I won't tell Cerys what you've done or what you've said. You'll be out on your ear then . . .'

'Cerys hates you. She won't believe a word you say,' he hisses maliciously. 'Because I have her exactly where I want her. She can't get enough of me, and you'd know how that feels, wouldn't you?'

And then he does something that truly frightens me, he glances around the room, as if mentally cataloguing all of its contents.

'I'm home, Beth. I'm back and you'll never be able to get rid of me now. Never. And it's about time you realised that. So, *call your fucking dog off*.'

# CHAPTER 24: CERYS

I sneaked out of the house while Mam was out on the farm with the dogs, so I was unlikely to bump into her. I've cooled down a lot since our fight in the graveyard yesterday, but I'm still upset. Although I understand how much she must have suffered as a result of what Dad did, I still can't bring myself to use the word paedophile in the same sentence as my father, she did well to protect me for so long. It couldn't have been easy for her, especially given all the mountain gossip that must have followed. But the way she went about telling me, with no regard to my feelings was selfish. She doesn't know how to have grown-up, honest conversations without resorting to anger. It's all about yelling and avoiding blame for her.

We both kept to our respective rooms last night after Luke left for work, so we wouldn't fight any more and say something we'd later regret. *If* he went to work, that is, as I continue to have reservations. I could have sworn his start date was today, the last Sunday before Christmas. He'd also arrived home considerably later than anticipated around 3 a.m. I pretended to be asleep when he came in, sensing he'd be annoyed with me if he found out I'd remained awake all night waiting for him to return. Since moving to the farm, Luke has become increasingly irritable and unpredictable.

Not the gentle, adoring, selfless lover I've grown accustomed to.

Although he fell asleep next to me in minutes, that same unpleasant smell lingering on his snoring breath, I tossed and turned until dawn, when I finally heard Mam stir. I'm ashamed to admit that before I left the room, I went through his pile of clothing left in an untidy heap on the floor and sniffed the black shirt between my thumb and fingers to see if there was any trace of an unknown woman's scent. But all I could smell was the aftershave he'd applied before leaving the house the night before.

A clucking brood of bedraggled hens follow me as I plod across the yard while Elvis scampers along beside me, this time on a lead so he doesn't bolt towards the barn. He keeps one wary eye on the chickens, who are almost as big as he is, while I keep a sly one out for Mam as I go over to greet my horse, whose glossy-black head is neighing to me from his stable door. The farmyard's unconcreted, non-gravelled areas are wet and muddy after yesterday's rain so I leapfrog those spots, as if I were a young girl again, to avoid clogging up my boots. Zorro's stable smells like damp hay, molasses, and musty horse.

'Hello, boy,' I say, holding out my palm for him to sniff. Recognising my scent, he instantly breathes warm air on my hand before flattening his ears when he detects a cowering, wiggling Elvis.

Then, for some reason I can't explain, as if I sense I'm being watched, I look back over my shoulder and up at the house, to Grandad's window, and there's Luke, bare-chested, staring down at me. Even from here, I can tell his eyes are scrunched up in irritation. When I raise a hand to him, he does not respond. Instead, he stands there for a few more seconds, before abruptly tugging the curtains shut and disappearing. This unsettles me, but I don't go back into the house to accuse him of ignoring me once again. He can wait. My conversation with Bryn cannot.

* * *

We're in the enormous, castle-sized, stone-walled, wooden-beamed kitchen, weighing each other up. Neither of us knows what to say to each other. When I first knocked on his door, Bryn appeared hesitant to let me in, but after rambling, 'You wouldn't ordinarily find me indoors,' I stood there long enough that he had no choice but to usher me inside.

He follows my eyes around the depressingly dark kitchen as I get to know my surroundings. There's a massive inglenook fireplace, a fading yellow Aga, dusty ancient furniture and blackened, oily parts of farm machinery. Thankfully, there are no pigs. The rumours were false. Given the ties between my family and his, I'm amazed I've never been in his house before. Why wasn't I brought up to think of him as an uncle, as is customary in rural Welsh communities? That in itself is odd. *Did Mam also suspect him of being a paedophile after Dad died? Is that why I was kept away from him?* She'd strenuously denied this at the graveyard, and I can hardly suspect her of collaborating with a known child abuser, she loves me far too much to ever put me in any danger, so I try to give him the benefit of the doubt, even though I've always sensed there was something strange about him.

'Does your mam know you're here?' he grunts at last, like one of his prize rare breed pigs.

'Does she need to?' I ask sharply. 'It's not like I'm a child any longer.'

'I've noticed,' he responds drily, then flushes as he realises this could be taken sexually. I don't react, since I know this is not how he intended it. It occurs to me then that he is just as awkward around me as I have been with him over the years. *Why is that?*

'Milk and three sugars, right?' he inquires.

I'm touched that he remembers my favourite childhood beverage. Who'd have guessed . . . 'Green tea if you have it.'

His expression tells me there's no chance of that. 'Builders it is then.' I offer him a one-shouldered shrug. 'No sugar or milk, thanks.'

When he turns his back on me to switch on the kettle, I walk over to the antique Victorian mahogany dining table and settle on one of the rickety chairs to watch him. A strand of blue wool hangs from a tatty hole in his jumper on the shoulder. His uncombed black hair has tufts sticking up from it, much like a moulting dog. In his own environment, he appears to be rather vulnerable. As a result, I no longer regard him as intimidating. Certainly not the feared ogre of my childhood and adolescence. I'm not really sure where I got that impression of him — except that Mam was always urging me not to bother him, since he had a lot on his mind. But she never said what. I had to find that out for myself, at school when all of us local kids got together and decided to mould him into something of a monster. Just for being socially awkward.

When he plonks a mug of tea in front of me on the table, spilling it and not caring, he leans back against the wall and slurps his drink. We stare at each other over our mugs, not saying anything, and I gather that standing up while entertaining visitors is a habit for him, normal even, but it makes me uncomfortable, so I get to my feet, cradling my mug in my hand, and ask, 'Shall we go into the living room so we can talk?'

I can tell he's surprised by this as it puts me in charge. After thinking about it for a second or two — *his expression is so readable* — he gestures for me to follow.

'It's a drawing room, technically.' He reveals this while fluffing up the cushions on the ox-blood Chesterfield sofa and signals for me to take a seat on it while selecting a green velvet-fringed recliner for himself, that happens to match his eyes. The red walls, dark wood panelling, and heavily swagged curtains at the floor-to-ceiling windows transport me to another century. I suspect nothing has changed in this room since he inherited Forest Farm from his elderly mother who allegedly moved in high circles.

'What did you want to talk to me about?' he asks, trying to regain control of the situation.

I take a deep breath and try not to look at his fly, which has come undone, but my gaze childishly keeps returning to it. He'd be so embarrassed if he knew. 'Mam told me about Dad and why he really killed himself,' I blurt out, hating having those words on my tongue.

'Bravo. Finally, she did the right thing.' He nods. 'I've been telling her for years that she should tell you the truth before you discovered it for yourself. I mean, no one should hear that kind of news second-hand.'

I'm both astonished and hurt that he's immediately on my side and seeing things from my perspective. Luke had been unable to do so, quickly jumping in to defend Mam, rather than support me.

'Why didn't you?' I challenge.

'Why didn't I what?

'Tell me.'

'That's not how we do things around here, Cerys. You know that.' He drains his tea and places the mug on a dainty coffee table with turned-out Queen-Anne legs that are not so different to Elvis's who is sitting at my side, bug-eyed, staring around the room.

I like the way Bryn says my name, with a soft lilting Welsh accent, not harsh the way Mam screeches it. I do believe he has never addressed me by my name before.

'On the mountain, we mind our own business and that's how it should be,' he murmurs, suddenly very distant, as if his mind is elsewhere. I can guess where . . .

I know all about his wife running off with another woman — the kids at school made a mountain out of a mole-hill out of it — and while it doesn't shock me, as it does some mountain folk, nobody, not even Mam, brings it up because he doesn't like to talk about it. Bryn is as private as they come when it comes to his personal life. My father was the only person he ever confided in, which is why I'm here now. I'd been hoping against all odds that Bryn would tell me none of what Mam told me is true. That she made it up just to spite me. Or that she got it wrong. My dad would never have done something like that. Never, ever, ever.

'I'll be honest with you, Cerys,' Bryn fumes. 'I would have killed Owen myself for doing what he did, and for putting your mam, and you, through something as diabolical as that. But the bloody coward beat me to it.'

# CHAPTER 25: BETH

Unlike at home, the church is festive and glittery. The cold stone walls are brightened by a sea of poinsettias and tall lit candles. Two Christmas trees glow on either side of the altar. Bryn would have dug up the trees on his farm and donated them to the church, as he does every year, even though he hasn't set foot inside it since losing his wife and daughter. I feel guilty, which is my annual contribution, that I haven't helped the church committee decorate, but my excuse is that I'm constantly tied up on the farm, and the fact is I'm not the flower-arranging kind. Unlike Cerys, I lack the ability to be creative. I suppose it wouldn't have hurt me to have volunteered to do some silver cleaning though.

The young reverend wears huge glasses and a life-is-good smile while clad in layers of vivid green robes that remind me of Bryn's eyes. His attire is significantly more colourful than anything I own. I'm not sure why Bryn is on my mind so much today when I have more serious worries, but he's the one I want to talk to the most — not my saviour. On that thought I remember to silently add a *please forgive me, Father,* just in case he's listening. The church is small, and we're crammed in like Emperor penguins in an icy huddle, shoulder to shoulder, beaks down. Despite the Christmassy ambience, the interior is cold, damp, and musty.

I've been coming here my entire life. I believe in Jesus and God, and I want more than anything to become a better person and live a righteous life, but I fail terribly at it. Bad thoughts. Terrible words. Selfish actions.

'In the name of the Father, the Son and the Holy spirit,' Reverend Green welcomes everyone to the eucharist service. I think of the Cluedo game whenever I hear his name. Ever since I was a young lass, I've always had my most inappropriate thoughts inside the walls of St Martin's. I'm not sure what that says about me as a Christian who regularly attends church.

'Amen,' we all mumble. There's a lot of neck craning and bum wiggling on seats. The church committee ladies adore a good-looking vicar, and I'm no different, except that I've sworn off men. Who could blame me?

'The Lord be with you.' Rev Green's young voice is clear and booming.

'And also, with you,' we reply.

'Almighty God to whom our hearts are open.'

My heart is open to Cerys, but I can't say the same for anyone else unfortunately, although I keep that thought to myself.

'All desires known and from whom no secrets are hidden . . .'

I fail spectacularly as a Christian from this point forward, since how am I supposed to enter his heavenly father's church with an open heart when I've never revealed my unholy secret to anyone, not even God? I rarely acknowledge it myself, even on my darkest days.

I don't join the congregation in the prayer of penitence because what I've done is not something God can forgive. I'm also not repentant. For that, I know I am going to hell. There is no mercy for us sinners.

'Let us pray,' Rev Green commands in the same elevated tone that all vicars use. They must study it at theological college.

*Here we go*, I think. Time for a good old chinwag. To get things off my chest privately. Following that, more prayers and forgiveness — *for some*. A Bible, Old Testament and New Testament reading, and a psalm, is followed by the vicar coming to stand in the centre of the congregation so we can all admire him. Rev Green is twenty-five years old and has bouncy, healthy, church-mouse brown hair. But he's here teaching us old dogs new tricks, so you have to take your hat off to him. I think the church committee ladies are wishing it was their necks when he kisses the book of the gospel before preaching the sermon. God help me for having such wicked thoughts.

I don't want him tapping me on the shoulder and exposing me as a sinner in front of these religious folk who've known me my whole life and believe I'm a devout, hard-working, God-fearing Christian, which I am, but I'm also the biggest sinner and liar on this mountain, so help me God.

A lump forms in my throat as prayers for our parish are read because many were spoken for myself and my family when Owen died. It took many months for me to be able to return to church knowing that some of the congregation would scrutinise and judge me. Not everyone sympathised with our circumstances. Some blamed us for the shame Owen brought upon the heads of our rural community. Most notably, mine.

Last prayers. Now we're talking. This is the part I've been looking forward to the most. Now, we're being told to turn to the side and shake the hand of the person standing next to us, and say, 'Peace be with you.' My neighbour is the toothless old boy who lives at the base of my mountain. When I take his hand, he winces as if in excruciating pain, the poor bugger. I make up my mind that I must do more for him. I hold his hand for a moment longer than is called for because I want him to feel loved, which must mean I'm not all bad, even though my daughter thinks I am.

'Let us first share peace before we share the body and blood of Christ.' Rev Green's voice reverberates throughout the church. Someone sneezes. Someone burps. Everyone pretends not to notice. Even the vicar.

When he uncovers the chalice and pours wine into it, I conjure up the memory of Luke's vampirish, red-stained wine lips. *Gross*, as my daughter would say. As the vicar relates the account of Jesus at the last supper with his disciples, with the breaking of bread and the pouring of wine, I recall the unpleasant tofu and jackfruit evenings I've had to endure and decide that Luke being in my house is the greatest sin of all. If anyone wants crucifying it's my son-in-law — the psychopath. When I realise the Lord's prayer is being said and I'm late to the table, I return my focus to the service.

'Our Father, who art in heaven, hallowed be thy name, thy kingdom come, thy will be done, on earth as it is in heaven. Give us this day our daily bread and forgive us our trespasses as we forgive those who trespass against us.'

Even as I repeat this, my mind is screaming — *never, ever, ever.*

'And lead us not into temptation but deliver us from evil . . .'

And what of the devil who lives in my farmhouse? How can I deliver my family from Luke's evil? Is that what God wants me to do to save Cerys, who is a heavenly angel if ever there was one?

'For thine is the kingdom, the power, and the glory. Amen.'

'Amen,' I mutter louder than I intended, and the vicar and my neighbours gaze at me as if they're wondering if I've finally surrendered to the Lord. If only they knew how much — because I swear, I've just experienced a heavenly intervention of some sort.

# CHAPTER 26: CERYS

The box of Christmas decorations full of old family favourites makes me nostalgic for the past and my perfect brought-up-on-a-farm childhood. Grandad used to say that I looked just like the beautiful, silvery-white, long-haired, fairy tree topper that came out every year as the showstopper. Then, there are the stouter, smiling, felt penguins, which Dad said reminded him of Mam. I brush away a tear from my eye at this point, sigh heavily, and proceed to decorate the living room — a snow globe on the coffee table, a robin on the mantelpiece and the wooden nativity set on the sideboard.

The living room is tired looking and in desperate need of some love. I wish Mam would do something with it. Get rid of the awful teal Anaglypta wallpaper and paint the walls a soft white. Change the sofa. Because it's still the same as it's always been, I'm expecting to see Dad and Grandad sitting there, each clutching a glass of black port, watching me and Mam put up the decorations as we did every year.

I reasoned that if I made the house more pleasant and inviting, Luke would be more likely to stay home and spend time in it with me. I'm kicking myself for forcing him to get a job so quickly; it could have waited until after Christmas, and now he'll be gone for the majority of it. He said that it was the busiest time of year for hospitality, and I had no choice but to accept this if I wanted him to keep his job. But he'd also implied that Mam was made of money and could help out more if she wanted to, which I know isn't the case. She's struggled financially for years, and the costly divorce didn't help, though I never mentioned this to him.

According to Mam, he'd dragged it out, and what should have cost a grand and a half ended up costing thousands more. Why didn't he just agree to the divorce and be done with it? I've never asked him. She had grounds (adultery), but he denied it, despite the pregnancy. Therefore she had to divorce him for unreasonable behaviour. This was before no-blame divorces came into effect. I can't imagine divorcing Luke simply for being unfaithful. He must be right about Mam not loving him enough to attempt to work things out. Luke claims I have unrealistic expectations about romantic love, but he only says this when he sees he isn't providing me with the life he promised me. I never imagined in my wildest dreams when I married him that we would land up living here, on the farm, although it suits me to do so, but I begin to suspect that this was his intention all along. The question is, why? Is he after Mam's money? He's never made a secret of the fact that he thinks she owes him. Or is he up to something far worse?

I stiffen as I hear the kitchen back door open, accompanied by the sounds of dogs barking, whining, spilling of bowls, and sniffing at doors, indicating that they have detected my presence — and I feel like a child caught out in some wrongdoing, like the time I crayoned all the walls in my bedroom. Elvis rushes to the door just in time to greet them as Mam enters, windblown and dishevelled, and without her boots, which she must have removed outside.

'I didn't think you were here,' I exclaim, embarrassed because I've been deliberately avoiding her, which is impossible given that we live in the same house. 'The Defender's not here,' I end lamely.

'Luke borrowed it for work,' Mam says, her eyes hitting the carpet.

‘He must be working his magic on you,’ is all I can say.

‘I didn’t need it today so it wasn’t a big deal.’

It absolutely is and we both know it. Even I have never been allowed behind its wheel! But I decide not to press her on it. That’ll have to wait until Luke gets home later tonight when I’ll force an explanation out of him. He has a long 12 p.m. to 10 p.m. shift today.

‘The room looks nice, love,’ Mam says, gazing around.

‘Thanks.’ I move away from her, concentrating on putting up more decorations. ‘I was hoping Luke could get us a tree for in here if that’s all right with you.’

‘Yes, of course, I’ll help you decorate it if you like.’

I can’t help but pull a face. When it comes to creative efforts, Mam is worse than a child.

‘I know I’m not particularly good at it, but I’ll give it a go. I could do the top branches, if you like, to save you from stretching,’ Mam suggests, motioning to my stomach.

‘That’s really sweet of you, but . . . it’s just that, well, it’s mine and Luke’s first Christmas, and I thought . . .’ I leave her hanging because I’m unable to squeeze the rest of my sentence out.

‘You thought you’d decorate it together?’ she states matter-of-factly as if it’s of no importance to her, but I don’t buy it. ‘Fine by me,’ she adds, unperturbed.

I don’t like the way she’s rolling her eyes, as if she knows Luke better than I do, and that he won’t want to help with the decorating. My shoulders go up. *We’ll see about that . . .*

‘Is everything okay, Mam?’ I ask, sensing that there is more to it than that. Now that I think about it, she appears on edge and jumpy.

‘What could be wrong?’ She smiles at me in an unsettling way, seeming to know something I don’t.

I’m tempted to tell Mam about my worries that Luke is drifting away from me, that he’s already bored with me, and that I suspect he might be seeing someone else, even though we’ve only been here five minutes so I know that’s absurd. And I would tell her all of this and more if she weren’t one of Luke's exes. How did things get so complicated? Instead of being married and pregnant, I should be finishing my university degree, focusing on my studies and my ambition of becoming a vet. It's not that I regret marrying Luke or having the baby, it's simply that things haven't turned out the way I expected.

When Mam shrugs off her wax jacket and walks over to the antique wall mirror, tugging at a stray curl, I find myself looking at her, *really* looking at her, as if for the first time. For years, Dad and I mocked her, saying she was more like a man than a woman, a workhorse, a grafter, everyone's favourite lumberjack — but she's actually extremely attractive in an earthy, natural way. Her eyes, which are a couple of shades darker than mine, are expressive and kind. As Luke had pointed out the other night, she has a wonderful body for her age. Despite having savagely short hair, it suits her. *My God, she's beautiful,* in a Keely-Hawes-the-actress way. How come I never noticed that before?

She's uncomplicated, not high-maintenance and needy to be around, like me, so I can see why she'd appeal to men, though I've never given her credit for this before because she's just, well . . . Mam. She may not realise it, but for years, half of the men on this mountain have been in love with her. Nor is she as unfeminine as I've unfairly described her. She may be super strong and independent but there's a vulnerability about her too. People are moved by her kindness as she goes out of her way to help others no matter who they are, even waifs and strays like me and Luke, who haven't always been deserving of her forgiveness. She might be blunt and to the point but she is genuine and always keeps her word.

Shame creeps up on me when I consider how I've always felt superior to her, what with my fancy private school education, but Mam was the glue that held our family together, not me, I realise now. There would have been no farmhouse, farm, prize-winning horses, or idyllic — *until it wasn't* — childhood without Mam. This fresh perspective on the incredible woman standing before me is humbling for me.

And now that I see her for who she is, she is a stranger to me. Not just somebody's mother, but a woman in her own right — competition even.

Because if I can see her that way, Luke will as well. Why had I never thought of her in that light before?

# CHAPTER 27: BETH

When I notice my daughter observing me from the corner of her eye, with an unfamiliar expression on her face, I'm intrigued. Something is clearly bothering her that she doesn't want me to know about. She's trying so hard to be casual, she gives herself away, which leads me to ask hesitantly, 'Where did you go earlier?'

Her lips open in surprise and she shuffles away from me, which is a defensive tactic if ever I saw one. 'It's okay, you don't have to tell me. I was just making conversation.'

'To Bryn's. I went to Bryn's,' Cerys blurts out, without looking at me.

'What did you do that for?' I say, immediately on edge.

'Because, understandably, you don't like talking about what happened with Dad, so I thought I'd ask him if he knew anything more,' she replies, sounding panicked.

'And did he?' I raise an eyebrow in disapproval.

'No, not really,' she sighs.

'I don't like the idea of you being alone in that house with him.'

'Why? He's harmless, isn't he?' Cerys's voice trembles with anxiety.

'I'd hardly have him come to the house if he wasn't.' No matter how hard I try, I can't get rid of the prickly tone. Cerys has touched on a sore subject. *She needs to stay away from Bryn.*

'That doesn't answer my question, Mam,' Cerys insists, with the subtlest stamp of a foot which reminds me of the stubborn, pampered little girl she used to be, whom I used to adore. And still miss.

'He's just a bit odd that's all. Too much time spent around pigs.' I attempt a joke.

Cerys has narrowed her eyes at me and appears to be trying to sum me up. *Good luck with that,* I think. I've inhabited myself for the last fifty years and I'm still no closer to finding out who I really am. *Does anyone?*

'You've always tried to keep me away from him, yet he seems nice. Like a friendly uncle.'

'You've changed your tune,' I observe dryly, thinking, *Uncle my eye — over my dead body*. 'But you needn't have bothered Bryn. You know you can ask me anything, Cerys.'

'Can I though, Mam?' This is said in a challenging tone.

'Yes. Haven't I always said so?'

'And if it was about Luke?'

I know my daughter. Tears are on their way. I wonder what Luke has done to upset her this time. I remind myself to be gentle with her and so I respond softly, 'Ask away.' Even though her marriage is the last thing I want to talk about right now.

She sighs, her shoulders unwinding. 'It doesn't matter.'

Instead of the ethereal, shining light I'm used to seeing reflected in Cerys's sky-blue eyes, I see nothing but sadness. This is torturous to witness when she has so much going for her. Didn't she get the grades she needed for her first-choice university? Isn't it true that she was voted prom queen three years in a row? When she was thirteen, she was offered a modelling career, which she declined, because it went against her values. Hadn't she won a slew of silver trophies on her horse, Zorro, for winning show jumping competitions? All of those achievements indicate to me that my daughter could have had an amazing life. It was hers for the taking. And now she's married to Luke with a baby on the way and has dropped out of university after diligently studying for her degree. Thinking about how much she has sacrificed makes me want to cry. And for what? A man like Luke Griffin who is unworthy of her. And who has abused her vulnerability.

Then, all of a sudden, I notice that Cerys's eyes are brimming with guts and determination. The first thing that comes to me is that my daughter has a strong backbone after all, which is something to be celebrated.

'What is it, Cerys?'

'Nothing,' she responds absentmindedly, snatching a set of keys from the sideboard. 'I'm just going out for a while.'

'Would you like me to come with you?'

'No. Thank you, though,' she says, remembering her manners. 'I'll be back shortly.'

And then she's gone. Leaving the Christmas decorations incomplete. The living room appears tired and dreary now that Cerys's beauty and presence are no longer in it. I should do something about it. Paint the walls. Change the sofa. If only life were as simple . . . Loathe your daughter's husband: change him; want him gone from your life, your farm: erase him — *which is how I interpreted God's words of wisdom this morning at church.*

I hadn't told Cerys the truth when I said I'd agreed Luke could take the Defender because I absolutely wouldn't have let him. She was right to question me.

'I'm taking the Defender,' he'd informed me earlier this morning, the keys already dangling from his hand. The challenge to my authority was a difficult pill to take, but I swallowed it meekly, without saying a word.

Now that I know he's a psychopath — he has to be to say and do the things he's said and done — and dangerous with it, he's left me no choice but to go along with his demands for the time being. My primary concern is Cerys's safety. My pride comes second to protecting her. Luke believes he has me just where he wants me, but he's in for a surprise. It'll only be a matter of time before I persuade Cerys of his true intentions, but I have to tread carefully . . . there's no telling how she'll react when she realises her husband is in love with her mother, *or thinks he is*. Luke was right when he said Cerys wouldn't believe me *now*; I don't agree that she hates me, but as they say, time will tell. Until then I'll have to put up with his snarling victory smiles.

He believes he has me terrified of my own shadow, but he couldn't be more wrong. The only thing I've ever been afraid of is losing Cerys, of her being wounded or sad. Cerys bouncing off a horse and fracturing her arm. Cerys cutting a finger and having it plastered. Only a mother physically and emotionally experiences the pain of her children, as if it were her own.

Men come and go in your life, loved ones die, and friends like Bryn temporarily fill the emptiness, but only one person truly matters to me in this world — my daughter. You can love certain animals, your dogs, maybe the odd cat or two, even a horse (not Zorro . . .) but it's not the same intense, protective, all-consuming love you feel for your child. Cerys will realise all of this for herself when her baby is born, and she will be wary of Luke then, knowing on a deeper, subconscious level that he will abandon and hurt them one day, using his power over her and the child to manipulate her — until all of her shining light has gone out.

I'll see him dead before that happens.

# CHAPTER 28: CERYS

Mam is nicer to me than I deserve, when I repeatedly have toxic thoughts about her, like just now, when she paused before saying I could ask her questions about Luke, which indicated to me she either didn't want to or had something to hide. Is she still holding a candle for him? Is it reciprocated? I'm not imagining things when I catch them exchanging glances that are meant to exclude me. But she's my mam, so she wouldn't . . . couldn't . . . entertain the idea of her and Luke getting back together. *Could she?* Even if she still loves him, she loves me more.

Knowing this makes me feel horrible about myself, which is a novel experience for me. Why, why, why did I think it was acceptable for me to marry my mother's ex-husband once I realised who he was? When I put myself in her shoes, which I've been unable to do until now, perhaps because I'm carrying my own child, I don't know how I could have convinced myself it was a moral thing to do. The uncomfortable fact is that I'm starting to discover new and challenging aspects of my personality, which I suppose is a sign that I'm finally maturing and getting to know the real me. Just as well, given that, I'll be responsible for a new human being in five months.

I'm on my way to see Luke at the Bear in Crickhowell. I intend to have it out with him. Make him tell me the truth. Admit any feelings he has towards Mam. I haven't thought beyond that, and don't want to. First things first . . .

The pink car smoothly slides down the mountain, but I know it won't be as easy to get it to go back up. It was not designed for this type of terrain and lacks power. I'll exchange it for something more appropriate when we can afford it. Perhaps a family hatchback. Luke was right to be dismissive about the colour and the vehicle type. It screams *Princess*, which I now find embarrassing as I lost the right to that crown when I married Mam's ex and paraded him in front of her broken heart.

But when we first met, I had no idea who Luke was, and by the time we figured it out together, it was too late — we were in love. Luke then insisted that we keep our relationship a secret from Mam, knowing she would flip out on us. He was convinced I'd cave under pressure and break things off with him which he claimed would break his heart. He'd joked that he wouldn't be able to recover if he were rejected by two generations of Williams women, which I found endearing at the time. Not so much now.

When Mam married again, I had already left for Singapore on the first leg of our college class of 2019 world tour, which Grandad had funded. I was eighteen at the time, and while Mam was concerned about my trip overseas and missed me dearly, she would never have thought of holding me back. We chatted frequently via text and FaceTime. It wasn't until I returned home that she admitted those years without me had been the worst of her life. Meanwhile, I was having a great time, and our trip kept getting extended as we all found work in Australia. My university was cool about keeping my course open indefinitely because I'd been such a fantastic student, receiving the highest grades possible. All was good.

Four months into my trip, Mam met this new bloke called Luke. And they had a whirlwind romance ending in a marriage that was doomed from the start, *unlike mine*. She revealed to me later that she never should have married him. It wasn't love, but lust. This was obviously long before I ever met him. I was devastated when she first told me she'd met someone else because it felt disrespectful to my dad.

Things were fine while she had me because I was enough for her, but once I got on that plane, Mam became lonely, and Luke was the result of that loneliness. Our gap year somehow turned into three which meant we had boyfriends, flats, jobs, and everything. I was seriously considering staying out there, because, of course, I was in love with my then boyfriend, Sam, or thought I was — *when wasn't I head over heels?* Except Luke was different. He was the real deal. *The one.*

But when Grandad died, it brought back the anguish of losing Dad, and I had to return home to attend his funeral and say goodbye. It was also time to say goodbye to my fictitious life in Oz, for as soon as my feet touched English and then Welsh soil, I knew I wasn't truly in love with Sam. It was time to return to my old life, to the farm, to Mam, and to attend university, so I could become the equine vet I'd always wanted to be.

Given their shared history, I decide not to hold it against Luke if he still has unresolved feelings for Mam. But because I love deeply, I find it difficult to understand how some people hurt those they claim to love the most. It does happen though. Look at Mam. Look at Luke. At the same time, I'm resolved that it will not happen to Luke and me. Sometimes you have to meet the right one to *know*, and then it doesn't matter who you were with before. Most people would understand this, but not Mam.

As I pull into the pub car park, I acknowledge even to myself that my emotions are a jumble of contradictions that exhaust me. For the first time, it occurs to me that showing up unexpectedly at Luke's workplace to ask him if he is in love with my mother would be not only unwise but insane. I decide to just pop in and say a friendly hello instead.

My first reaction on entering the pub is that everything is a glossy walnut brown. There are big squashy leather sofas, gentle lighting, and burnt-orange soft furnishings. Meanwhile, a log fire throws out toasty heat. I've only been here a couple of times with my family and we always sat outside because it was summer, so I've never seen the inside. Although traditional and nice, it doesn't seem the right fit for Luke, who prefers trendy neon-lit wine bars full of young people who look like me. The next thing I notice is that everyone on the crew is dressed in the same black uniform as Luke but he's nowhere to be seen. I'm immediately suspicious. Has he lied to me about his whereabouts? *Does he even have a job?*

My anxiety spirals as I search for his glossy blond locks amid all the drab brown heads in the lounge and bar areas, and my heart settles in my chest when I finally locate him seated in a bay window seat, heads together with a female colleague, who is also dressed completely in black. He must be on a well-deserved break. I'm about to approach them, and say 'Hi,' when I notice what they're up to . . .

# CHAPTER 29: BETH

The wind whips my face and cold rain clings to my eyelashes as I drop the heavy metal post knocker down onto the bent wooden post. *Once, twice, three times* . . . and rest. It's hard labour but it's necessary otherwise the sheep will soon be able to escape over the fence. This section of the field isn't electrocuted. As I look up at the dark clouds, I long for summer and warmer months. It's been a particularly harsh winter on the mountain — cold, wet, icy, bracing winds. In another three months, it will be the lambing season. I have thirty ewes, all pregnant, which means there's plenty of work coming my way — I could end up with sixty lambs on my hands. I love helping to bring new life into the world though. Just as Cerys used to.

Gypsy is herding the sheep and bothering them, I can hear their agitated bleating, so I yell, 'That'll do,' to call her off and she immediately comes to heel, although she doesn't stop eying them. Meanwhile, Toad hugs my side, his wet dog smell clinging to my jeans. I can't get my mind off what Luke said when he implied it was him who killed my old German Shepherd. Poor Wolf. He was so very protective of me. Could Luke really have done such a dreadful thing as to deliberately run him over? Or did he make it up just to intimidate me? I suppose I'll never know. He is capable of booting a dog, however, as I caught him in the act myself.

I can see the farmhouse in the lower valley from where I stand but it's the ever-watchful Gypsy who spots the pink car stampede into the yard first. Her stalking eyes dart to me, pleading for permission, which I grant. 'Away.'

As she races off to find Cerys, I'm not far behind. There's something about the way the small figure in the distance slams into the house that bothers me. *Now what's wrong?* When I notice Cerys has left the car door open, I speed up. She must have been in a state not to have shut it properly.

'Cerys,' I shout, frantically removing my muddy boots before entering the house. 'Cerys.'

I hurriedly wash and dry my hands in the kitchen sink before going in search of my daughter. 'Cerys, love. Are you there?' She isn't in the living room or the snug. I don't bother checking the dining room as we only ever use it on Christmas Day. I climb the stairs and peer into Tad's bedroom, I'll never think of it as Luke and Cerys's. My gaze is drawn to the bed, which Cerys has made beautifully, and I try not to picture what goes on in it. *Where is she?* I'm bewildered until I hear a faint sob coming down the hallway. I open the door to Cerys's old bedroom, hit once more by the shock of sherbet pink, as I am every time I enter this room.

My daughter is nose-down on the patchwork quilt, her eyes hidden in the pillow, her body heaving with sobs.

'Cerys, what's the matter?' I implore, moving over to sit next to her on the bed, my hand naturally settling in a patting gesture on her back.

'Mam,' she cries, turning around to hurl herself into my arms. I wrap my arms around her, feeling her pregnant stomach press against my waist for the first time. In that moment I'm overcome with love for both of them. I want to shield them from the world. Most notably from Luke.

'What is it, sweetheart? What's happened?'

'It's Luke.' She snivels into her sleeve.

I don't say, *I might have known,* even if that's what I'm thinking because I doubt it would be warmly received. Instead, I stroke her damp, clingy hair away from her red-rimmed eyes and whisper, 'Tell me.'

'I caught him . . .' Cerys bites down on her knuckle, unable to speak. I haven't seen my daughter this distraught in a long time, not since her grandad died.

'Oh, God, no,' I gasp, having come to my own conclusion about what Luke has done. It's what I've been hoping for and dreading at the same time. 'You caught him with another woman.'

'Mam, no.' Cerys angrily pulls away from me, turning to face the bright-as-popping-candy pink wall that has her name on it in lights. 'How could you? I mean why would you jump to that conclusion? I've told you before . . . Luke isn't like that with me.'

I shrug, indicating that I'm stumped, not sorry. 'So, what *has* he done then?' I demand, a slight edge to my voice because Cerys had implied Luke would cheat on *me*, but not *her.* I know how special my daughter is, but it was pretty darn insensitive of her.

'I know you think Luke is all bad, but—'

*I know so.* And I'd like to remind her I have good reason to think so. Not only because he's a liar and a cheater, but also because the bastard is using Cerys to get at me. But, of course, I remain silent.

'I'm listening, Cerys,' I prompt her.

When her shoulders slump and her eyes well up with pitiful tears, I forget about Luke and pull her back into my arms, thinking how I would die for her. I just want her to be happy and for the tears to stop. Seeing her like this makes me feel so helpless.

'Poor baby,' I mutter as I rub her arm.

'I went to the Bear in Crickhowell to see Luke,' she finally confesses.

I do a doubletake. 'You did?'

'And when I got there, he was on a break with a female co-worker . . .'

Ah. Here we go. Now we're getting to the meat of the matter. Luke's mask is starting to drop. Is this the beginning of the end, I wonder? If that's the case, praise God.

'And . . .'

'And?'

'Mam, he was eating a burger.'

'A burger?' I'm gobsmacked. 'That was the last thing I expected to hear.'

'I know.' Cerys misinterprets my reaction. She seems to think I share her outrage, but I don't. Not really.

'A beef burger.' Cerys is fuming. 'Not Quorn, but *proper meat*.'

After that, I pretend to be as offended as my daughter, who rants for ten minutes about how betrayed she feels. Asking herself over and over again why he pretended to be a vegetarian when he clearly wasn't. Describing how she feels unclean as a result of his lies. I realise how much this means to Cerys but in the grand scheme of things it's hardly significant enough to merit all this commotion, at least in my opinion. But she's only twenty-three and has a lot of maturing to do so she obviously sees things differently. I, on the other hand, have always known my former meat-and-two-veg husband was not the plant-based diet type. He was never going to be able to keep that pretence up for long.

As Cerys vents her anger, I listen faithfully, even as I smile inwardly — because that spoiled little girl is still in there — but feel my shoulders deflate as I recognise how disappointed I am that Luke's transgression isn't much worse.

'I knew he was lying about being a vegetarian when he said he had no idea what tofu was. I just knew it,' Cerys seethes as she grabs a fistful of duvet and wrings it. That's what I'd like to do to my son-in-law's neck. But not for eating a burger.

## CHAPTER 30: CERYS

I'm wrapping Christmas presents on the rug in front of the fire. One for Luke. One for Mam. And one for each of the dogs. Elvis, dressed in a green Elf outfit, chomps on a squeaky toy beside me. Every third or fourth heartbeat, the toy emits a high-pitched squeak, but I'm relaxed enough for it not to bother me. I've had plenty of time to calm down after catching Luke out at the pub as it's now late evening and he's due back from his shift at any moment.

He's already texted me dozens of apologies, to which I haven't yet responded. It won't hurt him to stew for a while. But I've already decided to forgive him for "falling off the waggon," as Mam refers to it. He obviously needs my help kicking the nasty meat-eating habit for good. At least now I know why his breath had been stinking for days. He needn't think about kissing me until he's returned to being a full-time vegan, or at the very least a vegetarian.

Because we don't have much money, Luke and I agreed that no extravagant gifts would be purchased this year; however, because it's our first Christmas together, I wanted to mark the occasion with something special, so I'd spent the last of my inheritance on an ethically sourced silver letter "L" pendant necklace for him from Wild Fawn. It cost slightly over 100 pounds, money we don't have, but I see it as an investment in our future together. I hope Mam isn't mad when she finds out. After all, we're not paying her any rent. I might make out it was a lot cheaper to be on the safe side. *Sorry, Mam.* Right now, she's drinking tea in the kitchen with Bryn. I hope he leaves before Luke gets home. Those two have never gotten along. It's almost ten already so he's cutting it fine, but I'm sure Mam is keeping an eye on the clock.

I sigh with relief when I hear the scrape of a chair being pushed back and the sound of the back door opening. When I told Mam that I'd been to Bryn's house, I was careful to avoid mentioning how disapproving he was of her not telling me about Dad sooner, as I didn't want to get him into trouble. It's odd that the man I used to dislike, not hate — that's far too strong a term — I now find myself protecting. I'm actually looking forward to getting to know him better and I felt strangely at ease in his dusty old house, complete with century-old furniture and blood-red walls.

I finish writing the gift cards on the presents and place them next to where the Christmas tree will go, over by the large bay window with the cushioned reading seat that nobody ever uses. I don't recall seeing Mam take up a book in a long time. Unlike Dad and me, she isn't a big reader. She doesn't even keep a Bible next to her bed, even though she is supposed to be a practising Christian. A few minutes later, I hear the sound of the Defender speeding too fast into the farmyard. Mam exits the kitchen as soon as Luke's hand lands on the doorknob. It brings me comfort to know she doesn't want to be around him. She wouldn't avoid him if she were in love with him. Or perhaps the reverse is true and she's trying to get his attention by ignoring him . . . except that doesn't sound like Mam. Whichever way I look at it I can't seem to win.

'I brought you a cup of your favourite herbal tea,' Mam says as she enters the room.

'Thanks, Mam.' I beam, appreciating how nice it is to be looked after, even though my cheeks are on fire from my earlier thoughts about her and Luke. She is so good to me: the lit fire; the hot tea; the vegan lasagne she made me for dinner; the squeaky dog toy for Elvis.

Mam then sits in her favourite recliner, picking up a magazine from a rack on the floor and pretending to read it. I get the impression she's merely here to function as a buffer in case Luke and I get into a fight. I'm about to reassure her that this isn't going to happen and that I'm not going to kick off again when Luke walks in, looking very apologetic.

'Hey, you,' he whispers, his gaze fixed only on me, which is all I've ever wanted.

'Hey, you.' I smile up at him to let him know he's no longer in the doghouse. I don't offer to make him a drink or ask if he wants something to eat, and nor does Mam because it'll all go downhill from there, as he'll probably say he's already eaten. Then I might go off on one, demanding to know *exactly* what he had eaten.

'It's very Christmassy in here,' he observes, glancing sideways at Mam.

'Don't look at me. Cerys did it all herself.' Mam exudes pride.

'Well done.' Luke nods his approval.

'I was thinking of getting a tree. We can go tomorrow on your day off if you like,' I suggest, but when I see Luke wince, I know something's up.

'Sorry. They're short-staffed so I'm having to go in.'

'That's a shame,' Mam mutters.

'Well, maybe we could go on Christmas Eve. There's still time.'

'Absolutely we can.' Luke collapses onto the sofa, exhausted. I notice he hasn't taken his shoes off, which is a house rule, and I know Mam's spotted this too because of her indignant expression. *Why doesn't he think?* It's me that gets it in the neck when he irritates her. Not him. She can hardly tell him off.

'Did you get my messages,' Luke asks quietly, flinching in annoyance whenever Elvis's toy squeaks.

'I did, thanks,' I say this noncommittedly.

Luke's mouth tightens into a grimace. 'How come you didn't respond? I was worried.'

I narrow my eyes at him and pull a face that suggests *not in front of Mam*, but his frown just climbs higher so I decide to change the subject.

'I saved a few last baubles,' I enthuse, holding out an assortment of Christmas decorations for him to approve. 'I thought we could finish them together tonight.'

'I can't think of anything I'd like more, sweetheart,' Luke replies.

I flash Mam a victorious grin. *There. See. I told you he would* . . . but she's staring at Luke, not at me. When I return my attention to my husband, I realise why — he's furious. I'd stupidly missed the sarcasm in his voice.

'I've just done a twelve-hour shift, Cerys, and you want me to mess about with poncy Christmas decorations?' Luke jerks to his feet, his eyes as mean as hell. 'Seriously? I don't think so.'

Mam walks out of the room with her nose in the air. She does not want to witness my humiliation, and for that I am grateful. I've been humbled yet again. And it's entirely my fault. She was right all along, about Luke not wanting to help with the decorations, and it's a bitter pill for any grown-up daughter to have to swallow.

'There's no need to raise your voice,' I sulk after Mam has left.

'Isn't there? I happen to disagree. You show up uninvited at my workplace, make a scene because you caught me eating a burger, and then ignore my texts all day . . .'

Luke pauses mid-argument when the toy squeaks again, three times in a row this time. It acts like a fuse, igniting his rage.

'Am I supposed to put up with this fucking squeaking all bloody night too?' Luke yells, lashing out with his foot and stamping on the toy, but also accidentally catching Elvis's leg. The dog cries out in fear, rather than pain.

'Luke!' I chastise, stooping to pick Elvis up.

'To make matters worse,' he continues hotly, 'neither my wife nor my mother-in-law can be bothered to offer me a cup of tea, let alone a bite to eat after I've been on my feet all day.'

'It's just as well you ate a high-protein meal earlier in the day then, isn't it?' I snap, getting back on my high horse.

'If you believe giving up being a vegan for one day is the worst thing that could happen, you've got a lot of growing up to do.'

And with that, Luke storms out of the room.

# CHAPTER 31: BETH

It's finally Christmas Eve. The New Year will be here soon. I, for one, am impatient for it. As far as I'm concerned, this year can piss right off. I've ridden Zorro to the top of the mountain, feeling that I deserve a break from the demands of the house and farm, as well as some respite from Luke's presence, which pervades the house even when he's not there.

I've spent the last day and a half slaving over a hot stove, preparing everything for our Christmas celebrations, if they can be called that. The turkey crown is in the cold store, so Cerys doesn't have to come face to face with it. It smells of lemons and herbs and . . . well . . . dead flesh. This morning, the mince pies came out of the oven in a lovely brown cinnamon glaze and the brandy-steeped Christmas pudding is ready to steam.

Cerys and I had a fun time preparing everything yesterday while Luke was at work. She'd kept me company by chopping vegetables and making the egg-free Yorkshire pudding mix at the kitchen table while I handled the heavier, hot work. We were listening to Christmas music in the background, and I sneaked a cheeky sherry or two while Cerys wasn't looking. She even allowed me to feel the baby kick. When that happened, my heart swelled in my chest.

Cerys had confided in me then, that the main reason she didn't want to find out the gender of her baby before giving birth was because Luke desperately wanted a boy. She didn't want to see the look of disappointment on his face if the midwife or doctor announced it was a girl during a routine scan. She's confident that he won't care what sex it is when he sees it being born, and I'm inclined to agree. Who couldn't fall in love with a baby, regardless of gender?

When I first mounted Zorro, he was on fire, flinging his head around, pawing the ground, and bucking, so I gave him his head as soon as his hooves hit the grass. After a long gallop uphill, I brought him back under control. He's frothing at the mouth and drenched in perspiration, but he's calmed down enough for me to take my eye off him long enough to look down into the dip of the valley where Pen-y-Bryn sits. The farmhouse and the land surrounding it have been in my family for generations and it means the world to me.

A thin mist, the colour of milky tea, clings to the rugged mountain ridges, but it has broken up in spots to reveal a dark blue sky beyond. Sugar Loaf Mountain's distinctive peak is not visible today. The magic of these black mountains never ceases to astound me — every time my gaze is drawn to them, it's as if I've never seen them before. They're in mine and Cerys's blood. The colours of the landscape range from green in summer sunlight to purple in late summer, then to russet when the bracken dies in late autumn, and finally to bright white in winter if snow has fallen. Tad always said that the best way to recall the layout of the mountains was to envision your right hand flat on a table with your fingers spread apart.

Cat's Back is your thumb. Hatterall is the name of your first finger. Ffawyddog is your second finger, with Bal-mawr at the knuckle. The Gader ridge is on your third finger. Your little finger is Allt-mawr, and your nail, *my favourite*, is Crug Hywell, which gives its name to the town of Crickhowell, where Cerys and Luke have gone to buy a Christmas tree.

*So, who is that in the farmyard then?* I lean forward onto Zorro's glossy-black neck for a closer look. He's seen the distant figure too. As a result, his ears are pricked and his nostrils have flared. He'll believe it's Cerys. But they can't possibly be back yet. There's also no sign of the Defender in the yard, which Luke now refers to as *his* in an attempt to get a reaction out of me. It doesn't work. The only vehicle I can see is the abandoned pink car that everyone's turned their nose up at.

'Come on, Zorro. Let's find out who it is.' I click my tongue and squeeze my calves against his ribcage — and into a canter, we go.

We're clip-clopping into the yard a few minutes later, but there's no one around, so I dismount and take him into his stable, where I untack him, lay a horse rug over him and leave him nibbling on a net of hay.

I'm uneasy about seeing a stranger on the property and them disappearing again, and I'm about to head over to the house to make sure no one has broken in, although that's unlikely with the dogs locked inside it, but when I turn the corner of the stable, I walk straight into a woman.

'Jesus Christ!' I squeal and leap backwards.

'I'm sorry, I didn't mean to scare you,' she exclaims, raising both hands in surrender, as if worried I might shoot her. She's lucky I don't have my gun on me today.

'You nearly gave me a heart attack,' I accuse harshly while weighing her up. She doesn't look like she comes from around here. "Town," is stamped all over her. From her heeled boots and faux-fur jacket to her strawberry blonde highlights that appear to be fresh out of foils.

'Well, if it makes you feel any better, I happen to be a nurse.' She laughs cheerfully, and I warm to her.

'Can I help you? I'm the owner of this house. I live here,' I feel compelled to explain, even though it should be obvious.

'Miss Parry.' She introduces herself by extending a hand that ends in too-long manicured fingernails, which I ignore, for now, and she drops it, on a long exhale.

'Mrs Williams,' I offer, finding it odd that a woman who is similar in age to myself should identify herself using her surname; not her first name. Each to their own, I suppose. 'Now, how can I help you?' Though I am curious as to what she's doing here, I do also have a hundred and one things to do.

She winces and wrings her hands as if she's nervous. 'I'm afraid you're going to be rather angry with me.'

'Why?'

'I heard it on good authority, and I won't say from whom in case it gets them in trouble, but I understand you have a holiday cabin that you let out.'

'Yes, that's right,' I confirm, curious as to who told her that.

'And I understand it's currently empty?' She poses this as a question.

'It is as it happens. Why do you ask?'

'I know it's incredibly short notice but I was hoping you might rent it to me for Christmas week. I'll pay you extra for the inconvenience.' She looks at me pleadingly.

'That's highly irregular. Normally, I use a booking agent to manage everything for me. Guest details. Payment, and so on,' I explain, but I can sense she's not paying attention to any of my concerns.

'I can pay in cash.' She pulls an envelope out of her shoulder bag and shows me the plethora of crisp notes it contains. My eyes boggle. A cash payment would mean no agency fee.

'You've left it a bit late,' I say cautiously, thinking we could do with the money, but the cabin isn't ready to be let. The bed needs making up. The log burner needs cleaning. It'll be very cold inside. Bad reviews are not worth the extra cash. They're not good for business.

'I'm a writer with a deadline to meet so I thought that if I isolated myself in the countryside with no distractions, I might be able to finish my book on time.'

'I thought you said you were a nurse,' I challenge.

'Both.' She shrugs helplessly, making deer-like eyes at me as if she knows I'm the mothering sort who can't stop herself from taking care of people.

'There'll be nowhere open this time of year. Not at Christmas,' I warn.

'I know, I brought my own supplies. I have everything I could ever want. My car is parked out on the road.' She flutters a hand in its direction.

'On one condition,' I bark, making a snap decision, not only because eight or nine hundred pounds, depending on how much she tips me, isn't to be sniffed at, but also because I'm genuinely intrigued by her.

She chuckles and makes a childlike clapping motion with her hands. 'Name it.'

'That you'll join us for Christmas lunch,' I barter. Anything is better than just me, Cerys, and Luke staring across the table at each other. I'm not even able to invite Bryn this year, because of my son-in-law. *And because I don't want him spending too much time with Cerys.*

'Deal.' She nods and extends her hand once again. This time I take it. And we shake on it.

## CHAPTER 32: CERYS

'Of course, Bryn must come for Christmas lunch.' I'm adamant. After everything Mam has done for me and Luke, it's the least I can do to persuade her. I hear Luke muttering something under his breath behind me, but I ignore him.

'I don't want there to be an atmosphere at Christmas and he and Luke have never got along,' Mam complains, continuing to peel the potatoes without pausing. It was meant to be my job, but she said we wouldn't sit down to lunch till Boxing Day at the rate I was going, so she took over.

'I'm sure they can manage one day between them,' I huff, turning to glare at my husband, who is pulling off his boots, after taking Elvis out to go pee-pee. 'Isn't that right, Luke?' I insist.

'I don't suppose it matters much since your mam's already invited one stranger to our first family Christmas together,' he huffs.

'What else could I do? The poor woman is all alone at Christmas,' Mam mumbles without turning around.

'And she's paying over the odds for the cabin,' I defend her decision. 'So, you'll invite Bryn too?' I persist, returning my focus to Mam.

'It's too late now. I can't go round there when I'm in the middle of everything.'

'You think he won't come, don't you? You don't fool me, Mam.'

'Not if he doesn't feel welcome,' she admits, bracing her shoulders as if expecting me to attack her.

'I'll go around there and get him,' I state unequivocally. 'He won't be able to refuse me. When I want to be, I can be pretty persuasive.'

Mam does turn around this time, her questioning gaze fixed on mine. 'Why would you do that?'

'Because he's your friend,' I explain, 'and he's all alone, like Miss Parry from the cabin. When they meet, they might even hit it off.' I chuckle, enjoying the idea of becoming a matchmaker. Even though Mam is flashing me daggers right now, it's not like she wants Bryn for herself. I don't believe she's had another boyfriend since Luke. Who could blame her? Nobody comes close to him. Now that we've made up, I can think this way again. Luke has blamed his recent angry outbursts on a combination of stress and financial concerns. He's started saying these things aloud in front of Mam too, which I believe is unfair, but he won't listen because he's convinced himself she's secretly loaded.

'It's not even eleven o'clock yet,' I mutter disapprovingly when I see Luke take a chilled bottle of sparkling white wine out of the fridge.

'It's Christmas.' He shrugs and smiles at me. 'And I still haven't had a Christmas kiss.'

Luke sets the bottle down and gently pulls me by the arm to stand beneath the mistletoe that hangs from the doorway, put there by him. 'Pucker up,' he commands while pressing his lips on mine. When he's in a playful mood, as he is right now, he's a joy to be around. Even Mam must be feeling it. The next thing I know, he's dancing me around the kitchen to Mariah Carey's 'All I Want for Christmas Is You.'

My laughter and good mood are cut short when I notice Mam glaring at the two of us. Luke sees the look too and pretends not to notice. But I'm not going to ignore it. Her gaze appears unguarded, and somehow suggests that Luke had acted out an identical situation with her before. Another Christmas ago. In this very room. Gypsy is stalking Luke before I can even process that thought, eyes fixated on him, hackles raised and growling. She clearly dislikes him being so close to me.

'Gypsy! Enough,' I box her ears and yank her back by her collar.

'That dog needs to be put down,' Luke sneers.

'Luke!' Both Mam and I turn on him at the same time.

'I was kidding,' he protests, his features contorted into a grimace. But when neither of us says anything, he sulkily grabs the bottle of wine and untwists the lid, before pouring it into his wineglass. 'If anyone needs me, I'll be watching *Love Actually* in the living room.' He walks out of the room, closing the door behind him so the dogs can't follow.

Mam and I exchange a smile and a roll of the eyes. We seem in agreement that Luke's behaviour is erratic. He constantly blows hot and cold, making us tread on eggshells around him.

'Right, I'll get off and go and get Bryn,' I tell Mam, snatching up my keys.

'Take the Defender,' Mam insists, handing me a different set.

'Are you sure?' I arch my brow at her.

'Yes, go ahead. And thank you once again for my lovely gift.' She raves, twirling the gorgeous gold Swarovski earrings that sparkle at her ears. I know how much she likes them because I saw her eyes light up when she opened her present this morning while we were all sitting around the Christmas tree.

'I'll just pop and see the child before I leave,' I giggle, which causes her to do a half smile, half grimace.

'Luke,' I say as I open the living room door. 'I'm just off to get Bryn. I won't be long.'

True to his word, he's watching the opening scenes of *Love Actually*, which he claims is his favourite film of all time because he's an incurable romantic. I'm not sure if romantic is the correct term to describe my husband but I've never explicitly said so. Who needs the conflict?

He shushes me as I go to sit on the arm of his chair, as he's engrossed in the Heathrow airport scene where families joyfully greet each other while Hugh Grant talks over them, stating, 'Love actually is all around.'

When I ruffle his hair, he pulls an annoyed face, which makes me laugh.

'What's funny?' he demands churlishly.

'You are,' I inform him. 'And grumpy too, but I still love you. And I adore this . . .' I touch the vegan banana yarn scarf around my neck. It's white and as soft as snow. 'I couldn't have chosen better myself.'

Luke nods, as if in agreement with me but when I initially opened my gift from him, he seemed more surprised than I was, as if he hadn't had anything to do with the buying of it, which I found odd. When I mentioned it to Mam later, her cheeks had reddened and she muttered something about it being, 'just his way.' After that, I shrugged it off.

'Where's the necklace I bought you?' I add as an afterthought. 'Have you put it on yet?

'Later,' he mumbles distractedly now that the movie has begun in earnest.

I sigh, trying and failing to hide my disappointment at how little enthusiasm he exhibited for the gift I had given him. 'Okay. You can show it to me later.'

# CHAPTER 33: BETH

Not long after Cerys had gone to fetch Bryn, despite my trying to make it perfectly clear I didn't want him here, Luke plods into the kitchen, dragging his feet in a depressed fashion. I don't turn around, but I pause in my work as his gaze burns into my shoulders. The chair scrapes back, and I become acutely aware of his presence, sensing that he is sitting down with his head in his hands. Since Luke moved back in, I've become finely attuned to his mood swings. Most of the time, I can predict them before he can.

He groans. 'We need to talk, Beth.'

I close my eyes tightly and feel my whole body stiffen. Although I've been expecting this, I'd anticipated he'd at least wait until after Christmas.

I shake off the water and potato peel from my hands and dry them on a tea towel before slowly turning around to find him staring at me with lovestruck eyes.

'Things can't continue as they are.' His voice cracks with emotion as he admits this.

'No, they can't,' I say sharply, defensively folding my arms.

'You agree?' His eyes light up with surprise. And hope.

'I do. So, when are you planning to move out?'

'I've told you before, Beth. I'm not going anywhere,' he growls, thumping the table with his palm, and causing the various pots on it to bounce.

'You and Cerys will never make a go of it as long as you live here, under my roof. Can't you see that?'

He sighs and rolls his eyes. 'What makes you think I want to make a go of it?'

'She's your *wife*,' I point out forcefully. 'And my daughter.'

'She's a child,' he insists, letting out a long shuddering breath he must have been holding for a long time. 'Look, Cerys is a great girl. But she bores me to tears. I could never be serious about someone like her.'

'You married her knowing this!' I gasp, taken aback. 'I can't listen to any more of this.' I storm towards the door.

'No. Please don't go, Beth. Stop!' He's on his feet, obstructing me. 'It's the age difference. We have nothing in common, unlike you and me.' His eyes wander to the mistletoe that's directly above our heads and then comes to rest on my mouth, as if he's thinking of kissing me.

'There is no you and me, Luke,' I grind out through clenched teeth, moving away from him.

'I know you feel the same way about me, Beth. I see it in your eyes.'

'How many times do I need to say this . . . I absolutely do not.' I'm yelling now and he's shushing me while restraining me with his hands on my arms. I shrug him off. 'Keep your hands off me.' Next to me Gypsy is back on her feet, hackles raised, lip snarling. Luke follows my gaze and removes his hands immediately, while I shuffle back to the sink, since he is blocking the doorway.

'Okay. Okay.' He holds out both palms and backs away, keeping one careful eye on Gypsy, who, although she has stood down, appears to still want to tear him apart.

'To me, Cerys is more like a daughter,' he elaborates.

'What?! You should have thought about that before marrying a girl so much younger than you!' I shout.

'Well, at least I'm not a paedophile like your *precious Owen*,' he combats, then apologises for going too far, 'Sorry. That was below the belt and none of it was your fault. Don't you see how much I want to look after you, Beth?'

'And you think hurting my daughter is looking after me?' I scoff.

'I could protect you both. We could also help Cerys with the baby when it comes.'

'*Your* baby.'

'*Our* baby.'

'What exactly are you suggesting?' I gasp, frightened of what he'll come out with next.

'Cerys could go back to university and finish her degree, while we bring the baby up. I've thought about how this would benefit all of us.'

'You need to get it through that thick skull of yours that I would never do anything to harm my daughter.'

'She didn't feel the same way about hurting you though, did she?' he retorts spitefully.

'I hold you responsible for that. I'm sure you manipulated her into it.'

We both jump at the sound of the front door knocker, so whatever he's about to say next is forgotten. My gaze darts between the door and Luke's eyes. 'That'll be Miss Parry. Nobody else would come to the front door.'

Before stepping out of the kitchen, he fires one last parting shot over his shoulder. 'I'll go let her in, but this conversation is far from over, Beth.'

My muscles relax once he's gone, but I'm shaking so violently that I have to perch on the edge of the chair for a minute. Now that Luke has brought his feelings into the open, I don't know what to do. If I tell Cerys what he said, he'll just deny it, and he has complete power over how she thinks. She'll believe him instead of me. I'm sure of it. I assumed time was on my side and that Cerys would eventually discover the real Luke for herself, but his increasing impatience and irritation with her are causing him to take risks. I don't kid myself that he's actually in love with me. I know exactly what he's after. This farm. And everything that goes with it.

Five minutes later, Luke has still not returned with our guest, which I find strange. The first thing he'd do is bring her into the kitchen to see me. But wait a minute, I can hear angry voices coming from outside. Is that them? Why has he not invited her in? What could they possibly be arguing about? Please, God, don't tell me he's turning away the poor woman at Christmas. Panicking, I make my way through the house to the front door, which has been left wide open, determined to find out what is going on.

That's when I notice them — Luke and Miss Parry — as if hiding from me, they are tucked away around the corner of the house. A red-faced Luke has a restraining hand on her shoulder and it looks like he's yelling at her. Meanwhile, she is giving as good as she gets. To say I'm flabbergasted is an understatement. I'm about to ask what the bloody hell is going on when those words are stolen out of my mouth . . .

'What the bloody hell is going on, Luke?' Cerys is yelling as she walks around the corner with Bryn trailing behind her.

# CHAPTER 34: CERYS

'Cerys, I can explain.' Luke's eyes bulge with alarm as his attention darts between the woman he has cornered against the wall, whom I've never seen before, Mam, and me. Something about this golden-haired, petite female's stance sends a silent scream through my trembling body. Her fists are locked by her sides, and her eyes are battling with Luke's as if it were a regular thing. Her chin juts obstinately giving the impression that she's ballsy. Not at all like me. Knowing this gives me an unsettled feeling. Beneath her faux-fur jacket and low-cut top, her loose shiny breasts rise and fall in rhythm with her breathing.

'I think you'd better,' I demand angrily.

No sooner have I opened my mouth than a thunderous cloud rolls over us, causing everyone's faces to darken. This is followed by a bone-chilling bolt of lightning that launches daggers of yellow light into the sky. While waiting for Luke's explanation, we all ignore the sudden downpour of rain.

'I didn't know she was coming. I wouldn't have . . . I never told her . . .' Luke's words come out strained as he casts a sidelong glance at the woman.

'Who is she?' I grind out, blinking away raindrops. But I can't prevent the anger from churning inside me.

'Less of the *she*,' the woman protests. 'I've got a name.'

'Do tell.' I'm being intentionally sarcastic. I hate her already without knowing why.

'Lynn,' she smarts, clearly rattled. 'When I told you my surname, I was only half lying as it's my mother's maiden name.' Lynn says huffily to Mam.

'Lynn,' Mam gasps, pressing her palm to her heart. 'Luke's Lynn?'

'She's not *my* Lynn,' Luke groans, throwing up his hands in a helpless gesture.

'What do you mean, *Luke's Lynn*?' I ask, my heart racing. When I glance at Mam, I notice that her steely blue eyes are locked angrily on Lynn's and vice versa, as if the two women have a history.

'She was the woman Luke had an affair with. The one he left me for when she got pregnant. I told you all this, Cerys, but you wouldn't believe me.'

'It's only an affair if you knew that the man was married, and I didn't. He told me he was single. I'm no homewrecker. And . . .'

'Shut up,' Luke yells in the woman's face, hands rigidly raised in the air as if he wants to close them around her throat. I feel Bryn tense by my side and take a protective step closer to me. He's got my back and I'm grateful for it. I could do with a strong, fatherly arm around my shoulder right now, but he doesn't go that far.

'Luke!' I bring his cagey-looking eyes back to me. 'You said you'd explain. I'm waiting.' I steal a quick glance at Mam then but she appears as perplexed as I am. She doesn't seem to know what's going on either or what Lynn is doing here.

All of a sudden, hail stones suddenly ping off the house roof, causing us to flinch as they pelt our eyelashes and cheekbones. They feel like cuts to the eyes. Every hair on my body stands on end as I dash under the overhanging roof for cover, Bryn mirroring me, but mercifully, the attack is brief.

'I've heard all about you, obviously.' Lynn stabs a finger in Mam's direction. 'But I have no idea who *you* are.' Her head whips around to face me.

'Hold your horses,' Mam commands, her face wild and almost tribal with rage. 'You're the stranger here. You don't get to ask the questions. Tell us what you're doing here first.'

'Cerys,' Luke cuts in furiously, 'I think you and your mam should go inside and let me deal with this. I'll explain everything later.'

'Why would I agree to that?' I gasp incredulously, watching him place a guiding hand on Lynn's arm, as if about to lead her away. I feel a jealous rage surge within me, making me want to claw her eyes out. 'What are you trying to hide, Luke?'

'Nothing. It's just a misunderstanding, that's all. Come with me, Lynn, so I can clear up the confusion . . .'

'Take your hands off me.' She aggressively shrugs him off. 'I haven't misunderstood anything. And I believe you're the one who's confused. Did you hit your head and forget your Aberystwyth address? I was wondering if you went back to your ex-wife's house because of memory loss.' She gives Mam a hard stare.

'Aberystwyth?' I feel a shudder rip through my body as I say this.

'Aye, that's where we lived together, in our flat, till he went AWOL five months ago.' She directs a livid glare towards Luke.

'You said that you lived alone in your flat and had been evicted for non-payment of rent,' I accuse Luke, noticing for the first time that his eyes are cloudy with drink. He must have consumed a lot of alcohol in the short time I've been gone.

Before he can answer Lynn jumps in, '*My* flat I'll have you know. And I pay my rent on time so nobody's going to kick me out. When I found out hubby here—' she motions to Luke with a stab of her hand before squaring up to Mam — 'had gone back to wife number one, even though you'd done the dirty on him by cheating on him with some pig farmer and robbing him of everything he owned, I decided to pay a visit. After all, it is Christmas.' She treats us to an unpleasant, fake little smile.

‘He told you that I cheated on him. Unbelievable!’ Mam is shaking her head and tutting in disgust, while Bryn’s eyes are on stalks. This instantly tells me that Luke has lied to Lynn. He’s lied to us all . . .

My teeth are chattering with the cold and I feel as icy and numb on the inside as I do on the outside. My world is collapsing around me. Everything comes to a halt . . . The barking of the dogs in the house grows muffled. The sound of the falling rain ceases. The clucking from the henhouse fades away. I can hear Mam, Luke, and Lynn bickering, but their words are distorted, just an echo in my thoughts, an inconvenience.

What did Lynn say? *Hubby here . . .*

# CHAPTER 35: BETH

'That's not true. I never said that,' Luke begs. 'Don't listen to her.' But he's pleading with the wrong woman. Why is he gazing at me when it's Cerys he has to convince? She's his wife.

'What did you mean when you called Luke "hubby"?' Cerys wants to know, as do I.

'What's it to do with you?' Lynn demands icily.

'I'm his wife,' Cerys argues.

'Don't be ridiculous.' Lynn cackles dirtily. 'You're just a babe in arms.'

'I'm a married woman and I'm carrying Luke's baby.'

'What? Hold on a second. I'm confused. What is going on here?' Lynn demands.

'I'm Beth. Luke's first wife . . . as you've already guessed. But he's now married to my daughter,' I explain in some embarrassment, realising how absurd that sounds.

'Fucking hell, Boyo. You've outdone yourself this time.' She flings Luke a furious look. But after a long pause in which her expression changes significantly, she then cries out, 'But he can't be married to you!'

'Why not?' Cerys snaps.

'Because he's still married to me and the last I knew, we hadn't gotten around to a divorce. He is still registered to my address because his mail comes to the flat. I've been checking his bank statements ever since he pulled a vanishing act to see where he was getting his money from, *since it wasn't me anymore*, but he hadn't taken any cash out until three days ago. I knew he'd gone back to wife number one the moment I found out the cash machine was in Abergavenny.'

'You're forgetting wife number three,' Cerys points out before turning on Luke. 'How could you?'

'She wouldn't divorce me, so what was I supposed to do?' Luke complains bitterly, changing his strategy now that his secret is out.

'Not commit bigamy!' Lynn takes him to task.

'You mean we aren't legally married?' The realisation causes Cerys to gasp. 'And, just as I suspected, you were living with another woman when we met.'

'I never intended to fall in love with you, Cerys, but I couldn't help it. It just happened,' Luke whines.

'Oh, don't mind me!' Lynn remarks while making a sour face. 'I'm just your wife watching you tell another woman that you love her.'

'That didn't bother you when the boot was on the other foot and I had to hear him say the same thing about you,' I observe, feeling like a bystander in this argument.

'By all accounts it didn't bother you that much either.'

She's right on the money — so I don't say anything — even though Luke had ripped out my heart when I discovered what a conman he was, I had been glad to see the back of him after all the lies and cheating. But, that's not to say he hadn't smashed all of my dreams at some point, as he is doing now to my poor daughter.

'I can't believe you'd let him marry your daughter. That's sick.'

'It's not like I had a choice,' I say frostily, thinking, *It is sick. And twisted.* I've always known this.

'What a family.' She shakes her head, aghast. 'Anyway, whether he comes back to me and the flat or not is by the by, but he's left me high and dry without any maintenance and I mean to get my money.'

'Maintenance for what?'

'For Evie, of course,' Lynn states as if we should all know this.

'Who is Evie?' As I ask this, my heart is in my mouth. I'm suddenly back in the mix and unable to look at my daughter. Even though I can feel her searching, perplexed gaze landing on me.

'Our three-year-old.' Lynn's chest swells with pride as she darts a quick look at Luke, who is presumably the father, before turning back to me. 'You should know. That's why he left you in the first place so he could be a proper dad to her.'

My head spins from this latest revelation. I can only imagine what Cerys, who still loves Luke, is going through. I instantly switch my attention to her husband . . . who happens to be my ex-husband. Lynn is right — what a family. Upon seeing my expression, he crumbles under my scrutiny and begins to appear pale, shaky, and lost — with panicked ocean-blue eyes.

'You told me she lost the baby! That she miscarried. You came back here three months later saying there was no longer any reason for you to stay and that you wanted to come home!'

'Fucking arsehole,' Lynn manages between clenched teeth.

'Lynn, what was I supposed to do? Back then, I couldn't handle the thought of being a father. It was all too much. The flat was so small and we argued all the time. I had to escape.'

'So, you lied about the pregnancy because you wanted your comfortable old life back,' I say, outraged . . . reliving the painful experience all over again. You never get over something like that.

'I never wanted to leave it in the first place, but she —' he casts an accusing glare at Lynn — 'got pregnant, on purpose, if you ask me. I never gave her the go-ahead to have my child. In fact, I told her to abort it but she refused.'

'But you went back to her anyway when I slammed the door in your face!' I yell.

'Where else was I meant to go?' Luke mutters, looking uncomfortable and shoving his hands in his pockets.

I was over Luke long before we separated and eventually divorced, but I feel the betrayal of what he'd done as if it were yesterday — as if he'd never married my daughter and we were still a couple. I want to kill him. For lying over and over again. For playing me and Lynn off against each other — neither of us guessing at the real truth. And now messing with my daughter.

When I turn to face Cerys, I am reminded that this is not about me or my suffering but rather about her. *She* is now married to Luke. My God, she's carrying that man's baby. If he could abandon one child, he could do so again. Some people don't deserve to be parents. *Haven't I always known this?* And haven't I known what Luke was capable of all along? Cerys stands there looking bedraggled and wet, her eyes sparkling with unshed tears and when I realise that she's in shock I feel a tug on my heartstrings. I'm about to approach her, when Luke, seeing how her face has now collapsed into tears, seizes his chance, and gets in before me.

'Cerys, sweetheart. Please don't look at me like that, as if I were a monster. I can't bear it.'

Her head snaps up to glare at him. 'Don't call me sweetheart.'

*That's my girl*, I secretly applaud. At last, it's over. She'll never have him back now. The pain of losing Luke will hurt like hell for a while but she, and the baby, will be much better off in the long run. I won't be celebrating that I've got my daughter back just yet though because doing so would be unfair to her. It will take months, if not years, for her to bounce back from this, but bounce back she will under my care and protection. Besides, she's young. She'll recover much more quickly than I did. If nothing else, she has inherited my resilience.

'Look, I need to speak with Lynn to see if we can work out an agreement over maintenance for the child.'

'*Your* child,' Lynn snaps. 'Her name's Evie, in case you've forgotten and she's been wondering where her father's been the past five months.'

Luke flinches but ignores her. 'I need to settle this issue once and for all so I'm taking Lynn back to the cabin to discuss it.'

Nothing can prevent me from shooting daggers at Luke when I hear this. 'Over my dead body. You're not taking that woman to my cabin.'

Ignoring me, Luke slouches pitifully in front of Cerys. 'Then we can be together properly,' he tells her, in full love-making mode. 'There won't be any more lying, I swear. You have no idea how hard this has been for me, having to keep something a secret from you, of all people.'

As Cerys's expression softens dangerously — *please don't let her be so weak as to fall for his lies* — she has no way of knowing that when he says this, his dishonest gaze travels over her head to fix purposefully on me.

# CHAPTER 36: CERYS

'I don't want her here,' I manage between sobs, wanting to fall into Luke's arms, and knowing I can't. Because he's a liar and a cheat. All the things Mam said he was, which I stubbornly refused to believe since I didn't want it to be true. And because I naively thought true love had changed him. Hadn't I taken pride in my unconditional love for this man? I even shamelessly boasted to Mam about it, saying I knew who he was. Despite feeling deeply humiliated and humbled, I still want to be able to forgive Luke and find a way to make things work, more for the baby than anything.

Having lost my dad at an early age, I refuse to think about the shameful circumstances surrounding his suicide, I'm aware of how important it is for a child to have a father figure in their life. Besides, aren't I meant to love my husband through good times and bad? This is definitely one of the bad times. But then . . . I remind myself I'm nobody's wife — even though I'm surrounded by them: Mam, and Lynn. But mine and Luke's civic ceremony was illegal, *another lie*, meaning I'm just a . . . I don't even know what I am — girlfriend, partner. An idiot. The baby I'm carrying is the only tangible thing to come out of my relationship with Luke and nobody can take that away from me, least of all him.

'It's just for one more night, Cerys,' he whispers, picking up my limp hand and holding it to his lips.

'You won't spend the night with her, will you?' I ask, suspicion flashing through my mind like the yellow bolts of lightning.

'No. Of course, not. What do you take me for?' Luke stretches his neck in a show of mock indignation.

*A liar. A cheat.*

'I just need to talk to her and sort everything out so I can concentrate on you and *our* baby.'

'How are you going to do that when you don't have any money?' My eyes sharpen as I object to the way he keeps forgetting that Evie is also his. Regardless of what happens between Luke and me, this is something I'll have to come to terms with as she will be a half-sister to my child.

'I'll find a way. I always do, don't I?'

I'm not sure that he does, but I'm too worn out to say so. 'Are you in love with Lynn?' I surprise myself by asking.

He shakes his head. 'All she cares about is money. You must be able to see that. I promise you I'll make things right again, even if it takes me the rest of my life.'

Despite feeling as I do, his words move me, and before I know it, I'm in his arms, sobbing into his chest, allowing myself to be comforted by him — even though he hadn't said the words I wanted to hear, *I don't love Lynn, or Beth, or anyone other than you, Cerys.*

'She's a funny, weak little thing. I don't know what you see in her,' Lynn pipes up observationally from somewhere behind me. The truth of what she's accusing me of has me hanging my reddened cheeks in shame.

'Don't . . .' Luke warns, his mouth tugging into a grimace, as he turns to scowl at Lynn.

'I find it hard to believe this snivelling creature is my replacement,' she observes to no one in particular, while inspecting her rainbow-coloured nail extensions.

'Say that again and you'll be staring down the barrel of a gun,' Mam threatens, her face as thunderous as the dark clouds in the sky.

'Are you threatening me?' Lynn tilts her chin upwards in a defiant gesture.

Mam's right eye twitches furiously. When she is livid, she is terrifying. 'For Evie's sake, you should shut up now.'

And Lynn does shut up. Miraculously. Because even she's unwilling to push Mam any further when it's clear from the intent in her hardened eyes that she is not lying about the gun. And nobody wants that.

'I'm going now, back to the cabin with Lynn. Are you listening, Cerys?' Luke says beside me, an anxious, urgent sound to his voice.

I'm still in shock so I'm having trouble processing everything. In situations like this, my attention is prone to wander and dwell on minor details as a way of escaping. The loose slate on the roof for instance or the pigeons paired up on the TV aerial. When Luke raises my chin with his fingers and lays his hands on either side of my cheeks I finally come to.

'Did you hear what I said?' he asks, concerned.

'She heard,' Mam hisses angrily near my ear while tugging Luke's hands from my face. She surprises us both as we were unaware of her approach. Mam has a stealthy, soldier-like quality.

As soon as I'm out of Luke's clutches and in Mam's arms, I become aware of Bryn's rapid, jabbing, boxer-like movements and before either Mam or I can yell at him to stop, he has punched Luke against the wall. Mam and I both cover our mouths in horror as Luke collapses to the ground in a huddle, leaving a smear of blood on the wall behind him.

'You've had that coming for years, Griffin,' Bryn bellows — bull-like — while glaring fearlessly down at Luke. 'That's for both of the Williams women.'

I tightly close my eyes, aware of how fast my heart is racing, thinking only of my father at that moment — his brain being blown out of the back of his head . . . leaving me forever. As I fear Luke is going to do now that he's hauled himself to his feet with the assistance of that woman . . . his wife . . . Lynn. The mother of his child. I'm taken aback when

Luke chooses to maintain his distance from Bryn instead of aiming a counterpunch at him. In addition to everything else, I never had him down as a coward. But am I being unfair? He's probably still feeling dazed by the punch to the side of his face, which is splashed with blood. I notice Lynn putting an arm around his waist to support him as he moves forward and I see red.

Mam must have noticed the panic in my eyes and been worried that I might do something stupid, like beg Luke not to go, or grab Lynn by the hair, because she firmly grasps both my hands in hers and states in a loud, steely voice, 'He's just taking her to the cabin.'

I feel a familiar sensation of loss as I watch them shuffle away, neither turning to look back at us over their shoulders. I'm conscious that the grief I'm experiencing has nothing to do with Luke and everything to do with my father, and yet the pain I'm feeling is very real. I can't stand the idea of being abandoned again. I realise I'm not like Mam, who exudes strength and independence. I, on the other hand, need to be loved by a man.

'He will come back, won't he?' Tears roll down my face as I say this.

'You can bet on it,' Mam growls, her gaze pursuing him like the telescopic sight on a sniper's rifle. 'And when he does, we'll be ready.'

Something about the way Mam mutters this makes me go cold all over.

# CHAPTER 37: BETH

I felt a wave of relief as soon as I slammed the front door and bolted it. It's over. He's gone. If I never see Luke Griffin again it will be too soon. But my daughter, who was trembling, pallid and sobbing hysterically, kept insisting on giving Luke one last chance. *She cannot be serious.*

As soon as we entered the hallway, Cerys dashed into the dining room to watch Luke through the window — nodding through her tears and repeating to herself, 'He's just taking Lynn to the cabin. He'll be back soon.'

I'm aware she's in shock but I'm unable to let go of my anger. I can't look at her when she says she will forgive him for the sake of the child, who needs a father, since this is a cop-out. She must sense my disapproval because I'm unable to conceal my feelings. Like Lynn mentioned, Cerys is weak where Luke's concerned. Part of me is ashamed. Doesn't she have any self-respect? She's doing it for the baby, she says, but I don't buy it. She is under his control. Sex. Lust. Call it what you want — I'm stomping mad with the pair of them. If it were me, I would have given him his marching orders. As I did once before.

'I need to get Cerys to bed. All this upset can't be good for the baby.' I make a face at Bryn, who since lashing out at Luke, has fallen back into a silent, thoughtful mode, and is following me around like a lost puppy. His presence only irritates me further. I was hoping he'd take the hint and leave but he isn't showing any signs of doing so.

I sigh and walk into the kitchen to get the first aid kit, saying, 'You'd better let me take a look at that hand first.' I want to let the dogs out, but I'm afraid that if I do that, they, as in Gypsy, will run straight to the cabin in pursuit of Luke, and that's another battle I don't need right now.

'Sit.' When I issue this command, Bryn immediately slumps into one of the chairs at the table and the dogs follow suit, parking their bums on the floor. 'I'm not known for my nursing skills,' I tell him, as I none-too-gently wipe clean his grazed and bloodied knuckles with a sterile wipe.

'I can tell,' he teases weakly.

I scowl. 'Whatever were you thinking, Rocky Balboa?'

'That I've missed you.'

When he says this, I pause what I'm doing but I don't respond. Best not to. Even though I can feel his concentrated gaze urging me to turn to face him.

'You need a man around.'

'Not now, Bryn,' I warn, feeling my hackles rise.

'You both do,' he persists.

'And look where that got us,' I hiss sarcastically. 'Besides, I can take care of myself.'

'Cerys needs a father, not a husband.'

'Just as well she's not *actually* married then. Besides, Cerys doesn't need a man at all. She has me.' I'm close to yelling now. I don't want to fall out with Bryn but he's got a nerve interfering in my business, my life, like this. Just because he punched Luke doesn't give him any ownership rights over us. I'm saved from saying so when Cerys enters the room, still sobbing and wringing her hands.

'You've locked the door. Why did you do that? How is Luke meant to get back in?'

'It's okay, Cerys,' I say in a voice that's meant to be soothing.

'No, it's not okay.' Cerys runs both hands through her hair and onto her face as if completely freaked out.

'You need some rest, love. You're overwrought.'

'Not until you unlock the door.'

Taking the key from my jeans pocket, I march through the hallway and unlock the door and then unbolt it. Cerys is on my heels behind me.

'There.' I hand her the key and she quickly wraps her palm around it as I say to her, 'He knows where to find you.'

'And you won't try to stop him?' Cerys looks panic-stricken.

'I swear,' I say, crossing my fingers behind my back, while ignoring Bryn's disapproving headshake, 'but only if you go and lie down for a while.'

Cerys's palm flutters to her stomach, as if contemplating what would be best for the baby, and her blue gaze returns to sanity.

'Okay.'

I extend my hand to help her up the stairs, offering, 'I'll come up with you,' but she stops me with a firm palm, forcing me to take a hesitant step backwards.

'Has anybody seen Elvis?' she asks, eyes swirling with panic.

'He isn't in the kitchen with the other dogs.' I observe, adding, 'I don't think I've seen him in a while, not since Lynn knocked on the door.'

'He must have got out. Sneaked past you.' Cerys's voice goes up a notch.

'It's okay, love. He'll be fine.'

'He's only little. Just a baby.' Cerys bites on her knuckles, worry lines appearing on her face.

Her anxiety is returning and I must do something to fix it, so I say in as reassuring a voice as I can, 'I'll go and find him just as soon as you've gone up to rest and I'll make sure he's here when you wake up.'

'Do you promise?'

'Hand on heart.' I cross my hand across my body, meaning it.

Cerys's shoulders drop as she puts her trust in me. 'Thanks, Mam.' But her gaze softens even more when it lands on Bryn's face. 'Bryn, would you mind helping me upstairs? I feel a little wobbly on my feet.'

'But . . .' I object, and I'm thinking about one very good reason why this isn't a good idea, when . . .

'Come on, love.' Bryn pushes past, without even glancing my way to check if it's okay with me — *which it bloody well isn't* — to place a guiding hand on Cerys's pointy shoulder. As I watch them climb the stairs together, my body tenses to the point where it is as sharp and knotted as barbed wire.

I'm miffed that Bryn seems to have changed his mind about my daughter. He never had much time for her before and that's how I preferred it. But now I've noticed him giving her worried looks. Which is all very well, but I could do with a bit of concern being shown my way. I would sacrifice anything for Cerys because I love her, but I can't pretend that she isn't to blame for a lot of things. We wouldn't be in this situation right now if she had paid attention to me when I begged her to give up Luke. She is currently paying for it, as I knew she would. Although harsh, that is the truth. And Bryn needn't be so soft around her either. Or he'll end up pissing me right off. He could be right though, about Cerys needing a father, but it sure as hell isn't going to be him.

Whirling around in a fit of rage, I stomp back into the kitchen and go to stand at the window. The cold rain has misted up the glass and I wipe a wet patch of it away so that I can see better. Luke and Lynn are no longer visible at this point. The black barn, however, can be seen in the distance near the summit of the hill. It summons me like a ghost. Cerys was much closer to her father than me and I've never got over the injustice of that, knowing that he intended to destroy our family by disclosing a secret so dark that it would be impossible to bury even on the blackest of mountains. But Owen and I had made a deal and I wasn't going to break it for anyone.

# CHAPTER 38: CERYS

'Do you think Mam will ever forgive me if I give Luke one last chance?' I sniff, dry-eyed from the comfort of my old bed. When he helped me upstairs, Bryn, quite correctly, directed me towards my childhood bedroom rather than the one I'd been sharing with Luke, which would have been unbearable knowing the sheets smelt of him.

Bryn murmurs softly, 'She'll forgive you anything. You know that.'

At that, I feel a grateful smile race across my lips and I snuggle further down in my bed, my toes curling up against the constrictive duvet wrapped around me. I've been able to relax thanks to the warm bed, a cup of calming camomile tea, drawn curtains, dim lighting, and Bryn's comforting presence. Not to mention Mam's promise to find Elvis. Now that I'm in control of my emotions again, I focus on this pig-farming friend of my parents, who I never paid much attention to before, but who is fast growing on me.

He doesn't sit on the bed next to me, sensing it wouldn't be appropriate, but instead wanders around the room, peering into the doll's house and moving some of the small figurines around. I catch him blushing when he comes across a framed photograph of me, Mam and Zorro at a show jumping event and his finger impulsively strokes the outline of her face. My jaw falls slack when I guess his secret.

'Does she know?' I exclaim.

He swivels his unguarded gaze on me. 'Know what?'

I raise an eyebrow. 'That you're in love with her.'

'Is it that obvious?' he grumbles, stuffing his hands deep into his pockets before moving over to sink into a slouchy pink beanbag chair.

'It is to me.' I chuckle, before adding on a sadder note, 'Not that I'm an expert on the subject . . . obviously.'

'You and me both,' he quips.

'For all you know, you might be the love of her life,' I gasp, suddenly not minding if Mam were to fall in love with another man. After what Dad did to her how could I object any longer?

'*You're* the love of her life. You always have been.' Bryn throws me a knowing smile.

'True,' I mutter, realising as I look down at my lap that I've never considered it that way before. *Will I feel the same way about my child?* 'You disapprove of Luke though, don't you? You always have.'

'If a man truly loves a woman, he sees only her.' Bryn's jaw flexes with determination when he comes out with this.

I recoil and grab a fistful of duvet, knowing he doesn't say this to hurt me. Even though it bloody well does. Too much. 'You're just like Mam. Did you attend the same school where you were taught to "say it like it is"?'

'We've lived on this mountain too long to have any fancy ways.' Bryn grins, and when a curl of hair falls across his eye, I'm reminded of how sad and melancholy he was before becoming Mam's friend. He was given the nickname "Heathcliff" by my friends and me after the brooding, tortured anti-hero in *Wuthering Heights.*

I wonder briefly if he's aware of this and whether I should let him in on the secret, but deciding against it, I urge instead, 'You should tell Mam how you feel.'

'That's not how we do things around here,' Bryn responds gruffly, adding, 'besides, she knows. Your mam's not daft.'

'Is she the one, do you think?' My eyes are bright with interest as I ask this, even though I'm feeling desperately sad inside, but the topic of real love has always made me excited.

'I reckon there are three ones in a person's lifetime,' he finally responds after being stubbornly mute for a solid minute.

'That's an interesting ideology.' My tea is still far too hot for me to drink, so I blow on it. 'Who was your first? Was it your wife?'

I recognise he's rankled when I notice his Adam's apple bouncing up and down agitatedly, resembling an out-of-control Welsh mineshaft, and I immediately regret having inquired about his wife. Everyone knows what a private person Bryn is and how he prefers not to discuss his marriage with anybody, not even Mam, so when he responds, with a harsh, 'No,' I'm lost for words.

'I may have loved her once,' he continues, 'but for the majority of our marriage she battled severe depression and acted like she hated me. It was difficult and, because she frequently threatened suicide, I dreaded returning home to find her dangling from a ceiling beam.'

My eyes widen with shock and I find myself gulping down the horrific images of my dad having his brains blown out. His dead body was zipped up in a bag and carried away. There were flashing red and blue police lights. The black tarred barn door was propped open as if it were sneering at us.

'I'm sorry, Bryn, I didn't know . . . I didn't mean to pry.'

'Didn't you?' His eyes briefly turn dark and distant before returning to normal. 'People around here like to think that when she left me for another woman six years ago, I was devastated, but in reality, I was relieved. After seventeen hellish years together, I wonder why she didn't do it sooner. She was always complaining about how miserable I made her.'

'It must have still been a terrible thing to go through,' I prompt, experiencing a hot thrill of triumph at Bryn's expense knowing that some couples have it worse than Luke and me. Even though it turns out that we are not married at all, at least we love each other and want to make our relationship work. Marriage is just a piece of paper anyway.

'The loss of my daughter was the worst part.'

'Didn't your wife take her with her when she left?'

'Who told you that?'

I hesitate, unsure if I should admit to this. I don't want to get her into trouble. 'Mam.'

'That sounds about right. She would have said that to protect you.'

'From what?' I'm baffled.

'The truth, of course. It's what your mam has always done with you. Not that I blame her. If I could go back in time, I'd have been far more protective of my child. If I had been, perhaps it wouldn't have happened.'

'I'm confused. What do you mean?' I come clean, sensing that if I dig deeper, I'm bound to uncover another secret Mam has deliberately kept from me. *But what exactly?* 'Are you saying your wife didn't take your daughter?' I persist doggedly.

'Oh, she took her all right.' Bryn's face collapses into his hands. 'Just not in the way you were led to believe.'

# CHAPTER 39: BETH

Knowing that Bryn is upstairs, alone, with my daughter makes me uneasy. I don't like it one little bit. *Should I be worried?* Why hasn't he come down by now? He has to have been up there for over an hour. If one man isn't worrying me to death, it appears that another one is. For all the grief that Bryn and Luke are giving me, they might as well be the same person in my eyes. I know that's an unfair comparison but I'm just, well, pissed off, and have resorted to lurking halfway up the stairs in an attempt to listen in on their conversation, even though I had promised my daughter that I would go out straight away and look for her dog. And I will, but first I have to know what they're talking about. It's torture not knowing. All I can make out though is Cerys's animated Snow White tone and Bryn's faint murmuring. Given the mess she's in, what with Luke and everything, I don't know what she's got to sound so excited and hopeful about.

Luke — that horrible, dreaded word — comes up once more. Should we expect him to return as he promised Cerys? Why doesn't he simply bugger off back to his rightful home in Aberystwyth with his wife and child? Everyone would benefit then. I'm not sure how I'll be able to keep my hands off him if he does come back. Not after the suffering he's caused my daughter, especially knowing that she's pregnant. The man can't keep it in his pants.

Christmas is ruined. There'll be no roast turkey with all the trimmings now, or mushroom Wellington in Cerys's case. I've shoved the turkey crown in the range anyway as it might come in handy for sandwiches over the coming days which I expect are going to be tense. They can't not be.

I sneak into the kitchen when I hear a floorboard creak above my head, whistling loudly and acting as casually as I can while flipping through a glossy cookbook. When no footsteps come down the stairs, I slam it shut, sigh heavily, and drum the table with my fingernails. Right now, I want to slam a broom handle against the ceiling and yell at Bryn to 'get down here,' but I know how my daughter would react to that.

Deciding to go out and do a bit of shooting with the dogs, while looking for Elvis — to take my mind off things as it's not as if I'm wanted around here — I slip on my wax jacket and Wellington boots, then go into the utility room, unlock the gun cabinet, and pull out Tad's gun, the one he inherited from his father and is now mine. Taking it to the kitchen table, I begin to clean it down, nearly falling off my chair when I hear the back door slam open and turn around to see a windswept Luke standing in the doorway, looking like a Marvel comic book anti-hero.

'You weren't long.' That is all I can think of to say when *idiot, knobhead, and dick* would be much better options.

'I haven't come to stay,' he announces, walking inside and closing the door after him, all the while keeping one careful eye on Gypsy, who is lying under the table with one eye closed and the other on him. 'I just wanted to see how Cerys is.'

'How do you think?' I scowl, pretending to concentrate on the rifle I'm cleaning. Anything is preferable to having to face him.

'Have you left her all alone? I'm not sure that's wise.' His eyes widen in surprise and he displays genuine concern. He almost succeeds in tricking me once more, since, based on our earlier conversation, I know he doesn't give a shit about Cerys. All he wants is the farm which he seems to think he's entitled to.

'Bryn is with her,' I tell him, gleaning satisfaction from his indignant expression. But as I watch him furrow his brow questioningly, as if deep in thought, I realise he's not as put out as I first imagined.

'You're mad at me?' he poses this as a question.

'You don't say,' I scoff.

'It's understandable, I get that.'

'That's mighty good of you.' I shoot a contemptuous glance his way.

'But you're not angry with me because of Cerys though, are you? This is about us. Tell me if I'm wrong.'

'Luke, you're wrong about everything.' I sigh, exasperated.

'You can say what you like. I know you still care about me.' Luke moves closer, his blue eyes locked firmly on mine. 'I told you before, I can see it in your eyes.'

'Hatred is what you see. Scorn. Even worse, the kind of pity I'd show to an injured animal before putting it out of its misery.' I grimace, but my hands are busy loading and cocking the gun the entire time. Sparks of rage fly in my skull as it makes a metallic flint-like snapping sound.

'I'm not buying it.' Luke vigorously shakes his head, never taking his eyes off my face. Luke, being Luke, thinks he can eventually win me over despite my clenched mouth and flared nostrils. Any other man would back away. Next to lying and cheating, his ego is his biggest flaw.

'Are you telling me—' I laugh sarcastically — 'that after this latest stunt you've pulled, you're stupid enough to still think that's the case.'

'You're forgetting something,' he reminds me coldly. 'You can't get rid of me when Cerys worships the ground I walk on and is determined to work things out with me.'

'Luke, *you don't want her*. You've already admitted it, so . . .' I try to reason with him as though he were a human being rather than a cold, unfeeling narcissist who lacks empathy,

'Why don't you go back to your flat with Lynn and be a proper father to Evie?'

'What about the child I'm expecting with Cerys?'

'You don't give a damn about them,' I point out.

This time he appears stumped. 'Look, none of this was my fault.'

'It never is, is it, Luke?' I utter in a worn-out voice.

'I didn't invite her here and I never gave her your address. I wouldn't.'

'Don't you see that none of that matters? She is your wife. She has every right to be here.'

'We'll see about that,' he hisses. 'But you're right. Lynn would never send me packing the way you did.'

'More fool her.'

'And neither would Cerys,' he taunts.

'Make the most of it while it lasts . . . Because you're wrong again, Luke. Whether you like it or not, I know my daughter better than you and she will grow tired of you in the end, just as she used to do with all her shiny new toys. She may seem like a Barbie doll to you, but my girl has a bigger set of balls than you. They just haven't dropped yet.'

He scowls disapprovingly. Am I getting through to him at last? But he quickly proves me wrong when he growls menacingly while stubbornly jutting out his chin and saying, 'I need to talk to Cerys.'

'Who is stopping you?' I pull a face and stand up, watching him as he's watching me — as if we were two opponents about to square off in the ring. And I suppose that's exactly what we are.

When his boots squeak on the flagstones, as if he's about to exit the room and fly up the stairs, I turn in his direction . . . and so does the gun. Luke immediately freezes, appearing afraid I might actually shoot him.

'You know what you are, Luke?'

'A dead man?' Even when he cracks a joke, it can't disguise the terror in his eyes or the sweat streaming down his bunched-up face.

'A fucking psychopath,' I sneer, my temper getting the better of me. Luke makes me angry just for being alive and in my house, and Bryn and Cerys have irritated me by excluding me — which is how it used to be with Cerys and her father. Everyone is driving me mad.

'You're the one holding a gun,' he points out and raises his hands in mock surrender, but when I approach him slowly and deliberately, he backs off as if he doesn't fancy his chances.

'Always the joker, aren't you, Luke?' I get into his space, nose to nose. My hatred matching his fear — one inhale at a time. And then, I'm gone, out of the door, into the cold, clinging-with-wet air, the dogs circling me, while Luke is doing a double take over his shoulder as if he thought today was his last and can't believe his luck. *Like I said, always the joker.*

# CHAPTER 40: CERYS

'And they never found her?' I exclaim in disbelief as I lurch upright in bed to protectively cradle my growing pregnancy bump with one hand.

In despair, Bryn shakes his head. 'The search went on for weeks but the police didn't find a single clue. It was as if our baby had never existed.'

'Oh, Bryn. I'm so sorry. I can only imagine how you must have felt.'

'Even then, I doubt it,' he mumbles. 'You see I have my own theory on what happened, as did the police, but they couldn't prove it.'

'What?'

'I believe Gwen hurt her, not intentionally, mind, but she wasn't coping.'

'Gwen, your wife?' I gasp.

'Aye. She had a difficult time bonding with the baby following a traumatic birth. The baby was born premature, you see, and came six weeks early. She was such a helpless, tiny, little thing,' he sighs heavily at this point, before continuing. 'The "baby blues," they called it back then, but Gwen's condition was much more severe than that. She'd always been predisposed to mental illness. It ran in her family, they said.'

'The poor baby,' I commiserate, my eyes welling with tears. I experience an overwhelming sense of love for my own baby when I feel it move inside me. Even if someone were to cut it out of me and then leave me to bleed to death, I cannot conceive a situation in which I would not love it.

'Despite having to manage the farm as well as care for the baby, so Gwen wouldn't have to, nothing I ever did made her depression go away. She tended to be on the delicate side. Not strong mentally or physically like Beth.' Bryn pauses to glance over at the photograph of Mam again.

I respond, 'No one is,' feeling wretched for him. What a Christmas Day this is turning out to be.

'First, she wanted a baby and then she didn't. The same went for husbands. And I don't pretend to understand women's hormones any more now than I did then.' He offers a feeble, regretful smile. 'In hindsight, I realise I was probably too hard on her because like many men of my generation I had been raised to suppress my feelings and didn't know how to deal with Gwen's destructive emotions. I guess I thought she was weak. And once I realised things were never going to improve it suited me to stay away from the farmhouse as much as possible.'

Because I've grown up in a completely different culture where emotions and mental health are discussed openly, perhaps too much at times, I try not to judge him, but it's hard not to . . . Despite his best efforts and taking care of the baby himself, his postpartum wife must have been losing her mind alone in that big, secluded house of his.

'How old was the baby when she went missing?' I inquire gently.

'Five weeks, two days and four hours.' Bryn gazes at me with haunted eyes. Naturally, his thoughts are on his child and the wasted years.

'How long ago was this?' I feel horrible for pressuring him but I'm shocked that I've never heard of this before.

'Same year you were born. If she had lived, she could have been your friend.'

'But you don't know that she didn't live?' I remind him while grieving the loss of a potential lifelong friend that I'll never meet.

'I do, Cerys. I feel it in here.' Bryn nods in time with his heartbeat as he thumps his chest. 'Gwen killed her. Maybe she accidentally dropped her or found her dead in her cot, who knows? But either way she hid our baby girl's body where nobody could find it. Not even me. And believe me, I looked. I spent years searching.'

'Oh my God, that is really horrible.'

'I ask myself sometimes why I stayed with her after that, but without proof . . .' Bryn's head sags onto his chest. 'And I suppose I knew deep down she wouldn't have meant to, and I might have been able to forgive that given the depression and all.'

I refrain from saying what first comes to mind, which is: *I bloody well wouldn't*, because I believe harming a child is the worst possible crime. Another reason why I'm struggling to come to terms with my dad's sexual preference for children. My mind is, as yet, unable to process the thought of him posting photographs of me, his only child, online for other perverts to see. Anger churns inside me when I consider what a huge betrayal that was, but I'm not mentally ready to unpick this yet. I don't know if I'll ever be ready. For now, I can only hope his fascination for child porn websites didn't progress to anything more.

'And now you know the story of the child who disappeared from the mountain,' Bryn states, standing up and absentmindedly patting his trouser pockets as if afraid he's lost something else, on top of his wife and child.

'I can't believe Mam never told me,' I snivel, fighting back tears because I don't want Bryn to think he needs to console me. Even though it's his pain rather than mine, I'm unable to hold them back and they fall anyway. I've never been more emotional than I am now that I'm pregnant.

'It's not the sort of story you'd want a child to know,' Bryn mutters while frowning. 'Your mam did right by not telling you. I bet you wish you hadn't asked now,' he adds apologetically.

'No. I'm glad you told me,' I reply shakily, but I do mean it.

'It's funny that the only two people I've ever really discussed it with in any detail are you and your dad,' he observes.

'I'm not sure if I should feel good or bad about that,' I complain, hating the fact that I can no longer be proud of any connection to my father.

'You know, the one thing that bothers me the most . . .' Bryn muses, rubbing his chin, 'is that nobody talks about it anymore. The local gossips were more interested in my wife's lesbian affair with a woman from Merthyr Tydfil than our missing child.' He shrugs, visibly upset, but manages to keep it contained — because that's what men his age do.

'What was your baby's name?' I whisper.

'She was called Eilonwy.' He beams as he starts to move towards the door. 'Meaning "deer." She was dear to me if nobody else.'

'Are you off now, Bryn?' I ask, noticing that his tweed cap, rescued from his pocket, is scrunched up in his hand.

'Aye, I think I'd better,' he replies, without moving.

As I observe him awkwardly standing there, I can't help but think that even though I've known him my entire life and he's as familiar to me as the mountains that surround us, up until this point we've kept our distance from one another. However, I sense that we have a genuine connection and that he understands how I feel. He has the same capacity for introspection and strong emotions as I do. He exudes an earthy, organic quality and kindness shines out of his soft green eyes. He's the complete opposite to Luke, I realise with sudden clarity, who has, shall we say, very different qualities, although I'd struggle to name a single one right now.

I jump out of bed on a whim and walk up to Bryn, kissing him on the cheek without having to stand on tiptoe like I usually do. I'm moved once more as I see the unshed tears in his eyes.

'You're a bonny lass, Cerys.' He hugs me. 'I've always thought so.'

'But never said so.' His woolly jumper, which smells like charred wood, diesel, and something else I can't place, muffles my laughter.

When the door clicks open, we both turn in unison, to see Luke standing there, his eyes apoplectic with rage and almost green with jealousy.

# CHAPTER 41: BETH

The farmyard is flooded since the rain hasn't stopped. As I plough through the mud, it clings to my boots, making them heavier than usual. I follow the dogs when they run to the chicken house excitedly barking and sniffing the ground, keeping my head low as a shield from the heavy rain.

'Toad, Gypsy, what is it?' I yell as I clumsily jog after them. And then: 'Oh, no,' as I see what's grabbed their attention. Three dead chickens. One white. Two brown. Feathers everywhere. Blood too.

'Fucking Charlie,' I mutter angrily, letting myself into the fence-and-wire outdoor coop and pushing the dogs' blood-inquisitive noses out of the way.

This is the fourth fox attack in as many months. The elderly rooster, who would have hidden rather than protected his harem of ladies, and the remaining hens are thankfully safe, if abnormally quiet and nervous. As there is no way Charlie would have left anything alive, he must have been disturbed during the attack. Because it was Christmas Day, I'd gotten up earlier than usual — to muck out Zorro's stable and feed him, then checked on the sheep in the dark, barrowing silage for the flock to eat — all before preparing a turkey roast and cleaning the house. The change of routine meant I'd got to the chickens around four thirty a.m. and they were fine then. I'd planned on letting them out a little later if the rain let up, but it hadn't, which means Charlie must have arrived after that, just before daybreak. I can see where he got in. The wire has been gnawed at again and he's stretched it wide enough to be able to crawl through it. That'll have to be fixed right away. Another chore to add to the never-ending list.

I stomp over to the workshop and fumble around in Tad's old toolbox until I find what I'm looking for, a pair of pliers. Then, grabbing a scrappy piece of wire from a pile of the stuff, I head back to repair the hole. By now, the dogs have grown bored and are whining at me to "come play."

'Stop that racket,' I grumble, my foul mood not improving.

Unlike a lot of folk, I know that foxes don't kill for fun. That's a myth. Usually, when a fox kills everything in sight and then leaves it behind, it's because he's planning on coming back for it. It's no different, in my opinion, from greedy individuals taking more from an all-you-can-eat buffet than they can possibly eat. That doesn't mean I'm not mad at Charlie, though; I'm furious, and if he were here now, I'd shoot him right between his cold, predatory eyes. To prevent the other hens from being disturbed by the smell of death, I remove the dead chickens, bloodying my numb-with-cold hands, and put them in a bin. Even though I don't have any sentimental attachments to my hens, I do have a responsibility to look after them, and the fox trespassing on my land brings out the warrior in me. I've always been too protective, that's my problem. A prime example of that is Cerys.

When the dogs' ears prick and their tails furiously wag, I look up to see Bryn leaving the house. His bouncy black curls turn this way and that as he searches for me. He can't see me from where I am, and I don't feel like talking to him right now, so I remain in hiding. When I hear his jeep start up, all I can think is, *Thank God he's gone.*

After a brief delay, I let myself out of the coop and trudge up the hill to my mountain with a gun over one shoulder and the dogs racing on ahead.

'Elvis. Elvis!' I yell until my voice cracks, but he is nowhere to be found. Not under the abandoned rusted-out tractor where he often likes to hide or in any of the sheep paddocks. As soon as they hear me call out the little man's name the dogs start to sniff the ground and appear to grasp that this is a search for their missing friend, but they also turn up nothing.

'This way,' I tell them, veering off to the left, in a direction I don't want to have to take, but am left with little choice. I promised my daughter that I would find Elvis and that he would be there waiting for her when she woke up and I don't want to disappoint her, not on top of everything else that has happened to her today. Where can he have gone?

Elvis has to be found. He wouldn't survive a night out here alone. He's still only a pup. He'd freeze to death. Or get taken by Charlie. The rain is getting worse, not better. The clouds are impossibly grey. The downpour has made my waterproof coat heavy, adding weight to my shoulders. The gun is slippery in my hands. Even the dogs seem miserable at this point and their eyes longingly swivel homeward. They have mud up to their forelegs, and the rain has flattened their coats.

I glance in the direction of the woods and the cabin, where Luke, the source of our suffering, is, and sigh at the misery of our situation. I picture the two of them either snuggled up inside as they reconcile or Lynn hurling plate after plate at him in a fit of rage. Their names go together nicely. Lynn and Luke or Luke and Lynn. I wish they'd go back to being a real couple. Or that Luke would go to jail for bigamy. Cerys cannot remain "pretend married," forever, so a solution will have to be found. I happen to think it's a good thing that she's not legally bound to him though. It's just a pity that the baby will forever tie her to him. Cerys may believe they can make their relationship work, but the more I think about it, the more certain I am that it is impossible. I'm relieved that Cerys won't have to experience a messy and costly divorce. Having your business and the intimate details of your marriage dragged through the courts to be pawed over by strangers was a humiliating experience for me.

I wouldn't wish that on anyone. Except for Luke to be on the receiving end for a change.

Even though I can't stop a string of vengeful thoughts going off in my head like fireworks, as I get closer to the barn — the only place I haven't looked — threads of anxiety gnaw at my insides. It stands abandoned, alone on the hill, with a sunken roof and a slight lean to one side. The tarred-black door is propped open as though to welcome me inside.

When I observe that the dogs are no longer following me and are hanging back and acting scared, adrenaline rushes through my body. They appear to be aware that something dreadful occurred here. Toad issues a warning bark at me as if to prevent me from entering. But go inside I must. I'm more afraid of not finding Elvis than I am of actually coming face-to-face with a ghost.

As I squeeze through the gap in the door while willing my heart to stop racing, I realise I left my phone on the table as I check my pocket for it. Even though I don't have a torch, I do have a gun, which I elevate to point precisely in front of me. A chill runs down my back as I am surrounded by the pitch-blackness of the barn.

'Elvis,' I hiss. 'Are you in here boy?'

When I hear a scrabbling sound, my eyes dart to the right. 'Elvis? Is that you? Don't be scared. It's only me.' I prattle nervously, not liking how my voice sounds so incredibly small like it could easily disappear.

As I stand there, motionless, I hear a sharp intake of breath that I know isn't mine and my heart beats so fast it feels as if it will burst through my ribcage. 'Owen,' I whimper, the sound of my heart growing ever louder. My skin prickles as I sense that somebody is standing next to me — their cold, invisible breath mingling with mine. *Owen?* Memories of the night he died flood through my mind. Everything is a blur. I can't breathe.

*'Do it.' I order fiercely, hurling a handful of photographs at him that land at his feet — Cerys aged around nine or ten with straw-coloured hair and delicate blue eyes smiles up at him. One picture shows her astride a white pony. Another of her cuddling a baby lamb. One*

*more of her in a swimming costume. Owen doesn't attempt to pick any of them up, but a low groan escapes from within him. Blinking away tears, he slides the barrel of the rifle into his mouth and seals his lips around it. Once he pulls the trigger everything will stop. I want that. I won't let him tear our family apart or harm our daughter. I would do anything to protect Cerys, including murder. One squeeze is all it takes . . . and then there will be silence.*

A new sound jerks me back to the present and one terror is replaced by another when I recognise the sound of a baby crying. It comes from another dusty, dark corner of the barn. The hair on my arms stands at attention and my jaw clenches as I stalk towards it, realising as I get closer that it's not a baby at all, but a trapped fox making that dreadful sound. *Charlie.*

When he notices me, his high-pitched distress call turns into a soft trilling. His glowing-in-the-dark amber eyes reveal his whereabouts. He is concealed between the barn wall and a stack of rotting, musty hay. I must have cut off his escape route when I entered the barn, trapping him inside. Even in the dark, I can see he's fully grown with a bright orange coat and a white underbelly. His intermittent whimpering is causing the dogs to go mad outside, barking aggressively, and scrabbling at the door. Their desire to protect me has overcome their fear of the barn and if I were to let them in now, they would kill the fox instantly. 'A good death,' Tad would have said. That was before he hung up his gun for his granddaughter. But I like to do my own dirty work and, if this is the same fox that killed my hens, it's also personal between me and him. If Cerys knew I'd killed a fox, she'd be horrified, but what she doesn't know can't hurt her. If I leave it to live another day there's a chance it will come back for more of my hens.

As I lift my rifle, the fox cowers and emits an unsettling screaming sound, once more like a child, as if it realises what I am about to do. As he stares mesmerised into my eyes, terrified and imploring at the same time — images of my dead husband flash through my mind — *his fear, his pleading eyes, the rain, the blood, his limp body* — and my desire to kill vanishes.

# CHAPTER 42: CERYS

Christmas Day has come and gone, and Elvis is still missing. Good riddance to Lynn though who returned to Aberystwyth this morning, but understandably, things remain tense between Luke and me. He's not acting exactly as I'd expected — he is nowhere near apologetic enough and seems distant. I urged him to put "missing dog," signs up in Crickhowell and the surrounding villages but he said he had to go to work today and, quite honestly, couldn't appear less concerned. The Luke I met and fell in love with six months ago, who would have moved mountains for me, isn't the Luke I see now. In the end, Mam and I went together, knocking on doors and searching outbuildings with the consent of our neighbours. Strangely, Bryn was the only one who objected to us searching on his property, saying he would do it himself out of concern for his pigs. Mam raised an eyebrow at that, saying, 'I never realised they were such sensitive creatures,' and his cheeks had blazed red as if he had something to hide.

Luke's expression was a picture when he came in yesterday and saw me in Bryn's arms. It's the first time I've seen him jealous, though I suspect this was more due to male rivalry than anything else. Fortunately, Bryn walked away before they could start posturing and arguing. One fight was enough for one day. Afterwards, I explained to Luke that it was just a friendly hug and how could it be anything else when Bryn was so old. Luke brought up the fact that they were essentially the same age and became even angrier. After checking on me, which I suppose demonstrates that he still cares, he'd gone back to the cabin to talk to Lynn and didn't return until several hours later, when I was ready to talk and all he wanted to do was sleep.

Because he refused to discuss our situation, claiming mental exhaustion, I told him I would be sleeping in my old bedroom for the time being, until that changed, and he agreed that this was a good idea. I could have murdered him for that because if we're not together, how are we meant to mend our marriage, sorry, relationship? Sometimes I think he doesn't want it to work and I know I shouldn't either, not when I consider the lies Luke has already told me, but I love hard. When I fall, I fall. And I find it so difficult to let go, perhaps because of losing my father at such an early age. Luke often used to tease me about having "abandonment issues" but we couldn't have known back then, when we were dating, just how much of a trauma I would be left with, after finding out the truth behind my father's reason for committing suicide. Perhaps Mam was right all along, and I *am* too trusting and naive when it comes to men. She's always saying I'm like a field of daisies or a basketful of kittens and that I need protecting. But I know Luke loves me because he told me so. He even kissed me on the cheek and whispered, 'To the moon and back' last night before I went to bed.

Although I've spent all morning with Mam, until I grew weary from trudging up and down our neighbours' hilly paths and she dropped me back home and carried on alone, I can't talk to her about Luke. It's too humiliating. So, we talked about anything but *him*. Elvis, mostly. Mam seemed quieter and more pensive than usual and I get that she blames herself for not keeping a closer eye on my dog, but how could she have when Lynn showed up at the door to sabotage Christmas? I'm really worried about my poor puppy. Where can he have gone? He usually comes when called, expecting treats, but so far there's been no sign of him, so that must mean he's out of earshot. Far away from here.

When Luke slouches into the kitchen, looking bleary-eyed, I'm working on a new "missing dog" poster on my laptop. This is the first time I've seen him today and it's 2 p.m.

'Good morning.' I'm deliberately sarcastic.

'Please don't start, Cerys,' he mumbles absently.

I look at him properly then, thinking he does look burnt out and we exchange sort-of smiles, making me warm to him. Perhaps things will be all right after all. *I do love him.* Even though I know I shouldn't. What can I say? Other than I'm hopeless when it comes to men. Especially the bad boys it would seem.

'Any news on Elvis?' he asks, sliding bread into the toaster.

'No.' I sigh. 'I'm really worried about him.'

'He'll be fine,' Luke comments indifferently, seemingly more interested in watching the kettle boil.

'But will *we*?' I ask tearfully because I am stung by his dismissive attitude and I want him to come over and hold me. To tell me that everything will be okay. That we'll find Elvis and everyone will live happily ever after.

'Try not to get upset, sweetheart. You know it's not good for the baby.' Luke comes over and lands a kiss on my head while stroking my hair. It's not enough. I want so much more from him. But is he capable of giving me what I want? I once thought so, because hadn't he promised to love me forever, to never hurt me and to keep me safe in his arms? Now, I'm no longer sure. He doesn't feel like my Luke anymore.

'And neither are these.' He scowls as he takes the family-sized packet of crisps I've been munching off the table and throws them in the bin.

'We need to talk, Luke,' I remind him testily.

'I know and we will. I promise.'

I cannot see his face because he is buttering his toast with his back to me, but at least he's starting to say the right things, apart from the dig at me over the crisps. I notice he doesn't offer to make me any tea or toast.

'When?' I press, raising my voice in frustration.

He turns to face me, surprising me all over again with how incredibly handsome he is. No wonder so many women throw themselves at him. Me. Mam. Lynn. And God knows how many others I don't know about. I think I could forgive him anything. *I may have to.*

'I'll try and get off early tonight, plead a family crisis.' He breaks into the most inappropriate grin I've ever seen.

'Only you could get away with saying something like that.' I roll my eyes, wanting to laugh, but resisting the urge. He's not out of the doghouse yet. 'What time?'

'Shall we say eight?'

'Eight it is,' I agree. 'You do want us to make a go of it, don't you, Luke?' I ask uncertainly.

'Course, I do, numpty.' He approaches me again and this time he puts his buttery, toast-crumbed lips to mine, before ruffling my hair as if I were an infant. 'What's that you're doing?' He gestures to my screen.

'A new poster for Elvis. Mam said she'd give me five hundred pounds as reward money for whoever finds him.'

I expect him to be impressed, grateful even, knowing how much Elvis means to me, but instead, his face falls spectacularly.

'Five hundred quid on a dog, when I can't even afford child maintenance payments for my kid,' he fumes.

'A kid we didn't know anything about until yesterday,' I respond angrily.

'I told you that your mam was loaded. I bloody well knew it. All this time she's been lying.' And with that, he crashes out of the room, his spiteful words ringing in my head.

# CHAPTER 43: BETH

I needed to get something off my chest so I've gone back to church. This time it's empty as there's no service on Boxing Day. It looks different without the burning candles and sparkling tree lights. The church was locked when I arrived but I know where the churchwarden keeps the key, so I helped myself to it and let myself in. It is so cold in here. Even though I'm wearing a knitted hat, scarf, and gloves I can't stop shivering.

For eleven years I've kept my secret to myself, sparing even God from the wrong I have done, and during that time I've been so focused on my daughter and then, for a short spell, Luke and my doomed marriage that I hadn't given enough thought to my actions. What would Cerys say if she knew her father hadn't committed suicide at all, but that I made him kill himself? Blackmailed him into it. The way I saw it back then, he had only two choices: go to prison for paedophilia or die — and he chose the latter.

I'm not sorry for what I did. If it meant defending my family, I'd do it all over again in a heartbeat, but coming to terms with having killed a person is a different matter. My husband died right before my eyes. And blowing your brains out with a gun is no ordinary death. I stood by as he begged for mercy, heartless in my desire to protect Cerys. However, a boulder of sadness had moved inside me when I gazed into that fox's eyes and saw my husband's terror reflected in them, afterwards staggering backwards, and dropping the gun. I'm not one for emotional outbursts as a rule, Luke having kicked me of that habit, but tears stream down my face as I stare at the statue of Mary cradling an infant Jesus in her arms.

I'd been eager to start a family ever since I married Owen as I was determined to have a child. It was what I was born for. Owen felt the same so when Cerys joined our family, we felt whole. After that day, we never again brought up the subject of all the lost babies. After a while, we even stopped visiting where they were buried. On this mountain, there are far too many unmarked graves. Dogs. Sheep. Horses . . . People.

From my seat in the first pew, I spare a thought for Bryn and the child he lost. How does he bear it? There was talk at the time that his wife Gwen might have killed her child by accident and then covered it up, but neither the police nor a distraught Bryn could ever find any evidence of that. Although she swore blind that she hadn't hurt so much as a hair on her baby's head, and never would, she was a strange, unnatural creature, in my opinion, to reject her daughter. But as I often say, some people don't deserve to have children. Some of the locals gossip behind Bryn's back, cruelly labelling Forest Farm the "farm people disappear from." *First his daughter, then his wife*, they insinuate, as if it were spooky folklore. When it suits them, they like to forget that Bryn's wife was meant to have done a runner with another woman.

Everyone was happy for me and Owen when Cerys finally came into the world after so many miscarriages, but at the same time the mountain folk avoided Bryn and Gwen who had tragically lost theirs around the same time. Unfair or what? The amount of suffering Bryn and I have endured over the years warrants some peace, and that's what I'm after today.

It's time to let the old guy in, which is my nickname for God, so I get down on my knees and kiss the St Christopher

I've had around my neck since Sunday school, before steepling my hands together in prayer.

'Lord Jesus Christ, you are the lamb of God. You take away the sins of the world. Through the grace of the Holy Spirit restore me to friendship with your Father, cleanse me from every stain of sin in the blood you shed for me, and raise me to new life for the glory of your name.' I recite from memory, continuing as fervently as possible, 'I ask this in the name of your son, Jesus Christ. Amen.'

Then, while I'm at it, even though it feels a bit cheeky, I add, 'And please could you make sure little Elvis is okay and that he is safely returned to my daughter, Cerys, who is already going through a difficult time. Amen.'

I scramble to my feet, feeling a little lighter in body and spirit, and I cross myself in front of the altar before leaving the church. Once outside, I march straight past Owen's grave without ever hesitating. If I were to express my feelings to God out loud, I think I would ask that no such forgiveness be shown to him. I'm also well aware of how hypocritical I am given that I have yet to confess my other, equally sinister secret and have no plans to do so. I can only handle one confession at a time.

# CHAPTER 44: CERYS

It's quarter past eight and there's no sign of Luke. He isn't answering his phone or replying to any of my texts, either. He would have informed me, surely, if he had been forced to stay late at work. Knowing that it will piss him off, and not caring, because of my rising anxiety, I phone the pub. It rings forever before someone answers. This indicates to me that they are busy, another reason for Luke having to stay on to finish his full shift.

'The Bear at Crickhowell.' A female voice, out of breath and not very polite.

'This is Cerys Griffin,' I say bluntly, in a nutshell wanting to know if she is the same co-worker that Luke had a beef burger with during his break. 'Can I speak to my husband, please?' No need for her to know that we're not as married as I thought we were. Besides, I tell myself for perhaps the hundredth time, a marriage certificate is just a piece of paper.

'He's not here.'

God, she's abrupt. I want to suggest that the hospitality industry might not be the right career choice for her, but of course, I don't, instead saying, 'Oh, has he left already?' Knowing that he's on his way home fills me with relief. I won't mention to him that I rang the pub. Hopefully, this girl won't either.

'No. He didn't come in today.'

'That can't be right.'

'I can assure you it is. We're all having to work longer shifts because of his no-show. The boss isn't happy.'

'You mean he didn't even ring in?'

'Nope. Look, we're really busy . . .'

'No, wait. If he does come in later, or if you see him at all, can you please ask him to ring me? I really need to speak to him. It's—'

'This isn't a marriage counselling line,' she interrupts rudely before hanging up the phone.

Hopping mad at both her and Luke, I fling a cushion across the room. I'd lit candles and opened a bottle of red wine, so that it would be at the right temperature when Luke arrived home, and Mam, taking the hint, had retired early to bed, but not before lighting the log burner in the snug for me. I can hear the TV on in her bedroom, vibrating down through the ceiling.

First, my dog goes missing. Then Luke. What the fuck is going on? And then I remember Lynn's words from yesterday: 'He is still registered to my address because his mail comes to the flat.'

Luke left the farm at 3 p.m. That was over five hours ago. Where has he been all that time if not at work? Could he have driven back to Aberystwyth to see Lynn and his daughter, hoping to make it back before eight? That would explain why he's refusing to pick up my calls. He wouldn't want to give himself away. The drive is just over two hours each way, so it would have been doable. Except he's not back yet, which must mean something has happened . . . Could he have left me? Gone back to Lynn, for *good*? Anger surges inside me, turning my mouth into a snarl and my hands into fists. This is what I now know to be *the Luke effect*. I'd seen the same righteous fury in Mam's eyes, then Lynn's and now it's my turn. I make a disgusted sound in my throat that does nothing to match how furious I feel.

But I'm not like Mam or Lynn, and I won't stand for it. I've had my fill of Luke's lies. He can't treat me like this. I'm expecting his child, for Christ's sake. Now I sound like Mam who blasphemes an awful lot for a Christian. Swears too. Much more than me. My shoulders slump when it occurs to me that Luke has already abandoned one child without giving her a second thought, so that he could run off and pretend to marry me. Nothing is stopping him from walking out on an as-yet unborn second.

Glancing shiftily around the room, as if it will provide me with the answers I'm searching for, I grab the full bottle of wine and taking it into the kitchen with me, I pour it straight down the sink. Then, tearing one of my "missing dog" posters in half and turning it over, I write on it:

> *Mam. Luke's not back and I think he's gone to see Lynn. I'm on my way there now to have this out with him once and for all. I'll be fine so there is no need to worry. Back soon. Love Cerys.*

I know this won't stop Mam from worrying the whole time I'm away and I feel bad for subjecting her to that on top of the day she's already had, spending the majority of it searching for Elvis in the cold and rain, while seeming out of sorts. I hope she's not coming down with anything. With a bit of luck, she'll remain in bed and be none the wiser that I've even gone. I'll be as quiet as a mouse when I leave so that she doesn't hear me.

Grabbing the keys to my pink car, I head towards the back door and I'm about to exit it when my gaze swings back to the kitchen — at the familiar, lived-in, dog-cluttered, farm-smelling, warm and cosy mess of it — wondering if we will ever sit down as a family at the old pine table again. But family life, as we used to know it, when it was just Mam and me after Grandad passed away — and before I went to university — has never been the same since Luke came into our lives, so who am I kidding? Only myself. And it's all my fault. What sort of daughter am I to marry my mother's ex-husband?

# CHAPTER 45: BETH

As soon as I hear the sound of the car engine outside followed by the dogs' quiet whimpers and the pattering of their paws clicking on the flagstone floor, I spring out of bed and dash to the window to watch Cerys drive out of the farmyard. Only after she enters the narrow lane that curves around the mountain, like an hourglass figure, do the car headlights come on. The sly little minx. Evidently, she didn't want me to know that she had left the house. But why? I thought she and Luke were meant to be having a heart-to-heart tonight to sort things out, which was why I'd made myself scarce in the first place. But his, *my*, Defender is not in the yard, making it clear he hasn't returned. What is he up to now?

Slipping on my threadbare dressing gown, I race down the stairs, shushing the dogs once I reach the kitchen to let them know there's nothing to get excited about, although I'm not sure that's strictly true because I'm stunned into helplessness when I read the note. Cerys travelling all that distance alone in the dark whilst pregnant bothers me. Once again, this is Luke's fault. Is he really at Lynn's as my daughter suspects?

Knowing there's no chance of me grabbing any sleep now, I go into the snug, leaving the dogs in the kitchen, and pour myself a large glass of whiskey before sinking into one of the squashy leather sofas to warm myself by the log burner. Fishing my mobile out of my pocket, I punch out a WhatsApp message to Cerys:

> *I wish you hadn't gone. I'll be worried sick all night now. Please let me know when you get there. Any problems text or ring and I'll come and get you. Drive safe and take care. Love Mam xxx*

It isn't until after I've hit send that I realise I have no means of transportation, but I make up my mind that I'll phone a taxi if necessary and sod the expense. I simply want my daughter to come home. If I'm being honest, that's all I've ever wanted. When she first left the farm to go travelling, fear had gnawed away at my heart and the hole in it became even bigger when she moved out to live in university dorms. After that, Luke came along, like a giant spider, to lure her into his deceitful web — and now we're both trapped in a toxic world of his lies, unable to escape.

Bristling with frustration, I tip the whiskey back into the bottle, deciding that I shouldn't consume any alcohol in case I end up being needed. Instead, I play a card game of patience to keep my mind occupied.

* * *

It's almost midnight and I'm flipping over the joker in the deck of cards, when I see car headlights sweeping across the window. For a moment, my mood lifts as I assume Cerys has come back but when I identify a diesel engine by its savage rumbling, I'm gutted it isn't her. I'm trying to figure out who it could be at this hour when panic digs its razor-sharp claws into me. If Luke is in Aberystwyth, it can't be him. Bryn, perhaps?

I brace myself for a knock at the door, but when it's wrenched open and the dogs begin to shuffle about and whine, I also hear an accompanying whistle that, to my ears, sounds too casual, forced even. I know then that it is my son-in-law. He hasn't been to Lynn's. That was an error on Cerys's part. I quickly send her another message letting her know this, but when I see that she hasn't read my last one, dismay lodges in my chest. I hope she's all right. Her being away from the farm makes me uneasy. Scooting forward in my chair, I wring my hands nervously as I gather myself for another round of Luke's lies and love bombing. *Please don't come in here. Go straight to bed,* I silently plead. My nerves spike at the thought of being alone in the house with him. With Cerys in Aberystwyth, I can't shake off the feeling that this won't end well.

My eyes are on stalks when the door handle moves slowly, first one way and then the other as if the person on the other side is debating whether or not to come in. When the handle stops moving, I strain my ears, only to be met with cold deafening silence and I almost pass out with relief. He must have gone. Deciding that I'll feel safer if the dogs are in here with me, I tiptoe discreetly towards the door and pause in front of it. Putting my ear to it, I listen once more . . . and hear nothing. The air is punched out of my body and I cry out in fear when I pull open the door to find Luke standing there — with a pinched face, intense eyes, and brooding expression.

'Beth, you scared the crap out of me!' he says, stumbling backwards but I get the sense that this is an act and that I didn't startle him at all.

The dogs are barking hysterically in the kitchen and hurl themselves against the door to get to me. They are in a panic as a result of my screaming. I wish they were in here to protect me.

'I was the one who nearly shit myself,' I burst out in disbelief while pressing a palm to my chest to stop it thumping. 'What in the world are you doing creeping about out here?'

'I thought you might be taking a nap. I didn't want to disturb you.' His face twists with fake concern.

'Only old people take naps,' I bark. I can tell by the way he's slurring his words that he's been drinking. While Cerys has been driving around in the rain looking for him, he must have been at the pub. *Arsehole.*

'Okay. Okay.' He raises his hands in surrender, a twitch of a smile tugging at his cheek. 'Let me make you a cup of tea for the shock.'

He then does a military about-turn and marches back into the kitchen. After having such a fright, I could use a bloody whiskey rather than a flipping cup of tea, I decide, collapsing heavily onto the sofa and filling the same indent in the buttoned leather that I left in it a moment ago.

The moment the dogs rush through to check me out, sniffing at my lap to make sure I'm okay before flopping at my feet with their tails wagging aimlessly and their eyes stretched vaguely in my direction, I instantly feel better. I'm even more reassured there's nothing to be concerned about by the everyday sound of the kettle crackling as it prepares to boil. I convince myself that this is just another typical night in our somewhat unconventional family. That I'm secure. There is no threat to anyone.

Honestly, what was he thinking to scare me like that? The fool. My gaze is drawn to the joker card that's lying face up on the coffee table. Its smirking face reminds me of Luke. 'Always the Joker.' That's what I'd said to him yesterday. My uneasiness returns when he enters the room holding a mug in one hand and wearing the kind of crooked smile that women find so alluring. For some reason I can't explain, a tiny voice in my head is urging me to run.

# CHAPTER 46: CERYS

The row of Victorian seafront houses in rock-stripe colours is well-lit even at night. Lynn lives at No. 3, the top flat of the imposing blue and white townhouse, according to Mam's visitor log for the cabin. I'd found it in a kitchen drawer while searching for a box of matches to light a candle before ever meeting the woman. Luke was lying when he said his flat was "squalid" since, at least from the outside, it looks incredible. Its windows look out over the promenade and the north beach, where my university friends and I would flaunt our flawless bodies in the tiniest of bikinis and object to old men gawking at us. The fit good-looking lifeguards, however, *were* allowed. While he was still living with Lynn, Luke might have been ogling me from the top window. Had he noticed the girl with the distinctive long, pale-blonde hair cavorting on the sand with her friends and set out to find her? I'm beginning to suspect our first meeting wasn't exactly the chance encounter that he made it out to be.

As I walk up the steps and see the illuminated doorbell on the exterior wall, I realise I'm going to have to buzz the flat first, meaning I won't be able to take Lynn by surprise as I'd hoped. When I see the name Griffin allocated to Flat 3, my insides churn, not with rage — as I'm all out of that

— but with something more like acceptance. But just then, as if good fortune still existed in the world, a man comes out of the door, holding it open for me in a gentlemanly gesture and I slide in, thanking him gratefully.

There isn't a lift, just three short flights of meeting-room-blue carpeted steps. Not ideal for a sometimes-single-parent of a three-year-old like Lynn. I don't feel anxious when I find myself in front of her door. She's already paid us an unannounced visit, so why shouldn't I? Is it possible that was only two days ago? It seems like a lifetime ago. No. Lynn hadn't considered our feelings when she showed up unexpectedly at our place and lied to Mam about who she was, so the feeling is mutual.

Behind the door, I can hear a child screaming. It must be Evie. Why doesn't Lynn do anything about it? I'm left wondering what sort of mother she is as a result. If my child were crying, I wouldn't ignore it.

Or is this a hint of what's to come for me as a single parent because it's looking more and more likely that's what I'm destined to be. I ask myself, am I ready for motherhood? *You bet I am.* Like Mam, I see it as the best job in the world — not the only job of course, because I'll still need to work to support my child. I fear I'll have to do that regardless of whether Luke is in our lives or not because the future doesn't look good with him not showing up for work or even telling his employer he was going AWOL. Like an unneutered tomcat, he would rather doss around all day and then go out on the prowl all night. A depressing thought . . .

Knowing there's no point waiting for the cries to die down before knocking because that might never happen, I let the knocker drop twice. In the fraction of a second that Evie stops sobbing, I hear a woman's voice exclaim, 'One minute,' loudly, followed by the sound of a dog yapping incessantly. At first, I don't give it much thought, but then . . .

I would recognise that high-pitched barking anywhere. It's Elvis. I'm sure of it. Blood boiling, I pound the door with my fist till it cracks open an inch and a set of blue, fake-lashed eyes stare back at me. When Lynn realises who I am, her mouth drops open in shock, as if to say, 'You!' but I'm already stabbing my finger at her overly sexy bosom and saying, 'You've got my dog.'

'What are you talking about? It's Evie's dog.'

I start to doubt myself, but then I hear Elvis's out of sight whining from behind the door, and I know then that he's recognised my voice and is desperate to see me.

'We'll see about that,' I murmur, opening the door with the flat of my hand and strolling past Lynn, who is slow to react because she's been taken off guard.

'Elvis. There you are.' I pick up my ecstatic puppy, whose tongue and tail are assaulting my body at racing-car speed. 'Let me look at you and see if you're okay.' I hold him at arm's length and shoot Lynn a furious glance, as I inspect his writhing body. He doesn't appear any worse for having been kidnapped.

'I can't believe you stole him.' My face twists with anger as I turn to confront Lynn.

'Hold your horses. Who said anything about stealing?' Lynn snaps.

'Why else would he be here?' I demand, noticing Evie for the first time whose confused gaze is flitting between her mother and me.

She's concealed in a pile of toys, kneeling on the floor with a little finger up her crusty nose. Her sobs have dried up but she couldn't appear less happy. She reminds me so much of Luke. There's no reason for a paternity test then, I regretfully conclude. She possesses the same dark blue eyes, a mane of golden locks, and a spoiled, downturned mouth. She will be stunning when she is older, and I have a feeling she will break many hearts. Like father like daughter.

'He was a Christmas present for her from Luke.' Lynn defensively folds her arms and, after pausing for a few seconds, she closes the door to the apartment, before hissing, 'If you must know.'

'We've been looking for him since yesterday, and all the while . . .' I tug at my hair, shocked by this most recent betrayal, but not all that surprised. 'I've had him since he was eight weeks old. He was an engagement present from Luke . . .'

'Mummy. Who is that lady?'

Lynn walks over to pick up Evie as her face drops and she looks like she's about to start bawling again, forgetting about me temporarily. I watch as she places Evie on her lap and settles into a beige corner sofa — the kind I would pick if I had my own apartment — while muttering, 'Just a friend of your daddy's. Nobody special.' She then soothes her child with numerous bird-peck kisses and gently dabs her snotty nose with a damp flannel.

I now realise how much Lynn loves Evie, and I regret my prior judgements of her parenting abilities. *Cerys Williams, lesson learned*, I sternly scold myself. The fact that I had a high-end education does not give me the right to judge others before getting to know them.

I want to loathe the child, which Mam used to refer to as *the miscarriage*, before she knew any better, but she is adorable. Besides, I couldn't be unkind to any child, no matter who the parents were. It's not Evie's fault that my so-called marriage came to an end so abruptly. It's not even Lynn's. It's Luke's. When isn't it Luke's fault?

The flat is immaculate and unexpectedly sophisticated. If I'm being really honest, I'm not sure what I expected from Lynn. Not quite a slum, but also not this. I can't help noticing that our tastes are surprisingly similar. I see that she enjoys reading, just as I do. Her bookshelves are full to the brim. A sly glance at the titles tells me we're fans of the same authors: Karen Clarke and Amanda Brittany, McGarvey Black and C.J. Grayson. She's into psychological thrillers and crime, again like me.

But when I notice the silver "L" for Luke necklace glistening around Lynn's neck, I realise it's just one too many coincidences.

'You have the necklace too!' I roar. 'The one I bought Luke!'

# CHAPTER 47: BETH

Luke sits across from me, appraising me over his glass of whiskey. I now regret not spitting in it. Gypsy is curled up at my feet, her pointy black and white muzzle resting on my slippers, but she seems unusually quiet and not at all like herself. On the other hand, Toad is sound asleep and snoring loudly. The mood is strained and I feel the urge to speak first to break the silence.

'You haven't asked where Cerys is,' I observe pleasantly enough, stealing yet another glance at the grandfather clock in the corner of the room. It's twelve thirty a.m. Cerys could walk in the door at any moment.

'Where is she?' Luke asks dutifully, but when his eyes swing away and he avoids looking at me, I can see he doesn't give a damn.

I narrow my eyes at him and cross my arms. 'Out looking for you. For some inexplicable reason she seems to want to give you a second chance.'

His gaze, when it comes back to me, speedier than super-fast broadband, has a searing quality from the flickering flames of the fire, and I can feel the hairs on my arms being scorched.

'It's a shame you're not more like your daughter, Beth,' he states simply.

Now it's my turn to look away and when I finally comprehend that Luke has grown tired of my daughter and that there is no turning back for him, I sigh heavily. Will he regret his decision at some point in the future, as he did with me? Who knows? Who cares? No one but Cerys, who foolishly believes she loves him, and can tolerate his lies and cheating, as I once did. But it's an illusion. Nothing more than a trick of the imagination. Luke has a magnetic quality about him, making it easy for women to fall for him.

In a rare instance of vulnerability, he once confided that he feared women only wanted him for his appearance and that no one had ever truly loved him. Nobody wants to hear that they are unlovable, not even Luke, therefore I refrained from saying anything at the time. But without his good looks and charm, he doesn't have much to offer. He doesn't even have a personality of his own; instead, he mimics the preferences of his numerous lovers by appearing to enjoy their tastes. He isn't inherently evil, in my opinion. He is simply different from the rest of us since something in his brain and heart is missing. Although he may appear to be a scared young boy in a man's body, I'm quite aware of how dangerous that makes him.

'You should know that I'm sorry for what I did to you, Beth.'

'It doesn't matter now.'

'You always were gracious. I wish I was more like you.' He shrugs almost apologetically.

I mumble, 'I wish that for you as well.'

'That's what I mean about you. Despite everything you've been through, you're still a decent human being.'

'I wouldn't be so sure of that if I were you,' I warn, darkly. 'You might think you know me, Luke, but you don't.'

'I wish I'd never left you. I was a fool . . .'

'That's the first thing you've said tonight that has a ring of honesty about it,' I quip, thinking of the "joker" once again. Then I say more seriously, 'Well, you did. And I've moved past that. As you ought to.'

'You don't mean that.' He lifts his brows comically, as if a woman could never be over him. It's inconceivable as far as he is concerned.

'You only want me because I rejected you,' I point out. 'Your ego can't stand it.'

'You could be right.' He frowns, as if disappointed in himself, and then he stares into the fire.

I don't fool myself into thinking that Luke is capable of self-reflection because I know it's not possible. Now that I come to think of it, he is being way too nice tonight, like he's trying to win me over. That alone convinces me he is up to no good. He'll be incensed when he finds out where Cerys has gone but he won't hear it from me. My loyalty belongs to my daughter and no one else.

'I made a mistake when I left you for Lynn. After only a few days in, I realised it, but I had already committed to the baby and her and didn't want to let them down.'

*Yet you did. Me too.* That is all I can think. But I remain silent.

He grinds his teeth, face darkening, as he mutters, 'For once in my life, I wanted to do the right thing but I couldn't hack it. Everything was too much. Lynn, lovely as she is, was too much. As for the baby . . . I mean I love Evie and all that, but being a full-time dad . . .'

He heaves a sigh that *almost* makes me feel sorry for him, but then I think about how he pretended to marry my daughter and convinced her that he was in love with her only to avenge me and my heart hardens.

'By then, I realised I wanted you more than anything but I knew I'd blown it, so after you refused to take me back even when I lied about losing the baby, I tried with Lynn instead. I really did. But there was no comparison. Beth, nobody comes close to you,' he whispers in an admiring but unconvincing way.

I will him to remain seated and not make any movement towards me as his eyes sparkle with unshed tears and he turns them on me as if they were a secret weapon. As he tries to lure me back into his magnetic web, the atmosphere between us is electric. I know it's a trap. He doesn't want me. Not really. It's the farm he's after. And revenge. Nevertheless, I stare transfixed at his partially open lips, which are already poised to utter sweet nothings and everlasting love if given the chance. But they won't be.

When I make a dart for the door, desperate to escape, he somehow manages to get there before me, gently pinning my arms against it. His nose is inches from mine. I inhale his aftershave. His coconut shampoo. His alcohol-fumed breath.

'No, I don't think so. You don't get to run away from me a second time.'

'You have to let me go, Luke. You had your chance and now it's over. It's been that way for a very long time.'

'Don't say that,' he pleads. 'Everything I've done has been for you. You're the reason I tracked down Cerys in the first place. She was my excuse to get close to you again.'

'An excuse you went on to marry and impregnate knowing it would kill me,' I rage, trying and failing to escape his arms. His spell. His wickedness.

Luke smirks. 'Exactly. Because you still love me.'

I don't respond to that because my eyes are flitting between him and Gypsy. Why isn't she protecting me from him? Her eyes, although half-open, are cloudy and unfocused. I go cold as I realise Luke has done something to her, and a shiver spreads through my entire body. Toad, on the other hand, has gone into hiding as he always does whenever someone raises their voice. He'll be cowering out of sight somewhere. Despite being a large, intimidating guard dog, he is a coward.

'What have you done to my dog!' I yell, tearing one arm free long enough to thump Luke on the chest, while tears sting my eyes.

'She'll be fine. Trust me.'

'Trust you! As if,' I hiss, adding, 'you've drugged my dog and you used my daughter to get back at me. I'll never forgive you for either of those things, Luke Griffin. Never.'

'Very well. Have it your own way,' he snaps abruptly, giving up far too easily, which leads me to think I was right all along and that he doesn't want me at all.

This increases my fury, and I manage to push him away using the muscles I've developed over the years from chopping wood and working on the farm. He is too stunned to want to manhandle me again after that, but his mood darkens. He keeps watch over my every move in case I should run away again, letting me know that wherever I go he's coming after me.

'But I think you should know that after Cerys told me about the reward money for the dog, I went to the bank and used your card at the cash machine,' he sneers. 'Imagine how touched I was to learn that you still use the date of our wedding as your PIN.'

Now that I am free of his grasp, I move away and rub my arm, wanting to erase his fingerprints from my skin. 'You had no right. How bloody dare you,' I fume.

'How dare you!' he retaliates, just as angrily. 'Fifteen grand, Beth! That's how much money you have in your account. I wonder what Cerys will say when she finds out I was right all along and that you *are* loaded.'

# CHAPTER 48: CERYS

Luke giving away Elvis and the necklace to another woman is more than a slap in the face. It's several punches as well as a stab in the eye. For the first time I'm relieved that I'm not married to the man. I ought to pity Lynn, who is furious, but I don't. Elvis won't stop yapping; Evie has resumed crying and Lynn is determined to use every expletive she knows.

'Fucking bastard. He told me he personally picked out that necklace for me. What an arsehole. I'm going to kill him when I see him.'

'You and me both.'

'God! Doesn't that sausage dog ever shut up? Take him. He's all yours. He's driving me crazy anyway. I don't even like dogs.'

'They're not called sausage dogs,' I retort petulantly. 'He's a dachshund.' When I consider how my puppy has been kept confined in this flat with people who don't care about him, I blink tears from my eyes.

'And you can have this back an' all.' Lynn rips the necklace off her neck and shoves it inside my palm. I stare at the piece of silver that has the letter "L" on it and another tear lands on my cheek. Then, as my trembling fingers find the soft folds of the white scarf around my neck, it dawns on me that it wasn't a gift from Luke at all and that Mam must have gone out and bought it once she realised he hadn't gotten me anything for Christmas. Knowing he'd given everything I gave him to Lynn hardens my heart.

'I would divorce him this second if I were actually married to him.' As I say this, I stomp my foot petulantly, as if I were still a child.

'You're forgetting one thing, love. He's still married to me,' Lynn scolds. 'And he's Evie's father, whether you like it or not.'

'And what about Luke? Does *he* like it?'

*Bingo.* I celebrate a small victory because that hit her where it stung. I don't know why I should consider this woman a threat to my happiness or feel the need to come out on top during an argument with her, but I do.

'You'd have to ask *him* that.' Lynn squints her eyes at me and juts out a chin in defiance. Her neck is stretched tall and slender, like a narrow vase, and she shows no sign of backing down as she did with Mam. I'm obviously not as intimidating.

'You don't know where he is, do you?' Lynn guesses at last.

'He's gone missing,' I admit despondently.

'Luke's always missing. What's new?' Lynn scoffs, jiggling her child on her hip in an effort to calm her down. Fortunately, it seems to be working because Evie, despite her mother's loud voice ranting in her ear, appears to be almost asleep. 'Oh, I get it. You thought he was here. Well, I can assure you he's not. And you drove all this way in the rain at night because of him! You must have it bad.' She rolls her eyes in disbelief.

I walk to the beige sofa and take a seat without bothering to ask for permission. I feel as though I'll crash to the floor if I don't take the weight off my legs, which after the long drive feel swollen and uncomfortable. I suppose my blood pressure must have soared when white stars swirl around in my head like glitter in a snow globe.

'Are you all right? Can I get you anything?' Lynn comes to hover uncertainly. She has changed her tone, showing that she is sympathetic underneath the brash demeanour.

'Some water,' I whisper, while bending my head and pinching the sides of my nose to drown out the sudden wave of nausea.

A sleepy, bleary-eyed Evie is placed next to me on the sofa, where she won't roll off, and Lynn then leaves the room and enters what I presume to be the kitchen. I can't look away from Luke's daughter. She is so like him. Belatedly, I realise that the mother and daughter are wearing matching bodysuits with Christmas trees and reindeer on them. How cute is that? Actually, I'd forgotten that the majority of people are still celebrating the festive period. Not the Williams or Griffins though. I wonder whether Luke has a set of identical pyjamas waiting for him in a drawer somewhere. I can't see him agreeing to wear them but who knows what he's like when he's with Lynn. It seems like he adapts to all of us.

With Mam he played landowner and rural gent, sporting gilets and tweed caps . . . even though he worked in a bar by night. With me, he became a vegan (allegedly) and pretended to care about the environment and human and animal rights. With Lynn, I imagine he played the doting dad, child bouncing on one knee. For a while anyway . . .

'Here you go. Drink it slowly,' Lynn orders, handing me a glass, which she helps to secure in my trembling hand. She settles down next to me as I take a thirsty sip.

'Why do you put up with him?' I inquire, as I study her worried expression. *I could ask myself the same thing.*

'It's him that can't keep away.' She casually shrugs off my question but I can see the hurt hiding behind her eyes. They swirl with grief. As do mine. As do Mam's.

'No matter what, he always comes back to me, so I suppose that must mean something. He's told me "I'm the one" enough times for me to believe that *he believes it* if you know what I mean.' Before continuing, Lynn puffs out her cheeks, as if mad at herself for falling for Luke's falsehoods. 'I bet he told you the same thing. But Luke promises I'm the real deal and that I satisfy most of his needs. He reckons I make up ninety per cent of what he looks for in a woman and that he only ever leaves me for the missing ten per cent he can't get from me but can from others.'

It strikes me as I hold Lynn's warm look that she's different from Mam and me. Her secret is that she's immune to Luke in a way that us Williams women are not. He says the same thing to all of us, and we, meaning Mam and I, choose to believe it whereas Lynn recognises it for what it really is, and she uses that to her advantage, taking everything he says with a pinch of salt. They get along because of the transactional nature of their relationship.

She supports my hypothesis when she says, 'I wouldn't call it love; to be honest, I'm not sure if I've ever experienced that, but we get along okay, and when he's here, he's good with Evie. He's funny, attractive, and, as you already know, pretty hot in bed.' Then, noticing my tense expression, she motions to her mouth and makes a zipping gesture, adding, 'I'll shut up, shall I?'

While I understand that what Luke is offering Lynn might be enough for her, it would never be enough for me. I view myself as a high-value woman, and I demand and deserve better than that. But even though Lynn has promised to stop talking, it's evident she hasn't, so I sit up and pay attention to what she is saying.

'I know you want me to stay away from him.' Lynn lets out a long and troubled exhale. 'And I've tried that before, countless times. But he won't let me go.'

'What do you mean he won't let you go?' I scowl, not understanding.

'He doesn't let any of us go. Not me. Not you. Nor your mam. He thinks we're his forever. That we belong to him.'

'Does that make him dangerous?' I gasp, suddenly fearing for myself and my child.

'Aren't all men?' She shrugs once more as if it were her answer to all of life's problems. 'Put it this way.' Lynn inches closer to me and lowers her voice to nearly a whisper with a razor-sharp edge. 'I wouldn't want to be your mam for anything. Luke has always been completely obsessed over that woman.'

Before I can respond, a message comes through on my phone, and to my ears it sounds like an urgent, high-pitched distress call, much like the flashing blue and red lights of the police cars the night my father passed away. I take my phone out of my pocket with the same ominous feeling I had that night and read Mam's first message.

As I realise that she's only worried about me, as one would expect from her, my body relaxes. But, when I read her abrupt second message: *He's here*, the bone-white walls of the flat engulf me until I am unable to breathe, and I feel something inside me snap. Is Lynn right about Luke being obsessed with Mam? And if so, does that make him dangerous? Have I played into Luke's hands by chasing him all the way out here, while he, meanwhile, is back at the farmhouse, alone with Mam?

# CHAPTER 49: BETH

Luke pulls a wallet from his back jeans pocket, opens it, and dangles a wad of cash in front of my face. 'The machine would only let me withdraw three hundred and fifty pounds of your secret hoard at a time but it's a start.'

'That's theft plain and simple.' I bristle, wanting to lash out at him, but not quite having the guts to. I've never seen Luke this angry before so I cannot predict what he would do. *Would he hit me back?*

'Ha.' He fakes a laugh and his spittle flies across the room. 'You mean like you stole from me. I left here with nothing two years ago while you kept everything. Everything, Beth.'

'You're forgetting one thing, Luke,' I caution.

'What's that?'

'You came here with nothing,' I remind him.

When Gypsy stirs and raises her head, growling softly, before dropping her jaw to the floor once again, Luke grabs hold of me once more and turns me to face the door. This time, though, his hold is firmer and I struggle to escape his clutches. 'Get off me. Take your hands . . .'

He pushes me in the direction of the door and opens it as I feel his palm pressing the middle of my shoulders. 'If you don't come through here, Beth, there's no telling what I'll do to your dog if and when it wakes up again.'

I allow him to guide me into the kitchen after that, since I know he means it. Once inside, he abruptly lets go of me and slams the door shut before heading over to lock the back door.

'Are you expecting trouble?' I raise an eyebrow.

'From you, nothing but.' He grimaces, keeping a close eye on me while leaning against the sink. 'I told Cerys all along that you could have helped us out more if you wanted to. Given how hard up we were, *your own daughter,* how could you have kept all that money for yourself?'

'What is it you want, Luke?' I get to the point, crossing my arms. After my run-in with the fox yesterday, I left the gun in the utility room, and I have to force myself not to glance in its direction now, in case Luke interprets the look and beats me to it. I remember that I hadn't locked it away in the metal cabinet. What if Luke got his hands on it and threatened me with it just like I had done to him yesterday, albeit unintentionally?

His eyes flash with a smugness I've never seen him display before as if he thinks he's finally won. 'How much are you prepared to pay me to leave here for good?'

I flinch at his words. 'You mean you'd abandon Cerys and the baby?'

'For the right amount, I'd do anything.' He gloats. 'Just as I would've done anything to get into your daughter's knickers if it meant getting my own back on you.' He looks like he's finally enjoying himself, especially when he sees the look of disgust crawling over my face.

'Is that what this is about?' I wave my hands around the room as if the entire farm were represented here. 'Money?' I bark at him while making a disgusted noise in the back of my throat.

'Only those who have plenty of it talk about it as if it were a dirty word,' he protests.

'Luke, the gold-digger.' I roll my eyes and glare at him like the vermin he is. 'What a fitting epitaph for your gravestone.'

I can see him blanche in response to my comments, but he immediately recovers and continues. 'How much?'

'Ten grand,' I tell him as if I'm plucking a figure out of nowhere.

'Fifteen,' he counters.

'I see that you want everything as usual. But you know what, it'll be my pleasure to give you it all. Anything to see the back of you,' I taunt. My eyes are mere slits when I add, 'For good this time.'

I slowly move away from the table where he left me, not far enough for him to notice, but I want to get my hands on that gun so I can somehow change the course of events. There's no way he's getting his hands on that money. Let alone my daughter. *Somebody would have to die first.*

'We'll go into town first thing tomorrow morning and you can make the withdrawal then. I want cash, mind,' Luke instructs, avoiding my gaze as if he is ashamed of what he is doing on some level. He wasn't raised to be a criminal or a horrible person but, as a result of his own shortcomings, that is exactly how he's turned out. He's scum and he knows it.

Luke, being Luke, and not the most intelligent person, wouldn't know that rural Welsh banks like the one in Abergavenny wouldn't give out that amount of cash without prior notice. It typically takes three working days. None of that matters though because we won't be going anywhere together tomorrow morning. I can guarantee it. Naturally, though, I don't mention this to Luke.

'You've always wanted what you can't have, haven't you?' I ask conversationally while taking another imperceptible step in the direction of the utility room.

'Why is that relevant now?' He narrows his eyes suspiciously.

'Because, Luke, it's not my money. It's always been yours.'

'What are you talking about?' He shifts his position and displays confusion.

'I'm talking about the money Cerys's grandad left her when he died.'

'I know all about that,' he mumbles dismissively, his melancholy eyes hugging the floor. 'That's long since been spent.'

'But neither Cerys nor you are aware that what she received was only the first instalment. She wasn't supposed to get everything at once.'

'You're lying.' His eyes reflect his shock and mounting discomfort.

In fierce defence, I shake my head. 'I agreed to hold it for her and give her some when he died and the rest later. That's why I transferred the cash over to my bank account a few days ago so it would be available because she's due to inherit her next instalment on her birthday, which as you know, is New Year's Day.'

'How much money was she left overall?' Luke demands to know. *Of course, he does.*

'I kept it a secret from Cerys because I knew I couldn't trust you with her money. And because I thought it would be a lovely surprise for her.'

'How much, Beth?' Angry veins throb across Luke's face as he yells.

'One hundred thousand.' I chuckle as I allow that sum to sink in.

He takes the news hard. His clenched jaw and stiff posture speak for themselves. I'm waiting for his eyes to fill with regret, as they're bound to.

'Luke, you've been chasing the wrong woman all this time. It's Cerys who holds the purse strings . . . who has all the money . . . not me. The farm is hers too. When I told you Tad was going to leave it to me, I lied. It was never mine. It was held in trust for Cerys. I merely served as its keeper and until you came along, I was happy to do so.'

He reels, staggering backwards and hitting his spine against the sink. 'Is this true?'

'You're nothing more than a fortune hunter, and now you've exposed your true colours, you've lost everything.

Once Cerys finds out about this, she'll never want anything to do with you again.'

Then . . .

From behind us . . .

A long drawn-out growl.

'Once Cerys finds out about what?' the voice demands.

Luke and I both jump in alarm and turn around at the same moment to face a wild-eyed, windswept, sodden Cerys, who is standing in the utility room doorway with a gun pointed at us.

# CHAPTER 50: CERYS

The shock of almost crashing the car on the way home, aquaplaning across a flooded section of the road till it skidded to an exceedingly dangerous stop inches from where the mountain ended, isn't the only thing making my hands shake. It makes sense that I've never handled a firearm before given what happened to my father. I can't bring myself to wonder if the gun I'm holding is the same one that was used to blow his brains out. Surely, Mam would have gotten rid of it. Wouldn't she?

When I let myself in the front door just now, which must have been left unlocked since yesterday when I insisted Mam leave it that way for Luke, and heard raised voices coming from the kitchen, I crept into the utility room's other door, accessible through the downstairs loo, so I could listen in without being discovered. Only when I heard Mam hissing at Luke that he'd been chasing around after the wrong woman, did I grab hold of the gun off the worktop. Don't ask me why. Rage probably. And a desire to scare Luke as much he was scaring me. My whole life was unravelling and he seemed oblivious to the fact. *Didn't care more like.*

I feel like I'm almost done with Luke now that I've spent time with Lynn and little Evie. Although Mam would describe Lynn as cheap and tarty, she has a heart of gold to match her highlights. Much to my surprise, I came away liking her, although I wouldn't admit that to Mam because she had thought of her for years as the woman who had stolen her husband from her — not that she had wanted Luke by that point. But no matter how you feel about someone, being cheated on is the worst thing you can do to another human being. It degrades you. And them. I ought to have looked out for Mam more. Been there for her when she was going through a painful divorce. Flying home for a month wouldn't have hurt me.

My worst crime though was choosing to believe Luke when he accused Mam of lying about all the affairs. I'm deeply ashamed of myself for that. How could I have been so caught up in my desire for him that I lost all sense? What was I thinking? I'm meant to be an intelligent, grade-A student. And I became a dithering idiot when I met him. A sickening version of myself. So much for feminism and the empowerment of women.

Luke crouches in dread as I peer through the gun's sight at him, and I find myself wondering what all the commotion was about. Long hair on a fifty-year-old somehow appears ludicrous to me now and next to Mam, he seems rather old. When he isn't smiling, like now, his jowls sag and there are age spots on his hands. All the things about him I used to find attractive now make me nauseous. The quick wit and easy humour I once credited him with I now see as nothing but sarcasm and a desire to belittle others so he could feel clever and important. I used to think he was such a kind and loving person, but after seeing the destruction he's wreaked on the lives of those who love him the most, I know that Luke is manipulative and cares only about himself.

'Cerys, love. Put the gun down, there's a good girl.' Mam reaches out a wobbly hand in a calming gesture but doesn't attempt to approach me. She's too wise for that. Like an old mare, bombproof to ride. Unafraid of passing traffic. Or circling dogs, like my husband.

When I swing the gun from Luke to Mam, so I can keep an eye on them both, I hear Mam's sharp intake of breath.

'You don't know what you're doing, Cerys,' Luke whimpers, holding a cowardly palm out in front of him. As if that will stop me. As if anything could.

'What if I do?' I protest hotly, cocking the gun so it's ready to fire. I may never have used a firearm before but I'm an avid reader of thrillers and I'm of the generation who grew up on real-life crime documentaries. Not only has Netflix taught me how to break a person's neck and make a body disappear, but also how to operate a bolt .22 rifle.

'Now, where were we?' I scowl, adding, 'Something to do with Luke chasing around after the wrong woman and this farmhouse being mine.'

'Cerys, I can explain.' This comes from both of them at the same time.

'One at a time,' I command, letting the gun come to rest on Mam's scrunched-up face. 'You go first.'

'I was going to tell you on your birthday.' Mam heaves a sigh.

She seems unafraid of the gun. And me. Even though I have no intention of hurting her, this bothers me more than it should. Next to her, I'm seen as weak and insignificant. A spoilt Barbie doll.

'Why not before then?' I jerk the gun at her. *Why isn't she afraid?* Am I that pathetic that I can't scare anyone even when I'm armed. This causes me to bark louder than I intended. 'Like when I had to practically beg you to let me and Luke move in.'

'It's my home too, love,' Mam asserts.

'Did you know Grandad was leaving the farm to me?'

'Yes, of course. It's what I wanted too.'

Deciding that I believe her — I mean why would she lie as she could easily have fought Grandad's decision or even challenged the will — I lower the gun a fraction. 'And what did you mean about Luke chasing around after the wrong woman and me holding the purse strings?'

'You mustn't listen to anything your mam says,' Luke interrupts. 'She has been lying the whole time—'

'One at a time, I said.' I remind him without once glancing in his direction before screeching, 'Mam.'

'Your grandad also left you some money. More than you were originally told. I know you were over twenty-one when he died, and legally an adult, but that was still incredibly young in his eyes. He didn't want you to have it all at once in case it went to your head. That's why he made the staggered payments a condition of his will. He made me promise to—'

'How much money?' I gasp.

'A lot.' Mam shakes her head, in shame or anger, I can't tell. 'Over a hundred thousand.'

'A hundred thousand pounds! Why on earth didn't you tell me?'

I watch her cast a side glance at Luke, before muttering, 'Isn't it obvious? He would have had it off you in a second.'

Given what Luke had done with Elvis and the necklace, she has a point. But I can't get rid of the impression that Luke took those actions out of desperation. He had no money, and Lynn was after him for child support. He might not have stooped so low if he weren't in such a tight spot. This makes me feel even more angry because that money might have been the making of us.

'But you were aware of how poor we were. Instead of having to move in with you, we could have used that money to place a down payment on a house of our own.' I steal a glance at Luke to find him staring at me with the softest and bluest of eyes that have a Jesus-like quality to them. In that moment, I feel my heart tug. I can't lie.

'She could have helped us, sweetheart, but instead she forced us to move in with her knowing how difficult it would be for us. For you,' Luke exclaims, shaking his head in bewilderment.

'I was going to tell you on New Year's Day in just under a week. It was all planned,' Mam combats, throwing Luke an evil look.

'But why didn't you tell me about the money when you found out I was pregnant and before we moved in here?' I ask shakily, sensing for the first time that Mam had an ulterior motive for wanting us under her roof.

# CHAPTER 51: BETH

'You're forgetting that *you're* the one who asked to move in with me, not the other way around,' I respond, furious that all of my past attempts to support my daughter are being interpreted negatively.

'But I didn't know then that it was my house — not yours — and that you should have been the one asking for permission to stay.'

I am taken aback by her attitude. 'Talk about ungrateful.' I recoil, fixing my steely eyes on her much-loved face, before softening as I concede, 'I admit I thought it might be better if you moved in here, for a while at least, but only so I could keep an eye on Luke. To find out what he was up to.' I narrow my eyes at my former husband, hatred oozing out of the pores of my skin and then return my gaze to Cerys. 'Can't you see what he's doing, twisting my words, and lying?'

'I don't know what to think anymore, Mam, or who to believe,' Cerys grinds out, tightening her grip on the gun.

It's not that I believe she'd ever use the gun on Luke or me. Ever. She is plainly upset and unable to think clearly, though. Why else pick it up on her way in? Something must have happened at Lynn's. Undoubtedly another dispute involving Luke. And then she caught me and him in the middle of another row and it sent her into a panic, especially when she overheard me complaining about him chasing the wrong woman and finding out the farm was hers. Hearing that must have shocked her.

As I watch Cerys's face crumple, I notice her hands are shaking. Her sky-blue eyes are dark with suspicion and full of thunder. My poor, delicate daughter has endured so much in the past few days and my heart aches to see her in such pain. But while she's holding the gun, I can't approach her, in case it prompts her to behave irrationally. I am more familiar than most with what happens following a gun crime — accidental or otherwise.

'Cerys, love, we need to sit down and talk.' I sweep another accusing sideways glance at Luke, intended for Cerys's eyes only. 'There are things I have to tell you.'

'Don't listen to anything she says,' Luke snarls. 'I'm sorry to have to tell you this, Cerys, but . . .' He swings innocent eyes in my daughter's direction, adding, 'She, your mam, came on to me.'

'What? No! I didn't, Cerys. I swear.'

'She's been trying it on with me behind your back ever since we moved in. With you being pregnant, I didn't want to tell you . . .'

'Mam?' Cerys raises a pair of sorrowful, beseeching eyes at me.

I can tell that she wants it to be my fault and not his. If I were guilty of the thing Luke is accusing me of then that would mean he hadn't betrayed her in the worst way possible and her life and relationship wouldn't be a lie. But I can't help her. She has to know the truth. And accept it eventually.

'It's not true, love. You know I'd never do anything to hurt you.'

'But Luke would? Is that what you're saying.'

'Luke would,' I admit, my eyes hitting the floor. I don't want to see the devastation on her face as I continue, 'He asked me for money so he could leave.'

'It was the other way around. She tried to buy me off when she realised that I wouldn't touch her with a barge pole,' Luke fires a spiteful sneer my way. 'She promised to give me fifteen grand if I left you and the baby.'

'Mam. How could you?'

I open my mouth to speak but Luke beats me to it.

Luke pulls a disgusted face. 'You've seen the way she looks at me. She can't take her eyes off me.'

Even though Luke has lied to everyone and Cerys must be able to see that, she still stubbornly refuses to believe it. He really does have that much of a hold over her. Sensing that I am losing the battle of trust with my daughter I close my eyes for a second, allowing the anger and pain to wash over me as I exhale long and hard. If I want to prevent Cerys from spending the rest of her life with Luke, I need to be completely convincing. *Why is it so hard when I'm telling the truth?* Allowing her to become estranged from me — the only person in the world who has her best interests at heart and who would die protecting her — would be the end of her. She needs me far more than she realises. She always has.

'Cerys.' I snap my fingers, assuming from her vacant expression that she's about to mentally depart the room, a habit of hers I recognise from when she was young. She's never been able to cope with real life, having been cocooned in a protective bubble for much of it by her doting father and grandfather. 'Listen to me,' I hiss, determining on letting her have the ugly truth, like it or not. 'Luke has never loved you and the sooner you get your head around that the better. He begged me to give him one last chance. He even suggested that you should go back to university so that he and I could raise the child together. He only got with you in the first place to get his own back on me for rejecting him. I know that's harsh and that you don't want to hear it, but it's the truth and it needs saying.'

'No. He wouldn't.' On that thought, Cerys spins around to confront Luke who is visibly shaken, silenced by my outburst. Guilt crawls over his face, making his darkest of blue eyes twitch. 'You wouldn't,' Cerys repeats.

'It wouldn't be the first time he's abandoned his wife and child,' I remind her sternly since I feel the need to step on egg-shells around her is over. Time to smash them for good. Until all that is left are wet feathers and underdeveloped tiny bones.

'Luke, is this true? Did you really try and blackmail Mam into handing over her money, *my money*, so that you could run back to Lynn? Is that what your plan has been all along? Lynn said that you always go back to her in the end and that you told her she was "the one." Just how many women have you told that to?' Cerys shouts.

Luke's mouth opens to say something, but he then seems to change his mind and his face returns to that of the Luke I met earlier this evening — the dangerous, trapped, brooding villain out for what he can get. I see Cerys's eyes widen with realisation as he nonchalantly shoves his hands into his jean pockets and tilts his head in a rebellious bad boy gesture.

'Okay, I admit it.' He shrugs as if he has nothing to lose. 'Because all this—' he throws up his hands in a lasso-like gesture intended to capture me and my daughter — 'is becoming so boring. Your mam can deny it all she likes, but I know she wants me as much as I do her. But she won't take me back on account of you, Cerys, even though you don't deserve such consideration after the stunt you pulled. You taking up with your mother's ex and rubbing it in her face always seemed selfish and cruel to me. I realised then that I could never love a girl like you. That you weren't a patch on Beth.'

'You used me.' Cerys stumbles forward, zombie-like, and leans onto the table for support. Her face is mangled with heartbreak and disbelief and is the palest I've ever seen it. 'You *bastard*. You used me to get back with Mam. You didn't love me at all.'

'Just give me the money as you promised, Beth.' Luke turns towards me, cruelly cutting off my daughter's words as well as her heart, before spluttering angrily, 'And I'll be out of here first thing.'

'You're going to her, aren't you?' Cerys asks, seemingly still shockable.

'Lynn loves me no matter what.' Luke tosses his curls in my direction, wanting me to know that this is a dig at me, rather than my daughter. 'She's not like you heartless Williams bitches.'

And then he's barging past Cerys, almost knocking into her as he storms towards the door. It's as if he's suddenly no longer afraid of the gun, leading me to assume that this was just an act before. It occurs to me, then, that he thinks her weak. As Lynn did. He really doesn't know my daughter at all. She has my resilience and determination if nothing else.

She proves this now, by screaming, 'You think you can just walk out!'

But he doesn't stop or glance over his shoulder. He keeps on going. Like she doesn't matter. The shock in her eyes is traumatic to see. Terrifying even. A veil of hatred settles on her face like morning mist.

'Let him go, Cerys.' I raise my voice to get her attention. And just as I'm about to add, 'Good riddance to bad rubbish,' there's a massive, deafening bang that leaves my ears ringing, causing me to feel disorientated and as if I were hovering over a mountain edge about to fall. It's like someone has hit me on the back of the head. Did Cerys shoot me? Her own mother? Although I am unable to hear anything, I can feel the echo of gunshot reverberating off the walls.

My daughter is staring at the ground instead of at me when I finally manage to focus my shaky gaze on her. I watch her release the gun, seemingly in slow motion, and it falls with a tinny, echoing clatter that jabs at my pounding eardrum. Cerys then jerks her gaze away from the floor and the large pool of blood that is gathering on it to look at the palms of her hands as if they too were covered in splashes of red. Then, with one word on her lips, she turns her horrified gaze towards me.

'Luke.'

## CHAPTER 52: CERYS

Dogs are barking somewhere in the house. My right hand feels hot and empty without the weight of the gun in it. But I won't look at Luke. I refuse to. Instead, I play a childish game in my head. *What I can't see doesn't exist. Therefore, it can't hurt me.* If I listen hard enough, I can hear the ticking of the grandfather clock in the snug. As the fire goes out, the final wood shards will fall to the hearth. Someone is screaming. Mam? From the corner of my eye, I notice her bending over something. Someone. Crying and pleading with God. Inside me, the baby moves and my hand immediately caps my stomach. Does he or she sense what I have done — that I killed its father — and is trying to punish me for it? Will my child hate me? Growing up, Mam would often lecture me about the sins of the fathers visiting the child, even on the third and fourth generation, but that stopped abruptly when Dad died. Am I now paying the price for what he did?

I realise now that I have been losing my mind up until this point, trying to figure out exactly what Luke wanted. Was it my mother or me? Or the farm to which he believed he was entitled? Even though he'd only been married to Mam for three years and had made no financial contribution to the household, despite having signed a prenuptial agreement, he felt cheated out of his share after the divorce. Luke was a liar, out for what he could get, and he might have been controlling and abusive and had revenge firmly on his mind but was he as bad as he made out? Did he never show genuine compassion? Did he really never have any love for me? If so, he was the most convincing imposter. That is very hard for me to comprehend, probably because I have been surrounded by love my entire life.

But, if I were to go by his actions rather than his meaningless words, he wasn't a good person. Luke was an illusion. A dream. The man I fell in love with doesn't exist. When I originally met Luke, he acted as though he were a perfect match for me by appearing to share my interests and even adopting some of my personality traits. Of course, at the time, I was not aware that these were strategies employed to get me to fall for him.

In addition to lying about being a vegetarian, he also claimed to be an animal lover, but if he had loved Elvis, he would never have given him to a stranger. Nor does he care about the climate or the environment the way I do, but he would have said anything to get where he needed to be at the time — in my underwear — but only to place him back in his primary target's life: Beth, the one woman who got away. Nobody could understand the trauma knowing this brings me, unless they had experienced it themselves, as I have.

If Lynn hadn't shown up to expose his lies, and if Mam weren't his ex, I wonder how long Luke would have played the adoring husband and doting father before getting tired and turning to gaslighting and emotional abuse, which are some of the toxic behaviours I've seen for myself. He had even tried to turn me against my own mother and had succeeded for a while, but it's true what they say, "There's no bond closer than mother and daughter." And if the baby weren't a boy, as Luke hoped it would be, would he have lost interest, as he had with Evie? Lynn was much stronger than me and could take care of herself where Luke was concerned, giving back as much abuse as she got, no doubt. But what about me? What would my long-term future have looked like with him? Would he have done anything to gain control over me and my money, such as isolating me from my friends and family or accusing me of being a bad mother?

Mam was right all along when she said Luke was no good. And I was aware in my head, but not in my heart, that I no longer wanted him in light of what he had done to the three of us. He had abused us all. Me. Mam. Lynn. And abandoned poor Evie as well. He was planning to do the same to me and my child, and I believe that's why he planned to run — now . . . before he was rejected and humiliated again — because he sensed, *knew*, that I was almost done with him and that it would only be a matter of time before he was kicked out of the farmhouse. Again!

He'll never understand how much worse my dread of abandonment — of being left by the men in my life — is than anything he could ever go through. I'm not the girl who gets left behind anymore. I won't tolerate it. I've worked hard my entire life to ensure it will never happen again. I was the most popular girl at school, prom queen three times over, and top of my class. My menfolk adored me. Spoilt me rotten. I avoid the subject of paedophilia when I think of my father.

All of the above meant a loser like Luke Griffin wasn't going to reject me. Even Mam got rid of him because he wasn't good enough for her. Where did that leave me if that were the case? At the bottom, that's where. And that's somewhere I've never visited before. I've turned into someone so pathetic and co-dependant that I've tolerated all of Luke's vile behaviour, because deep down I struggle with daddy abandonment issues and decided that no one can ever leave me, least of all my worthless, lying, cheating lover, whose betrayal was even worse than that of my father's.

Luke will never know any of this. Because he's dead. I shot him. Killed him. And I'd do it all over again in a heartbeat if I had to.

# CHAPTER 53: BETH

Amid the aftermath of the shooting, even while I'm still in shock, I'm relieved to know that my dog is recovering from whatever my son-in-law did to her and is unharmed, based on the barking emanating from the snug. Luke's body is spread out in a twisted, crumpled heap on the floor, a circle of blood surrounding it that makes me think of the red wine he liked to drink. His glassy eyes are open and seem to be resting on me as he stares ahead. I stagger backwards because I don't want to see the same look in his eyes as I did in my first husband's all those years ago. How could things have come full circle like this? The body count has just gone up. That's two murdered husbands now. "Like mother like daughter" has never been truer.

Cerys has killed the man she loves and is in pieces, but only I would know that because her odd behaviour indicates otherwise. This is typical of my daughter, who is broken but is avoiding dealing with what has happened. She refuses to even glance at Luke's body. Instead, she's away with the fairies. The men in our lives accused me of being unduly protective of Cerys, especially when she was younger, but what they couldn't see was that she had always been different. She had a propensity to run away from reality. To leave behind the people that had damaged her. As her mother, I'm aware that she uses this technique to shield herself from those who might hurt or abandon her, which is why I've never understood why she tolerated Luke's appalling treatment of her in the first place, alternatively devaluing and discarding her before love bombing her all over again.

I also don't want to confront the reality of what happened here today, but one of us has to. And that means having to touch Luke's body so I can check for a heartbeat to determine whether or not an ambulance is needed. I don't ask myself if I want there to be one, all I can think about is how I don't want Cerys to have to go to prison for murder. In a place like that, my ethereal, barefoot mountain child would perish.

'Dear God,' I fervently pray, 'please don't let him be dead.' *Don't let me lose my daughter.*

The way Luke is slumped against the door leads me to believe that the bullet, which would have been travelling at several thousand feet per second, had entered through his right ear, where blood continues to pump out, causing significant injury, and haemorrhaging to his brain. His death would have been quick but not usually this instant. When Luke's eyes make a tiny sideways movement as if he is aware of my presence, it confirms my suspicions. I was mistaken before. He *is* alive and is exhaling in wispy, moist breaths. I watch, in dread, as his head sinks further back and his eyes attempt to refocus. He's aware of who and where he is, then. And who I am. This is utterly heartbreaking. Cerys mustn't see him like this. As usual I feel the need to protect my daughter from the harsh truth, so I position myself in front of him, directing his gaze away from her and towards me.

Tears cloud my vision as I crouch down next to Luke to gently swipe a bloody strand of golden hair from his hazy eyes that have mostly lost their hypnotic blue colour. His mouth falls open and his boyish gaze slides over my face as though he were capturing it for memory's sake. This is followed by a lifting of one perfectly formed cheekbone as a faint smile appears. For a second, I see the man he could have been — *laughing, loving, giving, accepting.* One hand then shoots upward, as if intending to cup my face. But his strength is fading fast and the hand drops limply back to his side.

'Bethan.' He coughs, blood erupting from his mouth.

'Luke,' I whisper, so Cerys won't hear.

I realise that he is going to die in a few minutes and that there is nothing I can do to stop it from happening. Nobody deserves to die alone but I imagine the devil will be waiting for him at the black gates of hell when he gets there. I want his transition into the next life to still be kind though, so I smile consolingly and cover his hand with my palm. Poor Luke. The man-child. Did he love me after all? He seemed so determined that I should believe him. Maybe he loved us all in his own damaged way and didn't know it. I can't help but feel sorry for him because of how much he wanted to be loved and admired. And I did love him once.

One last breath, agonisingly lengthy, like a death rattle and I have the impression that his gaze has left me. His hand in mine trembles slightly before falling still. Then, there's nothing. I don't need to check for a pulse or a heartbeat to know that the man my daughter and I had loved and lusted after is no longer with us. The death stare tells me everything. He's gone. Tad would have referred to it as "a good death" and bitterly added that Luke hadn't earned such an easy exit. It had been his idea to leave the money to Cerys in case Luke took me to court and asserted a claim to the farmhouse. Despite having signed a prenup, neither of us knew enough about the law to be certain that Luke wouldn't prevail. Ironically, between the two of us, we had made sure that the money went to the one person that Luke would eventually have complete power over.

I sob as I realise that I've secretly wished Luke dead for years without really meaning it. During the previous six months, more so than ever before. As I struggle to my feet, I wipe away my tears on the sleeve of my dressing gown and when my eyes roam over Luke's dead-but-still-beautiful body one last time, I experience a humbling, overwhelming sense of sorrow that is completely unexpected. And I have to remind myself that it's God who ultimately takes lives. He decides who lives and who dies. Not Cerys. It can't be her fault . . . Or me. With one exception, of course — Owen.

How is it possible that Luke Griffin ended up dying in my kitchen, which up until now has been the centre of my home? And where all of the Williams females matured into women. Stupid women, it must be said, for falling for such a man. Didn't we deserve better? My heart hardens when I realise that this is yet again all Luke's fault. Because of him, my extremely sensitive, highly emotional, and pregnant daughter will go to prison.

She would never survive a stint in jail.

But I could.

# CHAPTER 54: CERYS

I feel Mam's grip on my arm. Her tea-fragranced breath on my face. I'm being led, as if I were a small child, over to the table and made to sit down. I notice that she has positioned me in the chair facing away from Luke and that suits me. I'm not yet prepared to face the consequences of my actions. I am a decent person. I have compassion for other people. I also have empathy. My friends at university would one hundred per cent back me up on this. How, therefore, could I, Cerys Williams, a passionate advocate for human rights kill someone?

'You're not to blame,' Mam is insisting, as she collapses into a chair across from me and grabs hold of my hands. 'This is Luke's fault. He had it coming. He pushed you too far. People will understand.'

'By people, do you mean police?' I ask in a quiet voice that isn't mine.

'You can't go to go to prison, Cerys. You're pregnant and—'

'I killed him, Mam,' I sob as the shock begins to wear off and reality sets in, like the reinstatement of the death penalty. 'I shot Luke.'

'What if you didn't?' Mam's eyes burn with intensity.

'What do you mean?' I protest, snapping my hands away from her grasp. 'You saw me.'

'The way he was shot. It could be made to look like he did it himself.'

I give her a wide-eyed look. Even though I'm a killer, Mam's suggestion has shocked me to my core. 'You mean make it look like suicide.'

'People would believe it. I don't want to speak ill of the dead, Cerys, but . . .' Mam leans forward in her chair, as if unable to contain her enthusiasm. 'He was a liar, a cheat, and a bigamist, and as a result, he was about to lose his wife and unborn child as well as his home. Plus, his ex was threatening to take him to court for maintenance. That would be enough to depress anyone.'

I groan, burying my face in my hands. 'Poor Luke.'

'Never mind, *poor Luke*. You have to put yourself first, Cerys, and we have to act fast if we're going to do this.'

'No,' I exclaim forcefully, cutting her off, 'I won't do anything like that. It wouldn't be right.'

'And shooting somebody is?' Mam barks, as she lurches to her feet to glare at me. Hands on hips, she adds angrily, 'Well if you won't, I will. Since there's no way any daughter of mine is going to prison.'

'Mam, what are you doing?' I panic when I see her grab a tea towel from the sink, briefly run it under the tap, and then walk over to where the gun is on the floor. 'Mam?'

'We need to clean the weapon before putting it in Luke's hand.'

'We can't.' I stagger to my feet as I observe her hunch over the rifle.

'We have to,' Mam mumbles, turning away from me.

Behind her is Luke's body. Although his eyes are still half open, they are lifeless and milky in colour. His gorgeous blond curls drip with coagulating blood. 'Oh, God. What have I done?' I moan while tearing at my hair.

'There's no time for that now,' Mam snaps, her elbow moving back and forth as she wipes my prints from the gun.

I wonder if she's right. What would be the point of me going to prison for killing Luke? It wouldn't change anything. He'd still be dead. And it isn't as if I pose a threat to anyone else. He had pushed me too far, as Mam had correctly stated.

'The police might not believe us. Nowadays, they have all kinds of forensic specialists who can identify the cause of death and establish whether it was a homicide or suicide right away. I've watched enough crime documentaries on TV to know this.'

Mam turns to look at me with a questioning expression on her face. 'Cerys, if that happens, I'll say I did it. They'd believe me given mine and Luke's history.'

'Why on earth would you do that?' I gasp.

'Because I'm your mother.' She points out matter-of-factly. 'And you're about to become one. Whether I'm in jail or on this mountain, I can stand up for myself because I'm as tough as old boots. Whereas you—'

She leaves the rest unsaid, but I can guess what she was going to say. She believes that I am weak, just like everyone else. Given that I just killed a man, how is it possible for her to still think this way?

'Let's just hope it doesn't come to that.' Mam's words come out strained.

She's finished cleaning the gun and is cradling it in the tea towel as she warily approaches Luke's body. I have to look away when she pries open his right hand to slide the handle of the gun inside it. Morbid curiosity from streaming too many murder scenes and even the occasional autopsy gets the better of me and I'm soon glancing back again. In time to see Mam repositioning Luke's bloodied face. I notice that her posture and technique are both incredibly effective. Like the pathologists, I've seen on TV.

'The entry point below the ear is typically seen in suicides so I think we stand a fighting chance of being believed,' Mam continues in the same vein. 'We'll be all right. You just have to do what I say, no matter what. Do you understand, Cerys?'

The phrase "You just have to do what I say no matter what" makes my heart flip over and a long-forgotten memory from deep within me stirs as I go back in time to visualise . . .

* * *

I'd woken up with a start in the middle of the night, knowing, just knowing, that something was wrong. Sensing that a noise — like a loud bang — had disturbed me, I sat up in bed and wiped the sleep out of my eyes. When the door opened a fraction and light poured in, I thought for a moment it was my dad standing there, coming to check on me to see if I was all right.

'Is that you, Dad?' I'd squinted at the shadow in the doorway, blinded by the light.

'It's me, Mam.'

Her voice sounded different. Tight, strained and somehow dangerous, I remember thinking. I wished then that I'd never woken up. She was soaked to the skin and her hair was wet, as if she'd just stepped out of the shower, but she was fully dressed. I watched her glance sentimentally around the room, at the pink walls, the doll's house, and my name in lights on the wall. Then, as her eyes lingered on my face, she appeared to want to come over and hug me but refrained from doing so.

'Cerys, you must stay in bed. You just have to do what I say no matter what. Do you understand?'

I opened my mouth to protest, but when I recognised that she had been crying, which was unusual for her, I sank back into the bed, thinking she looked tired, even if she did have her authoritative "I must be obeyed" voice on. Who was I to argue? No matter what was going on, I knew Mam had my best interests at heart. I never once questioned it.

I then turned over and drifted off to sleep once more, dreaming about horses and show jumping trophies. The second time I woke up, to an even louder sound this time, there were flashing red and blue lights in our farmyard that lit up my bedroom like fairy lights. They passed by my window in a disco ball of colour that went faster than a speeding police car.

Leaning against the windowsill, my chin propped up in my hands, I'd watched in confusion as the police outside battled against the rain while yelling orders at each other. The thrum of more serious conversations drifted up the stairs and under my door. There were raised voices one minute. Hushed the next.

The sounds I was most familiar with were absent — dogs barking, Grandad laughing, Mam muttering under her breath. When I heard the howling, I held my breath. At first, I thought it was the wind as a terrible storm was raging outside, making the walls of our farmhouse creak arthritically, but when I realised it was Mam, I was unable to shake off the fear that nothing in our world would ever be right again. I wanted my dad but his was the only voice I couldn't hear in the house that night.

# CHAPTER 55: BETH

Part of me wonders, *What now?* as I look up and see Cerys glaring at me as if I had killed Luke and she was an innocent bystander. I simply want this evening to end. Wouldn't it be fantastic if we as a family could undo the previous six months and act as though Luke had never returned to our lives? Instead, we will have to repeat the arduous, drawn-out process of a police investigation — as we did with Owen. My nerves are shot. I don't think I can stand it. Even though I had just told Cerys that I'm as tough as old boots, I'm not sure that statement holds true anymore. I'm so God-damned tired. I have to be strong for my daughter's sake, but if left to my own devices, I would throw myself off the top of the Sugar Loaf Mountain.

'What?' I demand spikily. Something about the way Cerys's eyes are scanning me, head to toe, makes me uneasy. 'What is it?'

'You look like you've done this before.' Cerys frowns and crosses her arms across her chest in a defensive manner.

'Done what?' I ask, lowering my eyes and moving across the kitchen to rinse Luke's blood from my hands under the tap.

'Two suicides in twelve years. I don't think so. You killed Dad, didn't you?'

I twist around to scowl at her. 'How dare you?'

'I believe I heard the gunshot that night, and then you came to my bedroom and told me not to leave my room.'

'You were just a kid. The last thing I wanted was for you to see . . .'

'But that was before the police arrived. And you were already crying.'

'I had just found your father dead, Cerys. Of course, I was crying.'

'I've never understood what you were doing out in the barn anyway.'

'Just like you, Cerys.' I continue to look at the blood dripping down the plughole while facing away from her. 'I heard the shot.'

'But when you came into my bedroom your clothes were wet through, as if you'd already been outside.'

'No. You must be misremembering. I heard the gun going off, went to check on you to make sure you were safe, and only then did I leave the house to find out what was going on outside.'

'But you just said you were crying because you'd found Dad,' she points out venomously.

'How am I meant to remember every detail of that awful night?' My voice sounds guilty to my own ears, so I inhale deeply, steadying myself. 'I didn't kill anyone, Cerys. Your father took his own life,' I say truthfully, relieved when I see uncertainty crawling over her face.

'Why didn't you call Grandad instead of going out there alone?' she persists, albeit less interrogatingly, but still with narrowed eyes.

'He was asleep in bed and you know how impossible he was to wake up after a few whiskeys.' I make a wobbly attempt at smiling but it feels wrong on my lips. There is a dead body in the kitchen with us. *Another ghost.*

'You were the one who gave him the whiskeys. I saw you,' Cerys accuses. 'And I remember because they were bigger glasses than usual.'

I will my heart to stop racing as I turn to face my daughter, while absentmindedly drying my hands on my clothes. My confident demeanour has begun to fray in response to her words. We are both aware of it.

'You did that on purpose,' she gasps. 'So Grandad wouldn't wake up.'

'After all I've done for you, I don't know how you can accuse me of such things.' I'm having trouble speaking because I'm terrified Cerys is going to wring the truth out of me. But on the other hand, a confession from me might help her see sense about her own dire situation.

'What exactly did you do for me, Mam?' Cerys says scathingly.

'The humiliation of others finding out would have destroyed us. Even God could not forgive what he did. Those images of you that he uploaded, Cerys . . . for others to see. I would never have let him hurt you. Never.'

Cerys's face contorts in rage. 'My God. You made him do it, didn't you? You might not have pulled the trigger yourself, but you killed him—'

'It was his choice. Not mine,' I insist, even as the scene in the barn plays out in my head once more . . .

*'Do it,' I order fiercely, hurling a handful of photographs at him that land at his feet — Cerys aged around nine or ten with straw-coloured hair and delicate blue eyes smiles up at him. One picture shows her astride a white pony. Another of her cuddling a baby lamb. One more of her in a swimming costume. Owen doesn't attempt to pick any of them up, but a low groan escapes from within him. Blinking away tears, he slides the barrel of the rifle into his mouth and seals his lips around it. Once he pulls the trigger everything will stop. I want that. I won't let him tear our family apart or harm our daughter. I would do anything to protect Cerys, including murder. One squeeze is all it takes . . . and then there will be silence.*

'Oh, my God. I can't believe you'd do something like that. To Dad of all people.' Cerys's hands cover her mouth.

I scream internally, incensed that Cerys should take her dead father's side in this when all I've ever done is try to protect her from him. 'He betrayed us in the worst way possible and was about to destroy our family. What was I meant to do?'

'I don't know,' Cerys admits bluntly while fixating on the ground. 'But not that. Couldn't you have gone to the police?'

'Are you insane? How long do you think your father would have lasted behind bars? A known paedophile? Suicide was a much kinder option.'

'And you watched him do it?' Cerys scrunches up her face in horror.

'I had to be sure,' I murmur, hanging my head. 'It was him or us, Cerys. Ask yourself what you would have done if it had been your child in danger.'

'I can't hear this. I won't . . .' Cerys wildly runs her hands over her face as she paces agitatedly up and down the room. 'I have to get out of here.'

'Wait, where are you going?' I yell in disbelief as she unlocks the back door and yanks it open, letting the wintry rain in. 'You can't go. Not in the middle of all this. What about Luke?'

'Do what you have to do, Mam.' Her eyes are mere slits. 'Just leave me out of it.'

'Leave you out of it!' My mouth drops open in shock. 'What sort of talk is that? You can't just walk out and pretend you haven't killed someone.'

At that, Cerys rears up. 'Haven't you been doing that for years?'

# CHAPTER 56: CERYS

I am aware that Mam is not telling me everything about what happened the night my father took his life. Don't ask me how I know this. I just do. I feel as if his ghost is trying to tell me something, no matter how absurd that sounds. Or, has my confusion over my feelings for Mam got in the way of reality? It's true that I hated her on and off for a while when I suspected her and Luke of still having feelings for each other. But now I know that it was only Luke who'd had trouble letting go of their relationship, shouldn't I admit that I was wrong and Mam was right all along? Hadn't she proved time and time again that she had my best interests at heart and would never hurt me?

However, this latest revelation about Dad, on top of just finding out that he was a paedophile, is too much to take. How much did Mam contribute to his death, and how could she have stood by while he blew his brains out? The mother I know doesn't sound anything like that. But she doesn't have a problem killing, does she? As a born and bred countrywoman, it comes naturally to her. Death plays a big part in farming life. I've always been told I wasn't cut out for it because I was overly sentimental, especially by Mam. Both Dad and Grandad would have gone to their graves believing that "Cerys couldn't hurt a fly" but I've proved them wrong, haven't I? In the worst possible way by murdering the father of my unborn child.

When the scariest thought eventually hits me, a sob escapes from my throat. 'You can't go to prison, Cerys,' Mam said in the kitchen just before I cut her off. 'You're pregnant.' I realise now she was implying that I might lose the baby. I seriously doubt that someone imprisoned for murder is permitted to keep their child. What would become of it? Would he or she be placed in foster care, or would they allow Mam to raise it? Do I want her to knowing what I know about her? As Lynn put it, 'What a family.' I could be sentenced to life imprisonment for killing Luke, I realise with a sickening thump in my chest. Mam's right — *again* — I can't go to prison.

As I bend my head against the torrential downpour, all of these thoughts accompany me to the car, like passengers hitching a ride. Elvis leaps from the rear seat to the one next to me when I get in, appearing deliriously happy to see me. As I try and fail to start the engine, his almost-smiling, whiskery face has me crying once more. As it stalls again, I slam my fist against the dashboard, but when I notice the kitchen door opening and Mam standing there in a halo of orange light, I try again — and this time the car roars into life. As I drive past the house, I force myself not to look at Mam. She is shouting after me, but I can't hear her because of the lashings of rain striking the car's roof. I imagine she's hoping I'll stop the car and go back inside. To what though? A kitchen full of deceit and death!

I had no idea where I was going when I first stormed out of the house, acting like the spoiled, overindulged, and overprotected child that I still am. But as my eyes hypnotically follow the swish of the window screen blades, it seems to me that I know where I'm heading. To Forest Farm. And Bryn. He's the only friend I have on this mountain.

I drive the short distance there cradling my growing belly as the car slips, stalls and slides down the flooded mountainside. Glancing often in the rear-view mirror, I wonder who the spaced-out woman is staring vacantly back at me. I feel different inside but it's the same reflection I see. Long, straight, pale-blonde hair. Sky-blue, wide-set eyes. Severe cheekbones. A small mouth. When I look again, more closely this time, I see a haunted, trauma-bonded expression lurking behind my eyes. This is what Luke has done to me, to us all.

* * *

Bryn hands me a mug of steaming tea and thoughtfully leaves a towel beside my elbow, which I pick up and use to unenthusiastically dry my hair. The fabric is scratchy, worn and smells of diesel but it does the job. At least I'm no longer dripping rainwater all over the dull, unpolished mahogany table. When I first hammered on the door, I waited ages in the pouring rain for a response but eventually, there was a tugging of the curtains in a window upstairs and a few minutes later I heard a variety of locks being opened.

'Good God! What are you doing here at this time of night?' was the first thing Bryn said to me, but after seeing my distraught face and red, puffy eyes, he opened the door wide and without saying a word invited me inside.

'Are you warm enough? Would you like a blanket?' he kindly inquires while keeping a wary eye on me from a distance.

'I'm fine,' I lie, shivering anyway. Elvis and I are both drenched to the skin, but at least he's toasty because he's parked right next to the yellowish Aga, which, from what I can tell, radiates heat day and night.

'No, you aren't.' Bryn rubs his chin and frowns. He then motions for me to stand up as he moves my empty chair over to the Aga and parks it close to my dog. 'Sit down,' he orders and I do what I'm told because that's what I've become accustomed to. First, it was Mam bossing me around, then Luke. Now Bryn. But at least he's grinning, which kind of implies that this isn't something he's used to.

He nods and moves another chair over for himself, saying, 'That's better,' before unlocking one of the oven doors with an oven glove to let the heat out. My whiter-than-white cheeks are immediately given new life. Sinking into the chair next to me, he motions for me to drink my tea and I take a sizeable mouthful, only to finish up swirling it around my mouth since I've lost the ability to swallow. Because how am I supposed to do that knowing what I've done? I have no right to be warm or have my thirst sated after taking another person's life. *Oh God, Luke. How could I have hurt you?* And I don't deserve the kindness the man sitting next to me, who has known me all my life — but doesn't know me at all — is showing me. He proves this by asking, 'I'm sure whatever has happened to make you come out in the middle of the night can't be all that bad, Cerys, but . . .'

He surprises me by extending his hand and, in a rough but well-intended gesture, wraps his thick fingers around mine. 'When you're ready to tell me about it, I'm here to listen.'

When I hear this more tears fall, but I try to contain them by focusing on his ragged, blackened fingernails. I fear that I might go completely nuts if I give way to my emotions, so I switch to joking instead. 'I can do your nails for you if you like.'

'When you work as a pig farmer all day there isn't much need for manicures,' he responds in kind, his dark green eyes glimmering with amusement. And another thing that I can easily recognise. Compassion.

'Bryn . . . I . . .' A wave of nausea comes over me as the roar of gunfire repeats in my ears. I hate what I am about to do. But Mam was right when she said I had to put myself first.

'Luke's dead. Mam killed him.'

# CHAPTER 57: BETH

I'm at a loss for what to do now that Cerys has left. Should I carry out my plan to make it appear as if Luke committed suicide so that I can continue to protect her, or is she likely to deny it once the cops arrive and admit to shooting him herself? I can't put them off much longer. If we wait too long to report a sudden death, they'll become suspicious, which will only lead to more questioning. After seeing Cerys's car headlights leave the farmyard, I returned to the table and let my head rest on the edge of it, crying till I was spent. As a result, my eyes and throat feel as dry and scratchy as sandpaper. Where can she have gone? Surely, she's not foolish enough to have driven to the police station in Abergavenny.

Clasping my hands together in prayer, I implore God, 'Please don't let her hand herself into the police,' knowing that if she does, it's all over and there's nothing I can do to protect my daughter. She'll end up going to jail for Luke's murder, and the baby will be taken away from her.

Would they let me raise it? Is that an option? Life doesn't always mean life nowadays which means Cerys could be released from prison eventually, in another twenty years or so. But I'd be seventy by then, and I don't think I have the energy to raise a child on my own. Not without my daughter.

Heaving a sigh, I force myself to my feet, cursing myself for wasting time and energy on things over which I have no control. There's no point in worrying because I have no idea where Cerys is. I console myself by imagining she'll be back shortly. She'll come around to seeing my way is best in the end. She knows I have her best interests at heart. And now that she's aware of what really happened to her father, she's bound to understand why I did it. To protect her, of course.

But as I stretch my arms above my head and crick my neck, my muscles feel like they'll never unwind. My entire body aches as though I'd aged ten years overnight. Perhaps it's a hint that I'll inherit Tad's rheumatic bones. It's difficult not to look at Luke's body again; he appears deader than he did a few minutes earlier. Unlike mine, his bones will never rise again. As that thought rolls around in my head, I go and check on the dogs in the living room. Gypsy is up and wagging her tail but still seems a little dazed. Toad won't come out from his hiding place at first, but eventually, I coax him out and he comes to be patted.

Now that I know they're okay — *God knows what Luke did to her* — I plod up the stairs to Tad's old room and gingerly push open the door, not sure what I'll find. It's surprisingly neat and tidy, unlike our lives. The bed has been made. The floor is clear of clothing. When I remember Luke undressing at night and leaving his jeans, tops, and socks where they fell, knowing I'd pick them up from the floor the next day and they'd magically reappear washed, ironed, and put away in his drawer a few days later, a tear stings at the corner of my eye. Humans have this amazing ability to resurrect their "unloved dead ones" into saints when they're no longer around and I'm just as guilty of that.

'But it's Cerys I have to think about, not Luke,' I try to convince myself, only to collapse onto the bed howling as I remember our first date when he had me laughing so hard, I thought I would pee myself. He was eager to please back then, like an exuberant puppy. We'd spend entire afternoons in bed wrapped in each other's arms, something I'd never done before and felt guilty about. Luke, the chatterbox, would talk my ear off about anything and everything . . . which got on my nerves in the end . . . as did everything else, especially the lies and the cheating. But those early days were filled with happy memories that I'd forgotten about, until now. The way he'd toss his golden curls like a male model. His eyes, like the first glimpse of a shiny blue sea, would sparkle with amusement at something he couldn't wait to tell me about. Him tearing off my clothes, admiring my body, and putting his kissable mouth to my skin. My collarbone. My ear. Right between my shoulder blades. I've been worrying about Luke and Cerys for so long, I'd refused to admit that not all memories of him were as horrible as I believed.

That image of him fades and is replaced by the sneering, cruel Luke of a few hours before, who humiliated my daughter in the worst way imaginable by saying he'd never loved her and had set out to use her from the beginning merely to get back with me, *or at me* . . . I can never be sure which. Thoughts of Luke, both dead and alive, continue to plague me and I squeeze my eyes shut to keep the tears at bay, even as I take down his suitcase from the top of the wardrobe and start packing his clothes inside.

Cerys should be the one sobbing over her late lover's belongings as she packs up his only possessions. Not me. His favourite denim jacket. Three pairs of trendy torn jeans, numerous black designer T-shirts, a chambray shirt, a bottle of expensive aftershave, dark shades, a pair of trainers and black laced-up shoes so shiny I can nearly see my face in them.

I zip up the suitcase and check around the room, but all traces of Luke have been erased, so I haul the case down the stairs and into the back of the Defender, not caring that I get completely soaked in only a few minutes. I finish by brushing my hands together. The case is proof that Luke was on his way somewhere. That everything had got too much for him and he intended to run away from us all — just as he said. After I caught him out in his first affair, he had begged me not to abandon him and sobbed because he hated being him. Nobody, not Lynn, Cerys, or me, could hate Luke as much as he hated himself.

Back in the kitchen, I have to touch his body again. Just long enough to ease his mobile phone out of his trouser pocket. This time, I avert my gaze from his, not wanting to see the marble-like emptiness in his eyes. I gulp bile once it's in my hand and I realise it won't open without Luke's fingerprint. The hand without the gun is cold to the touch, his flesh no longer sparking with electricity as it once did when it came into contact with mine. When I forcefully press his left digit to the back of the screen and it lights up, I immediately drop his hand and feel as if someone had stomped on my grave, even though it's the other way around.

Cerys, Lynn, his mother, and the Bear at Crickhowell's phone number are the only names in Luke's contacts. He had no real friends. Just a bunch of acquaintances. People who were most useful to him. I punch out a quick text to Lynn:

> *It's me. I'm not wanted here. They're kicking me out even though I've done nothing wrong. I'm broke and have nowhere else to go. Can I come home? Love Luke xxx.*

I go back into the living room, holding the phone close to my breast as if it will stop my heart from hammering, and pour myself a large glass of whiskey before collapsing onto the sofa. A text like that will undoubtedly irritate the hell out of Lynn. 'Please, God, let this work,' I mumble, since I don't know what else to do. As the message is returned, I feel the responding beep vibrate through my ribcage. When I read her reply, air enters my lungs and my shoulders visibly relax:

> *Not this time, Boyo. Not after that stunt you pulled with the dog and the necklace. You've made your bed and you can lie in it for all I care. And I'll see you in court over the money you owe me.*

I'm not sure what she's talking about when she mentions the dog and the jewellery, but I silently applaud Lynn for finally having the balls to say no to Luke. This has really fallen into my lap. The plan I hatched is taking shape. When the police question us about the shooting, I'll be able to show them the evidence that Luke had planned to return to his wife after being thrown out of the farmhouse, but when that avenue was closed to him, he had nowhere else to go, so he did what many middle-aged, bankrupt, white males do when their selfish, miserable lives catch up with them — he committed suicide.

I hear another ping as I slide the phone back into Luke's pocket, but this time it's not from his phone, but mine. I dig around in my dressing gown pocket for it and pull it out.

It's from Bryn. *She's here*, it simply states.

## CHAPTER 58: CERYS

'You should be able to find something to fit you in there.' Bryn motions to an enormous walnut wardrobe, and shrugs when he sees my confusion. 'My wife, Gwen, left a few things behind when she moved out which I never got around to getting rid of,' he explains, reddening. 'At the very least, they'll be warm and dry.'

'Thank you, Bryn,' I reply, imagining that he kept the clothes out of sentimental value, despite the fact that he previously confided to me that their marriage was not a happy one. I see he doesn't come inside the room but instead hovers uncertainly in the doorway.

'Was this her room?' I blurt out without thinking, only to regret it when I notice his eyes turn distant.

'Yes. We kept to our own rooms for years.'

As he discloses this, I watch his gaze swivel to a photograph on a Victorian writing desk, then fall quickly away again. 'I'm going to call the police now, Cerys, to tell them what happened. Are you okay with that?'

I nod without saying anything, but he catches the panic in my gaze and adds, 'It's not what either of us wants. You know how I feel about your mam, but she's left us with no choice.' With that he is gone, quietly closing the door behind him, leaving me alone in the middle of the vast room.

I can't think about Mam without feeling overcome by guilt and fear, but Bryn has stated that if I don't want to, I won't have to see her at all. *I don't want to.* How could I face her knowing I had deceived her after everything she'd done for me? It makes no difference that she volunteered to take the blame for Luke. That was the shock talking. Nobody, not even Mam, would attempt to cover something like that up. Or would she? After all, this wouldn't be the first time.

I tell myself I'm not like her, but . . . how can I, everyone's darling, go from being pro-life to killing my lover and blaming it on my mother — all within the blink of an eye — knowing she'll go to prison for it? I convince myself that I'm only doing what Mam would do in my situation. She would do anything to protect me, including encouraging my father to commit suicide to avoid the disgrace of being exposed as a paedophile, and I'm following in her footsteps by safeguarding my unborn child. I will not have it taken away from me under any circumstances. He or she needs me.

Rather than dwelling on the impending arrival of the police, who I know will want to question me at length and may even tear my story to shreds, my gaze sweeps the room. I'm more than curious about the woman who once inhabited it, sensing that there's more to their relationship than Bryn has revealed. Is he another Luke who obsesses over his first love, even though his feelings for her were not reciprocated?

Dark walnut Victorian furniture dominates the room, as do the overhead beams that I imagine are crawling with insect life. The bed, complete with an old-fashioned fringed bedspread has an intricately carved solid headboard. Next to it is a tiled washstand with a vintage rose-patterned jug and washing bowl. A dusky floral rug covers most of the wooden floor that creaks beneath the woollen fibres when I walk over to the wardrobe and pull open the door. I'm truly surprised to find it overflowing because based on what Bryn had said, I expected there to be only a few unwanted items remaining.

Perhaps a dress that no longer fitted or a blouse with a stain that couldn't be washed away. His wife had expensive tastes is the first thing I notice. Lots of cashmere and lambswool. A Barbour jacket. Tweed culottes. A herringbone gilet. Not what I imagined at all.

I take out a sand-coloured crew neck jumper and dark olive cords that look as if they might fit and change into them while hiding behind the wardrobe door, just in case Bryn walks back in. They still smell of her, I realise . . . geranium and cedar wood. Very pleasant. Bryn's right. I feel much better now that I've changed into something warm and dry. Even if I don't deserve to when Luke is lying dead and cold on our kitchen floor.

I then pull a heavy paisley shawl off its hanger and slip it over my shoulders. As I walk over to the writing desk to view the dulled-silver photograph that Bryn's eyes had wandered to, it cuddles me like a gigantic bear. The woman in the picture is sitting up in bed holding a baby, and my gaze is drawn to *it* rather than her. This must be Eilonwy, Bryn's daughter. The poor thing. I'd say she was a few weeks old when the photograph was taken, and her downturned lip suggests she's about to cry. I recognise the Victorian bed because it's identical to the one in this room.

When my attention returns to Bryn's wife, Gwen, my body goes limp and every hair on my body stands on end. It isn't possible . . . and yet . . . Although her hair is darker than mine, her eyes are wide-set and sky-blue in colour, mirroring mine. Her features have a softness to them that I'm used to seeing in my own reflection. I feel a massive tug on my heart as I stare open-mouthed at the woman in the photograph. Gwen's mouth though is drawn in a thin line and her eyes have no light in them. I imagine that I must look like this after the night I've experienced. Worry lines crease her face and the way she's holding her daughter away from her, as if terrified, confirms what Bryn told me about her struggling to bond with it.

Suddenly, everything becomes clear. All my life, my family has pointed out how different I am from them — both mentally and physically. "Their barefoot white-haired mountain girl" they called me. Because of my love of animals and desire to protect them, Mam lost hope that I would ever grow up to be a proper farmer's daughter. I was unlike all the Williams women who came before me. When Bryn described his wife as being "on the delicate side. Not strong mentally or physically like Beth" he might have been referring to me.

On that thought, my hands flutter to my mouth. Threads of anxiety continue to pull at my insides when I hear the light tapping on the door. When I don't answer, Bryn opens it cautiously and glances around it, whispering, 'Cerys? Can I come in? Are you decent?'

When I still don't respond, he creeps in anyway but halts when he sees my stunned, disbelieving expression. 'What is it? What's wrong?' he asks, appearing deeply concerned.

'Her eyes,' I stammer, pointing to the photograph. 'They're just like mine.'

Tears sting my eyes, blurring my vision, as he comes over to stand by me to have a closer look at the picture, oblivious to what I'm talking about. At that moment, I happen to catch a glimpse of our reflection in the wall mirror, and seeing us together for the first time, side by side, I realise we share the same well-defined jawline, and I know then without a doubt that it's true . . .

'Your daughter never left this mountain,' I tell him.

# CHAPTER 59: BETH

The third glass of whiskey reaches me in ways that God has never been able to. It loosens my tongue and relaxes my inhibitions, allowing me to self-reflect in ways I can't or won't when I'm sober. But what it can't do is cast out the devil in me. I'm just as guilty as Cerys is of murder. Even more so because what I did was premeditated. I'd meticulously planned my husband's suicide right down to the finest detail. On that reminder, the room falls away and everything blurs as I travel back in time. . .

To the night Owen and I struck our deal. One he later attempted to break, but it was too late by then. We'd lost six babies by this stage. This seemed unfair when other people, such as Gwen Morgan, *could* have children but didn't *want* them. Baby Blues, my eye. I didn't believe that postnatal depression existed. But, then again, she'd always been a highly emotional, some-would-say unstable, woman. I never understood why a man as down-to-earth as Bryn would marry such a highly-strung creature who by her own admission, suffered with her nerves. Or anxiety, as it's referred to today. Owen, Bryn's closest friend, however, could. He suspected that Bryn's mother had encouraged the marriage because Gwen came from a prominent family. God bless his mother, but she was a snob.

I was in my fifth month of pregnancy, so in the second trimester, and this was the longest I'd ever been pregnant which meant Owen and I were hopeful. But on that fateful day when our lives changed forever, I went into labour at home and lost the baby. Although I didn't know it at the time this would be my last ever miscarriage. It came quickly. Too fast for me to try to call anyone. After five dead babies, I knew the drill. It was not my life that was in danger. But theirs. It wasn't unheard of for mothers to give birth at home without a midwife in these remote parts of Wales.

Owen was with Bryn at a machinery auction at the time, having to listen to him rant on about how cruelly Gwen had rejected their little lass. So, when he came home to check on me and found me sobbing in a bloodied bed and clutching our tiny, underdeveloped dead baby in the palm of my hand, something inside him must have snapped. After helping me to get cleaned up, he took our baby girl and buried her on the mountain, marking her grave with a large stone — as if she were a pet dog rather than my entire world. My living, breathing flesh and bone.

He was missing for several hours after that, and I mistakenly thought this was his way of dealing with what had happened. I imagined him climbing to the peak of the mountain, trying to make sense of it all. He was a known thinker and ruminator, and he was just as desperate for a baby as I was. I also knew how much it pained him having to witness my grief over the loss of our children. When he eventually arrived home and came upstairs to see me, he presented me with a beautiful, healthy baby girl wrapped in a blanket. She had delicate white skin and the bluest of eyes. Her head was covered in fine hair the colour of cloudy lemonade.

I knew she was the daughter of Bryn and Gwen Morgan, and that Owen had kidnapped his best friend's child. I'd raised my eyes in disbelief at my husband, whose steely blue stare was set firmly on the baby. I knew then that we weren't going to give her back. It was a done deal. She was ours.

While Gwent police knocked on doors and searched the mountains for the Morgan's missing baby who had been stolen out of their farmhouse when no one was looking, I remained in my bedroom, claiming I had high blood pressure and saying that I had been advised to stay in bed for the duration of my pregnancy. Nobody questioned this due to all the other miscarriages. If I had to go out at all, which wasn't very often, I padded out my stomach to make myself look pregnant. It's impossible to stop a baby from crying though, no matter how hard you try, and even though Tad was partially deaf, he couldn't pretend he didn't hear little Cerys's cries. But Tad, being Tad, turned a blind eye and said nothing. He'd heard about Gwen too and was on our side. He knew how much we wanted a child.

When enough time had passed, we made out the baby had come early and we laughed it off, saying we must have gotten our dates wrong, and what idiots we were because I was clearly further along in my pregnancy than I thought. As Cerys had been born prematurely, she was already underdeveloped, which meant she was still a tiny little thing, and we could pass her off as a newborn even though she was officially two months old by then. We knew that the midwives and doctors were not fools, but due to our medical history and a little bit of luck, we somehow managed to pull it off. We waited another month after the search for the Morgan's baby had all but fizzled out, before registering her birth. We named her Cerys, because it came from the Welsh word "*Caru*" meaning "To love" and, for as long as I lived, she was never going to have to go without that again.

I was shocked to get a pink congratulatory card from Gwen, who showed an interest in swinging by to see the baby one day. If it had been the other way around, I would have refused to visit Gwen because I couldn't find it in my heart to sympathise with her. She reminded me of the female ewe we'd sent to slaughter for abandoning every single litter of lambs she gave birth to. Unnatural, I'd labelled her. But, according to Owen, Gwen wanted her baby back now that it had vanished, but that was her tough luck, I'd thought meanly, refusing to open my heart to her. I knew Bryn suspected Gwen of harming the baby, and if he thought that about his own wife, there had to be something terribly wrong with her.

Every day I persuaded myself that some people didn't deserve to be parents, however, this wasn't true of Bryn because he wore himself out searching for his missing child in those mountains. You had to feel bad for him, but not enough to give Cerys back. Men, in my opinion, do not and should not raise children. That's a woman's job. As far as I'm concerned, it's the best one in the world.

Nobody suspected us because when wasn't Beth Williams pregnant? And Owen was Bryn's best friend. Our entire community rejoiced for us when news got out that we'd finally had a baby, which they thought was well-deserved after all our suffering. But Bryn and Gwen were avoided at all costs, because where there was smoke, there was fire, and it wouldn't surprise the locals if the Morgan woman, who was known to be mentally ill, had suffocated her child to death. Unfair or what?

What was even more unfair was when Owen had an attack of guilt years later and wanted to confess the truth of what we'd done so that Cerys might get to know her real family. Seeing his closest friend in such distress, broken even, had worn down my husband over the years and made him remorseful. Bryn confided in Owen which made it even harder for him.

'Over my dead body,' I'd warned Owen, reminding him of our deal.

He should have minded me, I fume, still enraged after all these years. Slamming my glass on the coffee table, I decide it's time once again to take my daughter from Bryn Morgan, who has become a thorn in my side.

# CHAPTER 60: CERYS

My head spins from this latest revelation and I watch mesmerised as Bryn, who I now know is my real father — not Owen, the man who abandoned me by committing suicide — scratches his brain as if trying to recall something.

'But you can't be my daughter,' he stutters, as if about to crash to the floor.

I snatch up the photograph and hold it under his nose, furious. 'Tell me I don't have the same eyes as her. You must be able to see it if I can.'

'But you can't be,' Bryn repeats, and I realise then that he's in shock, just as I was, so I put a firm hand on his arm and direct him over to the bed where he sinks upon it.

'Is this where I was born? In this bed?' I demand, returning my stubborn gaze to the photograph of my mother holding me in her arms. As soon as I saw her face, I felt an immediate, unfathomable connection that could not be denied. I'm like one of Mam's lambs, born with the ability to recognise its parent in a field full of sheep.

'Gwen gave birth in the hospital because it was her first . . . and only baby,' he says this while raising a pair of troubled eyes.

'How could you not have known? Have you not noticed the resemblance before? Our eyes are exactly the same.' I go on, determined to get to the bottom of this mystery. 'You watched me grow up.'

'I don't know, Cerys. I mean, you were just always there, Owen and Beth's little girl. I found it hard to even look at other children after what happened. I never imagined . . . and Gwen left years ago. She didn't look like that after she had the baby. She was depressed and had let herself go, becoming overweight and unrecognisable. That's how I remember her, not looking beautiful, as she appears here,' he continues thoughtfully, thumbing his wife's face.

'They must have kidnapped me and passed me off as their own.' I jerk to my feet, unable to remain still. I'm restless for the truth. I dismiss the voice in my head that says I've always known I was different from the rest of my family. I don't even resemble Mam.

'We don't know anything for sure,' Bryn mumbles, shaking his head. 'Beth and Gwen were pregnant at the same time. I'm sorry, love, I understand how upsetting this is for you, both of us actually, but I believe you're mistaken and that it's simply a coincidence. Owen would never have done such a thing. We were like brothers.'

'But Mam would,' I counter, and his head bounces on his shoulders in acknowledgement that I'm correct.

He sighs heavily. 'You're neglecting one thing though.'

'What's that?'

'She would have needed Owen on her side to pull it off. Besides, why would they when they were having a child of their own?'

Doubt enters my head for the first time, and I wonder if he's right. Is this something I'm making up to distract myself from the even more shocking fact that I killed Luke and I'm blaming Mam for it? Believing she kidnapped me and pretended to be my mother all these years would certainly give me a get-out-of-jail-free card. But on the other hand . . .

'What if she lost the baby.' I pounce on the possibility like a cat would a mouse. 'And they couldn't have any more. What then?'

'I think we would have heard about it. Owen would have told me, just as he had with the others. Besides, people around here made a right song and dance about it when you came into the world, when all the while we were going through the loss of ours,' Bryn grinds out bitterly and I sense that he's resigned to the fact that I am not his daughter. I need to do something to persuade him, but then it hits me what he just said.

'What do you mean "others"?'

'She didn't tell you?' Bryn's frow burrows.

I shake my head, willing him to go on. *What hasn't Mam told me now?*

'I'm not certain of the number, but she miscarried at least three or four of what would have been your older brothers and sisters before you came along. They're all buried on the mountain.'

I'm hit by a wave of dizziness so strong I feel as if I have been kicked in the stomach by a horse. My hands go white at the knuckles as I clench them and my brain swirls from so many secrets. 'But if she lost the baby she *was* carrying, they wouldn't have said anything if they planned on stealing yours, would they?' I exclaim.

Bryn stares at me as if I am insane. He could be right. Feeling like I have one last chance to convince him, I sit down next to him on the bed and gaze into his liquid-algae eyes.

'You once told me you feared Gwen had harmed the baby and that you spent years searching for your daughter's body. Do you still believe that?' I persist.

'I don't know what to think.' He leans back, avoiding my eyes.

'Yes, you do, Bryn,' I insist, stabbing a finger at the picture frame. 'Does she look like a woman who would harm anyone?'

'Well, no, but—'

I inhale a deep, trembling breath as I fight to rein in my frustration at him. 'Do you remember saying that you knew your baby was dead because you felt it in here?' As I say this, I clasp my hand over my heart.

He nods, and I see that his eyes are glistening with unshed tears. He wants it to be true then but is too scared to admit it. But do I? Wouldn't my entire universe come crashing down if that were the case? 'Then, lay your hand here, on my beating heart, and tell me if you still feel it.' I continue, deciding that my world will implode anyway, because of Luke.

When Bryn doesn't do as I've instructed, I lift his palm and forcibly press it on my left breast, watching his face for any sign of recognition. My heart is racing so fast at this point that I'm surprised it doesn't shock him.

Confusion flashes across his face and I steel myself for the inevitable denial. But then, his eyes gradually scan my face, seeming to take in every last detail and I hear his sharp intake of breath as it dawns on him who I really am. I'm deeply moved, and shocked, when he clasps a palm against my cheek, gently cupping it, before whispering one word, 'Eilonwy.'

Unexpectedly, I find myself in my father's arms, sobbing into his shoulder, but then we are just as suddenly jolted apart, as if the pounding on the front door had given us both an electric shock.

'Is that the police already?' I gasp.

'It can't be. It's too soon.' Bryn frowns as he gets to his feet and walks over to the window. I notice his shoulders rise as he exhales sharply. All of this contributes to my anxiety.

'Who is it?' I demand to know.

'It's your mam.'

'What? No? It can't be. How could she have known I was here?' I roll my eyes as the answer dawns on me. 'Oh, Bryn, you didn't?'

He pulls an apologetic face. 'I texted her before I knew about Luke or any of this, so she'd know you were safe.'

As a heavy feeling settles on my chest, I purse my lips. 'I don't believe I've ever been safe.'

# CHAPTER 61: BETH

'Bryn Morgan, open this door. Do you hear me?' As I shield my face from the wind and pouring rain, I yell, glancing up at the yellow light emanating from the room upstairs. An even bigger storm is brewing, I realise with dread. Just like the night Owen died. The wind has increased in strength, causing the black silhouette of the trees behind the farmhouse to perform a torturous dance. Only when I see the curtain twitch and catch a glimpse of Bryn's darkened face behind the glass do I stop pounding on the front door. I glare at him, thinking, *How dare he meddle in my business. My life. My child. He should have sent Cerys straight home rather than inviting her in. For years, he has been like a dark menacing shadow circling the farm, watching us. Like Charlie!*

Bryn's head appears in the window as it glides up a little, becoming stuck along the way because it is rarely opened. 'Beth, go home,' he orders, with a catch in his voice.

'I've come for my daughter,' I shout stubbornly, refusing to budge from the doorstep. I imagine the two of them whispering behind the glass and recall how it used to be with Cerys and her father, who always excluded me — *her mother* — who would have done anything for her. I still would.

The window then falls in a sudden guillotine-like motion, and the light goes off. 'So, I'm being ignored, am I?' I grumble to myself, like some old woman who can't reach her cobwebs and hates everyone as a result. 'We'll see about that.'

I stomp over to the enormous steel farm building that houses Bryn's machinery and flick open the key box screwed to the side of it. He'd given me the code in case of an emergency. I suspect our friendship is over and a part of me is disappointed because, despite everything I know about Bryn, I'm genuinely fond of him. I'd convinced myself that no one was perfect, least of all myself, so I'd disregarded his dark secret just as much as I'd overlooked mine. For the first time, I'm beginning to regret it. *I don't want a man like that anywhere near my precious daughter.*

It's harder to see the numbers and match them up in the funereal blackness, but I somehow manage it after entering the correct combination code 1234 and seize the hidden key. Bryn, like me, isn't the imaginative type. That's how Luke guessed my PIN, knowing I wouldn't have bothered to change it. Folks like me and Bryn are resistant to change.

As I march towards the house, this time heading around the back to the kitchen door, I feel the wind hurrying me along — its angry fist firmly in between my shoulder blades. My hair also ripples with it as if it were infested with headlice. Nights like this spook me no end. It's almost as if Owen had summoned the storm to punish me. I pray to God that he isn't waiting for me in the afterlife.

*'Do it.' I order fiercely, hurling a handful of photographs at him that land at his feet — Cerys aged around nine or ten with straw-coloured hair and delicate blue eyes smiles up at him.*

I take a deep breath and count to three as I slide the key into the door lock since I have no idea what's on the other side. Will Bryn have second-guessed my next move and rushed downstairs to bolt the doors, preventing me from entering his house? The metallic scratch of the key turning and the door opening begs to differ. I have outwitted him as I have done so many times before without his knowing.

Once inside, I notice that the softly lighted areas of the house, such as the fringed floor lamp in the drawing room and the green glass banker's lamp in Bryn's study, leak into the kitchen through purposefully left-open doors, to create shadows on its walls. I am one of them. Because the rifle I'm carrying is projected onto the wall, I recognise myself, thinking that I appear like a covert soldier on a mission. And maybe I am.

I stumble into a freestanding oily piece of machinery that smells of diesel and curse beneath my breath. The open door of the Aga warms the room. There's a bowl of food on the floor that shouldn't be there as Bryn doesn't own a dog. That's when I hear a faint bark from upstairs. It sounds exactly like Elvis. But how did he end up here? Had Bryn kidnapped him and held him, like I had done with his daughter? But why? I trip over Cerys's wrinkled brown leather size seven boots, deciding that makes no sense.

When I hear a creaking floorboard above my head, I swivel around, and the gun involuntarily points upwards at the ceiling. I then visualise a tall man passing by the window and my finger trembles on the trigger and sweat trickles down my brow. Owen's ghost isn't going to leave me alone tonight. In my head, I hear his voice imploring, 'Please,' as he begged for mercy that I couldn't . . . wouldn't give.

As I reach the foot of the twisted oak staircase that has the names of generations of Morgan children etched into it, I hear a door softly open and another dagger of light shoots out at me, as if it were a bullet aiming at my guilt-ridden skull. 'Cerys?' I whisper.

I put one booted foot on the first step and am about to take another when the landing light comes on and I see Bryn at the top of the stairs, looking ludicrous in an old-fashioned set of striped pyjamas. His eyes are on stalks when he sees the gun.

'Beth, put the gun down.'

'Not until I have what I came for.' I narrow my eyes at him as he nervously takes a step down, then another . . . 'Stay where you are,' I bark, not wanting to — but cocking the gun anyway. It seems like my daughter is not the only one who has gone gun-crazy tonight.

'Don't you think one person dead is enough for a single night?' He calmly raises both eyebrows as he comes to a stop.

'Stay out of this, Bryn,' I caution, climbing the rest of the stairs and stopping only when I'm a few feet away from him. 'You shouldn't have got involved. This is none of your business.'

'I think you'll find it is.' His voice darkens.

'Send Cerys down and we'll be on our way.'

'That's not going to happen.' He shakes his head firmly and his face twists into a grimace, which reminds me of Luke.

This isn't the Bryn I know. Normally, he is docile and does what I tell him without hesitation. Tonight, something other than my daughter has got to him. I ask myself, what do I know of Bryn anyway? I've always known he has a darker side so his change of attitude shouldn't come as a surprise.

'Is it true that you killed Luke?' he asks in disbelief.

'Is that what Cerys told you?' I gasp in surprise.

When I see Cerys, who has come to stand behind Bryn, my heart rolls into my mouth. I lower my gun slightly, hating to see how her head is bent low as if in shame. Her waist-length hair hangs down to obscure her beautiful face, which is forever imprinted on my heart. All I feel for her is love. I couldn't be angry with her if I tried. Even if she had misled Bryn and purposefully framed me for Luke's murder. Who knew she had it in her!

I'm furious with Bryn though for quite literally getting in the way of me and my daughter. How dare he shield her from me? While she cowers behind him as if I were a monster, he acts like the protective parent he is not. He had his chance and blew it by leaving his baby daughter alone and uncared for in the hands of his lunatic wife.

'Luke had it coming,' I mutter angrily because I would never, ever, in a million years, expose my daughter as a liar.

## CHAPTER 62: CERYS

'Give me the gun, Beth,' Bryn pleads again, like Mam had earlier with me, but he does not raise his voice. 'My house, my rules, remember.'

'My mountain,' Mam retorts defiantly, one eye on Bryn and the other on me. I can't meet her stare, despite knowing what I know about her. Have I always been frightened of her or is this something new? So far tonight, I've learned that she was involved in my father's death and that she, him, or both of them had kidnapped me and raised me as their own. Was she never going to tell me?

'Except it's not your mountain, Mam,' I blurt out, not knowing or caring where I got the confidence from to hurl that at her. 'It's mine.' Observing Bryn's bewildered expression, I explain, 'Grandad left the farm and his money to me. Not her. It's what we were arguing about when . . .'

'When what?' Bryn urges, squeezing his forehead in uncertainty.

'When Mam shot Luke,' I yell, feeling like a rebellious teenager all over again by standing up to my mother and daring to lie to her face.

Ignoring me, Bryn fixes his gaze on Mam, and I can tell he still cares profoundly for her, even though she has deceived him in the worst way possible. 'The police are on their way. They know about Luke. So, you need to put the gun down. The last thing we want is for anyone else to be harmed.'

Mam and I both notice his sidelong glance at me, and we both interpret it the same way. Bryn's implication that she would hurt me is like a red rag to a bull in her eyes.

'Do you think I'd hurt my own daughter?' she stutters, her eyes wide with disbelief.

'Except Cerys isn't your daughter, Beth, is she?' Bryn snatches the words out of my mouth before going on to remark, 'She's mine.'

'What?' Mam's jaw drops open, and her fierce eyes lock on his.

'We know, Mam. When I saw Gwen's photo, I immediately recognised myself in her. That's why you've been so insistent on keeping me away from this place and Bryn, who is my real father, all these years.'

'That isn't the only reason,' Mam snaps, less shocked than I would have expected considering the circumstances. I'd say she still has some cards to play. When it came to dealing her hand, she was always patient.

'Was Owen involved? Did he know that Cerys was my daughter?' Bryn asks, his voice breaking.

'It was his idea,' Mam laughs sarcastically, sounding like the kind of evil witch I had nightmares about as a child. At that moment, I believe I hate and fear her in equal amounts, but as I move closer to Bryn for protection, I notice he has shuffled away from me slightly and is inching towards Mam, obviously intent on getting his hands on the gun. He has already taken one step down without her noticing. As a warning, I roll my eyes at him and he nods as if to reassure me he won't do anything rash.

'You were meant to be my friend,' Bryn laments. 'I trusted you. How could you?'

'How could I not? I'd just lost another baby,' Mam manages through clenched teeth, but her eyes are full of remorse.

'What sort of life would Cerys have had in this place with a mother who didn't want her?'

I may not have met my biological mother, and I'm not sure if I ever will, but hearing that she didn't love me still stings.

'She was ill, Beth. She would have recovered in time, but you robbed her of that opportunity. And it's your fault she left because she never dealt with what happened to her child. Everyone blamed her for Cerys's disappearance, believing she'd hurt her. Jesus, I was guilty of that too.'

'And more.' As she says this, Mam's eyes flash with danger. She then addresses me sharply, catching me off guard. 'Cerys, get your coat and boots. We're leaving.'

I shrink backwards, conscious that Elvis is scratching at my birth mother's bedroom door, trying to get out. Gwen must also have felt imprisoned within that room after I disappeared. Bryn had stated that she never recovered, implying that she must have loved me after all. Knowing how much anguish Mam and Dad inflicted on the poor woman enrages me.

'I'm not going anywhere with you, Beth.' I use her first name on purpose, aiming to inflict as much pain on her as she has me. 'Not now I know what you're capable of. First Dad. Then Luke.' I avert my eyes from her gaze when I say this.

'What about Owen?' Bryn jumps in.

'She forced him to kill himself,' I blurt out. 'She watched her husband blow his brains out so no one would find out he was a paedophile.'

'Oh God, is this true? Beth, tell me it isn't.'

Mam's eyes deepen with guilt as I observe her. 'I didn't have a choice,' she owns up. 'I was afraid he'd do something to Cerys. And that we'd both have to live with the shame for the rest of our lives.'

At this point, a sob escapes my mouth, and for the first time in my life, I'm relieved Owen wasn't my father and that the man standing next to me — as if he's got everything to live for now that he has me — is, because I have a feeling that he'll never abandon me.

'But that doesn't make sense,' he says with a frown, 'because the police found out anyway. Why didn't you hide the evidence if you were so concerned?'

Mam flinches at his words and does not immediately respond, which is unusual for her because she always knows what to say and do. However, what Bryn said makes sense. Why hadn't I considered that? I'm meant to be the queen of crime. Bryn and I exchange a concerned look before returning our attention to Mam.

'I didn't know about the folders on his computer.' She grimaces. 'You think you're clever, don't you, Bryn?' Mam angrily puffs out her chest. 'But when it comes to secrets, I can go one better. You see, Cerys—' she fastens her eyes onto mine — 'what Bryn hasn't told you is that Gwen, like her daughter, never left this mountain.'

'What are you saying, Mam?' I'm a child again, seeking comfort after seeing Bryn stagger backwards in horror. His face is a living hell.

'She didn't run off with another woman at all. He—' Mam jabs a vicious finger in Bryn's direction — 'killed your so-called real mother,' she delivers her final killer blow, while glaring at Bryn. 'And fed her to his pigs.'

# CHAPTER 63: BETH

'No, that can't be true,' Cerys stammers, fluttering her fingers to her mouth. But she must see the horrible truth in Bryn's eyes when she looks at him. Their greenness is tinged with shock at being discovered.

'So much for being the perfect father, huh?' I can't stop myself from cracking a joke directed more at Bryn than at my daughter, even though I know it must upset her to hear it. Am I losing my mind? Going mad?

Then again, tonight has driven us all insane with fear. Who would have guessed that Luke's death, as tragic as it was, would be the catalyst for all of our secrets to spill out? The moment I dreaded . . . that Cerys would discover I wasn't her biological mother has finally arrived, and it has shocked us all, but Cerys the most. I've wanted to tell her for years but couldn't. They would have arrested me and returned her to Bryn, which I couldn't allow. He had committed murder while all I was guilty of was assisting someone — my husband — in their death. There is a difference. And no one could possibly have loved my daughter more than I did. Certainly not Gwen Morgan.

Bryn, on the other hand, seems to have recovered slightly. He pulls his gaze away from Cerys, realising that he has already lost her, and directs a fierce stare at me as if it were a weapon. I want to point out to him that he only had her for an hour, but I'm afraid this would be too below the belt even for me. It also occurs to me that I am now looking into a killer's eyes. Is this the expression he turned on Gwen the day he murdered her? Should I be afraid? Of Bryn Morgan? *Never*, I tell myself.

'What makes you think that?' Bryn finally asks.

'Because I was watching you,' I point out reasonably, thinking that if this is his attempt to fight back or plead his innocence, it's a feeble one.

I see bewilderment flash across his face as his eyes dart back and forth between Cerys and me, as though debating whether or not to confess.

'Fight or flight. Make your mind up,' I urge him while noticing that Cerys remains motionless, even though every inch of her tense body is turned towards the stairs, as though she desperately wants to escape. In this instance, she reminds me of a trapped fox. Once again, I'm reminded of Owen right before he died . . . *his fear, his pleading eyes, the rain, the blood, his limp body.* It feels as if my eyes are bleeding.

Bryn remains mute and avoids eye contact with both of us, preferring to look down at his old man slippers. So, I help him out. As a good friend should.

'It was Cerys's seventeenth birthday, and I'd taken the dogs out for a walk, thinking I'd drop over a slice of cake for you. If you recall, I never brought her to your house — because I didn't want your unnatural wife getting her hands on my daughter — so I always came alone. I saw you barrowing your wife's body over to the piggery that day. You knew they were always hungry and would eat anything. Even Gwen.' I finish with a long sigh and a disgusted shake of my head.

He had no idea what he was getting himself into when he welcomed my daughter inside his house, which she had previously been forbidden from visiting. He had to have known I'd exact my vengeance when his house and Gwen Morgan's ghost gave up its secrets.

'You're lying.' He scowls at me, before his frantic gaze flicks to Cerys, who is holding her face in her hands and staring out through her fingers. 'She's lying, Cerys. Making it up. You can't trust anything she says after what she did to you.' Turning back to me, he resumes his attack, 'You would have said something if you saw me doing that. Called the police.'

'In light of what we did, how could I? I didn't want them looking into things and dragging up the past any more than you did. We'd kidnapped your child.'

When I realise that I've lowered the rifle, I raise it again in case Bryn tries to wrestle it from my grasp, although to be honest he looks like a beaten man. 'I figured we were even after that,' I say softly.

'That's why you wouldn't let us look for Elvis on your property and insisted on searching for him yourself in case we found any remains. You were afraid her bones would show up years later, as skeletons sometimes do,' Cerys interrupts, clearly horrified.

Her eyes are filled with tears, and she's so pale that I fear she'll faint at any moment. I want to reach out to her, but I'm afraid to let go of the trigger. Bryn may appear to be a peaceful middle-aged farmer, but I know just how dangerous he is.

'After that, I made it my business to keep an eye on you. I felt better that way, knowing you were capable of murder.'

'You're only saying this because Cerys has finally learned the truth about her biological parents.' Bryn sticks out his chin in a defiant posture before saying in a rattled tone, 'My daughter. Here on my doorstep the whole time. How could you possibly have done that to me. To Gwen?'

'She didn't deserve her.' My voice is tight as I say this because, while I still believe Gwen didn't deserve to keep her daughter on account of her being an unnatural mother and everything, I wonder if Bryn is right and that she would have recovered over time. If that were true, it would make me a terrible person. I'd convinced myself for years that rescuing Cerys from an unloving home was the Christian thing to do, but what if I was wrong? Does this mean I'll be going to hell with Luke? Does God intend to punish me by making Luke my lifelong companion in the next life? And that the devil himself will be waiting for me at the black gates when the time comes for me to leave this world. This thought frightens me more than God's wrath, leading me to shiver in terror.

'But *I* did,' Bryn cries and lunges for the gun.

He catches me off guard, and, almost forgetting that I'm still standing on the stairs, I stumble backwards onto the next step, which isn't there, so I hover, unsure of where my feet are. I hear Cerys scream as I scramble to locate solid ground and my eyes lock on her as I feel myself falling and Bryn getting further away from me. I see him stretch out a hand as if to pull me backwards, but there's nothing there when I reach out to grab it.

My descent happens in slow motion. Isn't that always how these things turn out? And it's true what they say: my life flashed in front of my eyes before I hit the ground. *The babies buried on the mountain. The underdeveloped dead baby in the palm of my hand. Owen standing in the doorway, windswept, clutching Cerys in his arms. Cerys as a funny but spoilt three-year-old. Cerys astride her white pony. Cerys in a swimming costume playing in a paddling pool. Cerys bottle-feeding a lamb. A white-haired Cerys roaming around the mountain, barefoot.*

Cerys, Cerys, Cerys . . .

# CHAPTER 64: CERYS

Mam, of course, did not die that day. She's too tough and obstinate for that to happen. A survivor, if ever there was one. Armed police arrived shortly after her fall, and a slew of red lasers were aimed at her crumpled body at the bottom of the winding oak staircase. The paramedic had assured me and Bryn that she was unconscious but breathing. We both glanced at each other as if we weren't sure if that was a good thing or not. Then I remembered Bryn was my father, and that he'd murdered my mother. I hadn't believed him when he said Mam made it all up. It must have shown on my face because he turned away from me as if he couldn't see me, burying his face in his hands — leaving me as Owen and Luke had.

After suffering a head trauma that resulted in bleeding and swelling of the brain, Mam's skull fracture turned out to be less severe than expected and she made a full recovery. Although I had so much to process and wasn't sure how I felt about her anymore because my feelings alternated between anger and hatred for what she had done and love and compassion, also for what she had done, I still visited her in the hospital because she was my mam at the end of the day and had raised me. Also, I feared she wouldn't make it out of there alive. I hadn't considered her incredible willpower.

She kept her word and confessed to killing Luke so I wouldn't have to go to jail and lose my baby. When the police and courts learned of the emotional abuse we had undergone at his hands, they were sympathetic. Mam's top defence lawyer, who was paid for with Grandad's money, was able to get the murder charge reduced to voluntary manslaughter based on diminished responsibility. The judges were surprisingly lenient, sentencing her to a maximum of nine years in prison, which means she could be out by the time she's sixty. Sooner, if she behaves herself. I don't want to think about where she will go when that time comes.

When I asked Mam one day, while she was still recovering from her skull fracture and before she was put on trial, why she claimed to have killed Luke instead of pointing the finger at me, she'd looked at me with such love in her eyes as she said, 'I would do anything for you, Cerys, anything, and because I owe you for what Owen and I did.'

I thought so too. Nonetheless, this was the closest she'd ever gotten to apologising for taking me from my biological mother. If I press her on it, she withdraws into herself, avoiding the discussion and insisting that 'Nobody could have loved you as I did.' I believe she could be right. Because I wouldn't have been safe in Gwen's arms even if her maternal instinct had returned and she'd grown to love and care for me. I've since learnt that she was prone to mood swings and irrational outbursts, which explains why Bryn and everyone else was so quick to criticise and accuse her of injuring her baby. This makes me concerned about my own mental health because hadn't Mam always commented on how fragile and sensitive I was. "Away with the fairies" she used to call it. Could it be hereditary?

My parents are both in prison for killing another human being. But only one of them is serving a life sentence for murder. I paid Bryn a visit in prison right before he was sentenced. He'd lost a lot of weight and his hair had turned grey from shock. Unlike Mam, the courts showed him no mercy. He had brutally murdered his wife in cold blood. They claimed it was premeditated. That it was an act of revenge for allegedly harming the couple's baby that had mysteriously vanished from their home years ago. Bryn had paid for his own legal representation, but because he lacked conviction, their attempts to reduce his sentence to manslaughter failed. Put on the stand, Bryn sobbed out a damning confession, admitting to strangling his wife in a jealous frenzy when she threatened to leave him, afterwards feeding her body to his pigs. To put the police off his trail, he coldly made up a narrative about her leaving him for another woman.

The truth, however, was quite different. Bryn was now eager to confess his role in Gwen's death to me. I believe he saw it as therapeutic. Gwen had always been innocent of harming her baby, but Bryn had privately condemned her as a child murderer, so his anger at her had never gone away.

'I swear on my life it was an accident,' he pleaded. He wasn't allowed to reach out and hold my hands while the guard was watching. Instead, he reached out with honest eyes. 'We had this horrible row in which we both said things we shouldn't have. She was clawing at my face with her nails, yelling at me that she was relieved our baby was gone because I would have been a terrible father. When I heard that, something inside me broke, and I wrapped my hands around her throat to prevent her from saying anything else. The next thing I knew, she was dead on the floor.'

None of us chose to reveal details of the kidnapping and Mam's role in Owen's death to the police to safeguard what remained of our family and to avoid complicating matters — or, in other words, to protect me from the mess the adults in my life had made. It's not like it would have helped Bryn or Mam's case, quite the opposite in fact, so no one was any wiser that the child who had vanished from the mountain had returned home.

It was mine, Bryn's, and Mam's secret. I had married my mother's ex-husband and I had to pay the price for it. Just as Mam and Bryn are paying for their sins. This means I'll always be Cerys Williams. Not Eilonwy Morgan.

Some days it's difficult for me to comprehend that my real father and fake mother are both in prison, while my real mother and fake father are both dead, having perished at the hands of my real father and fake mother. You really couldn't make it up, could you? 'What a family' as Lynn would have said. I don't know what I'd have done without her. We've become close. She's like a second mother to me. Mam would be horrified to learn this, so I don't tell her. She still regards Lynn as the enemy, but this couldn't be further from the truth. She and Evie are now my family. And as heartbroken women, we are free to reminisce about Luke and try to recall his good qualities, but only because we're his children's mothers and they need to have some memories of him to grow up with. At least he's not a paedophile, like Owen, I console myself. I'm glad now that I don't share any of his genes.

I'm about to inherit two farms. Luke would be gutted to know this as I think he'd have liked playing the local squire. He really did pick the wrong Williams woman. Bryn has already signed over Forest Farm to me, claiming that it's my birthright. But now that I know what happened there, I have conflicting thoughts about it. The police searched everywhere for Gwen's body, even bringing in cadaver dogs to sniff out her remains, but they were unable to find anything. During the search, the piggery was demolished and destroyed. I had no qualms about sending Bryn's pigs to the slaughterhouse. They had devoured my real mother. It was personal.

For now, I'm living at Pen-y-Bryn farmhouse, which is the only home I've ever known. Lynn refuses to enter it, claiming it is haunted by Luke, so I visit her at her flat and sense his presence there as well. I don't think we'll ever be able to escape him. It's as Lynn remarked, 'He'll never let us go.' He's there on Evie's face every time I look at her. It's the same when I gaze into the eyes of my daughter, Eilonwy. She's incredibly beautiful and my heart breaks whenever I catch her smiling or saying 'Mama,' while blowing milky bubbles from her mouth. To my ears, it sounds lovely. I'm sure Mam felt the same about me. She was right when she said having a baby was the best job in the world. It most emphatically is.

Now that Mam is no longer around to protect and guide me, I've gotten considerably stronger. For the first time in my life, I feel empowered and I'm finally making well-considered decisions that will never include unsuitable partners again, as well as accepting responsibility for my actions. I always suspected that I was as tough and resilient as Mam, but I had never been allowed to grow into the strong woman I knew I could be. If Mam could see me now, with a rifle over one shoulder, roaming my mountain and counting my lambs while the dogs run around me, she would be immensely proud.

The little one comes everywhere with me, strapped to my chest in a toddler carrier. I won't let anyone other than Lynn mind her. I'm protective that way. The mist on the hills and the smoke seeping out of the chimney with logs chopped by my own hand soothe me as I walk back to the house. I've long since realised that I don't need a man to care for or love me. All I require is my daughter. Thanks to Mam, I'll be there for her at all times. The farmhouse will serve as a lighthouse for her wherever she goes in the world, whether she's on a gap year in Australia, at university, or married with children and living away from me. It will lead her back home.

On that thought, a niggling doubt works its way into my head. What if Mam wanted me to be "weak" for the rest of my life? Could she have preferred it that way, wanting me to stay childlike and dependent on her forever so she could mother and protect me as if I were still five? Her heart was broken when I left the farmhouse, and her, to live my own life. Is that how it is with mothers?

I decide that I don't have to be like her and that my very genuine fear of turning into her doesn't have to be a self-fulfilling prophecy. Without recognising whose words I'm repeating, I say aloud to myself, 'It's my mountain. My house. My daughter. And my rules.'

# CHAPTER 65: BETH

At HM Prison Styal, I'm no longer Beth, but Prisoner A1120NS. I'm imprisoned in a shared cell for twenty-three hours a day, and I'm only allowed out for one hour at night to shower and make phone calls. They say this is my punishment for murdering Luke, but the true penalty is not seeing Cerys or my grandchild. I keep a picture of little Eilonwy who looks uncannily similar to Luke inside my Bible, which was given to me by the prison chaplain. Eilonwy will soon be a year old. I expect she'll have a party, with cake and everything, just as Cerys did. I wish I could be there on her big day but simply by being here, in jail, I'm doing the very best I can for Cerys and her daughter. By taking Cerys's place as Luke's killer, I've given her back her life. The one I stole from her. She now has a chance to be the wonderful mother she was born to be.

I feel awful for Bryn because he got life, whereas I will be free in eight years. I've written to him multiple times, but he is yet to respond. I know he blames me for notifying the police about what he did to his wife, but he's completely wrong; it was Cerys who told them. Not me. I would have kept my gob shut, as I had done for years, because what was the point of both of us going to prison? Cerys, on the other hand, was insistent. She has better morals than Bryn and I put together. Perhaps because of this, she'd been taken seriously by the police. Even though they never recovered Gwen's body — *there's fat chance of that happening with those ravenous pigs* — the fact that she'd never been heard or seen of again was significant. Bryn was unlikely to see our beloved Welsh mountains ever again, thanks partly to my coerced confession. It was a shame they couldn't get his sentence reduced to manslaughter like mine was because it was a spur-of -the-moment crime of passion, in my opinion.

Bryn almost figured out my secret the last time we spoke on that fateful night, shortly before I fell down the stairs. 'That doesn't make sense,' he'd said on learning that I'd encouraged Owen to kill himself to avoid the shame of being labelled a paedophile, and me and Cerys by association. 'Because the police found out anyway. Why didn't you hide the evidence if you were so concerned?' That's where things get complicated because I needed the police to uncover the evidence, which I'd planted myself, to provide a motive for Owen's suicide. Otherwise, how would anyone believe my devoted, caring, and family-loving husband would do such a terrible thing?

God forgive me, but it was me who searched for and found the paedophile website on the dark web. Me who uploaded Cerys's photographs. Me who blackmailed Owen into killing himself because I would never have pulled the trigger myself. I am not a killer, unlike my daughter and Bryn. Overwhelmed with guilt and remorse for taking Cerys from his best friend, Owen had insisted on us owning up to our crime. By then my daughter — *and she was my daughter in every sense of the word* — was twelve and had never known a day without me. As a result, I gave him two options. I would either expose him as a paedophile, which he most emphatically was not, but I had evidence to the contrary, or he could end his own life by shooting himself. Being incarcerated as a known paedophile was not something that a mild-mannered, introspective man like my husband would have survived. As far as I was concerned, we had made a deal the day he stole Cerys and there was no going back on it years later. *She was mine.* He chose the second option. Job done, as they say.

Except it wasn't because I'm now paying the price for what I did to Owen. I am convinced that God sent me here to be punished for that reason. The prison chaplain claims that if I confess my sins and truly repent, God will be faithful, which means there can be no forgiveness for this old sinner because I cannot risk Cerys finding out what I did to her father. Besides, it's her forgiveness I crave. Not God's.

I haven't seen her since the trial when I caught sight of her weeping as my sentence was announced. She and I both lack the ability to turn off our feelings for one another. She tries, but she can't. She will always be my daughter, and I will always be her mother. Unlike Bryn, she does write to me though and I spend many hours re-reading her letters. My heart twists inside my chest whenever I see her familiar handwriting. Every letter begins with a *Dear Beth* on purpose, but when she goes on to describe how she and Eilonwy spend their days, she forgets and starts referring to me as "Mam" once more. She currently has no plans to pick up her studies again and is putting all of her attention into becoming a stay-at-home mother.

She boasts about being strong and independent and is planning to make some modifications to the farm. Another holiday cabin is going up, because, as she correctly points out, 'Grandad's money won't last forever' and she now has two farms to maintain. Our living room has apparently had a makeover and has finally succumbed to boring beige. When I read that section, I laughed aloud. The old black barn has gone too, I'm told, even though it lost its ability to terrify Cerys the instant she realised Owen wasn't really her father. Most of all, I like hearing about my precious little granddaughter. I've already missed her first steps and her first "Mama."

Although I haven't yet met this new Cerys, I am confident that I will adore her just as much as ever. She could never do anything wrong in my eyes. Girl or woman. However, it brings me comfort to picture her as my white-haired, barefoot mountain girl once more, cantering on her white pony and bottle-feeding the lambs. Every waking moment is taken up with thoughts of Cerys. Eilonwy too, who I long to meet. By the time I finally get to see her, she will be eight. It will feel strange returning to Pen-y-Bryn knowing I'm no longer mistress of it, but I'm sure we'll work things out between us. I can recall thinking, when Luke was still alive, that if it weren't for him — myself, Cerys, and the baby could be quite happy living together on the farm. Hopefully, one day, this dream will come true.

If there's one thing I know for sure, it's that those eight years will pass quickly. I can't wait. I miss Cerys so terribly that it hurts physically. They say that I might be released earlier for good behaviour so I plan on being a model prisoner. I'll do whatever it takes. Time would go even faster if Cerys were to visit me, but I can understand why she wants to focus all of her attention on her daughter and the farm. She takes after me in that respect because I was just the same. Nor do I want her to go through the anxiety of prison visits and the emotional drain they cause. They're not for someone like Cerys, who is, shall we say . . . on the delicate side. It's enough that she writes to me and hasn't completely cut me out of her life.

I long to be back on my mountain, surrounded by a mix of green and brown hills, inhaling the crisp mountain air. I also pine for Gypsy and Toad and wonder how they are. They'll be wondering where I have disappeared to, but at least they have Cerys. And Elvis. Nothing is stopping Charlie from coming back for my hens now though, I realise. Cerys has only ever fired a gun once, and after what happened to Luke, is likely to never pick up one again, so they no longer have any protection. No one misses my son-in-law, not even Cerys I imagine. Or does she think of him still when she opens the door to Tad's bedroom and sees the bed they once shared?

I hate to think of Cerys toiling away on her own, having to take care of a baby and two farms. When I eventually return home, we can do things together. As mother and daughter. Just the two of us and little Eilonwy. No Owen. No Bryn. And no Luke. It occurs to me that the sheep will have lambed by now, which is hard labour for two people, let alone one. It's the second year in a row I haven't seen them come into the world. We bonded over it, Cerys, and me. Much in the way a sheep and her lamb bond at birth. But if a ewe unnaturally rejects her lamb, another can typically be persuaded to adopt it. I like to believe that this is exactly what I had done with Cerys, whose birth mother rejected her. And those are the laws of nature. Not my own.

**THE END**

# ACKNOWLEDGEMENTS

This story came to me in a dream in which my youngest daughter texted me to say she was planning to marry my ex-husband (not her biological father) and that she'd secretly been seeing him behind my back for the last five months, which is why she'd been missing from my life. Imagine how I felt when I woke up, not knowing whether it was a dream or reality. When I glanced through my phone and saw no new messages from her, I was overcome with relief, but the idea lingered, and I began to wonder what it must be like for a mother and daughter to have to go through something like that, and *The Son-in-Law* was born.

Beth was an excellent example of the type of strong female protagonist I enjoy writing and developing. Her secrets were as dark as her black mountains, yet her love for her daughter was unwavering. Throughout the writing process, I kept wondering what I would have done in her shoes (i.e., my daughter marrying my ex). I still don't have an answer but I doubt I would have been as understanding as Beth. As for Luke, I've met enough men like him to know they exist, which is why I didn't try to soften him. Please accept my apologies for not including a single moral male character in this book. To be honest, the womenfolk didn't fare much better.

Being half-Welsh, I spent most of my childhood summers in Wales (Cwmbran mostly) and my relatives came from Croesyceiliog, near Abergavenny, so I wanted to set *The Son-in-Law* there. I once stayed in a cabin on a lake surrounded by the Brecon Beacons on a farm, and I enjoyed returning there (metaphorically speaking) while writing this book. One day, I hope to retire to Wales, and live on a smallholding with sheep and chickens, taking long walks on the mountains.

I'd like to dedicate this book to my own mam (Valerie James that was) who died in 1997. On our car journeys into Wales, she'd cry whenever she saw the Severn bridge, and we'd all laugh at her, but now I'm the same. I think of her whenever I see the sign, *Croeso i Gymru* that greets you when you enter Wales, which means "Welcome to Wales." She was known for being feisty so "Welsh dragon" became her nickname. I'd also like to commemorate my three Welsh uncles who were important figures in my childhood: Uncle Fatty (whose house we stayed at, and yes, we did call him that as they were different times), Uncle Joe (who had a toy factory), and Uncle Dilly. The James's made me feel like I was part of one joyful extended family, and when we returned to England at the end of each summer, my mam's Welsh accent was stronger than ever. I miss that.

I want to say a massive thank you to everyone at Joffe Books for all their hard work in getting this story ready for publication. They have been an absolute pleasure to work with and I'm both proud and pleased that they took home the prize of Trade Publisher of the Year in 2023. A well-deserved win. Special thanks go to Kate Lyall Grant, Joffe's publishing director.

If you are not from the UK, please excuse the English spelling. Oopsy Daisy, it's just the way we do things across the pond. Apologies also for any swearing but this is down to the characters and has nothing to do with me. Lol. The same goes for any blaspheming.

Now for the best bit where I get to thank my lovely readers for all their support, especially my ARC reading group. You know who you are! Your loyalty and friendship mean everything. As do your reviews. ☺

# THE JOFFE BOOKS STORY

We began in 2014 when Jasper agreed to publish his mum's much-rejected romance novel and it became a bestseller.

Since then we've grown into the largest independent publisher in the UK. We're extremely proud to publish some of the very best writers in the world, including Joy Ellis, Faith Martin, Caro Ramsay, Helen Forrester, Simon Brett and Robert Goddard. Everyone at Joffe Books loves reading and we never forget that it all begins with the magic of an author telling a story.

We are proud to publish talented first-time authors, as well as established writers whose books we love introducing to a new generation of readers.

We have been shortlisted for Independent Publisher of the Year at the British Book Awards three times, in 2020, 2021 and 2022, and for the Diversity and Inclusivity Award at the Independent Publishing Awards in 2022.

We built this company with your help, and we love to hear from you, so please email us about absolutely anything bookish at feedback@joffebooks.com

If you want to receive free books every Friday and hear about all our new releases, join our mailing list: www.joffebooks.com/contact

And when you tell your friends about us, just remember: it's pronounced Joffe as in coffee or toffee!

**ALSO BY JANE E. JAMES**

NOT MY CHILD
HER SECOND HUSBAND
THE SON-IN-LAW

Printed in Great Britain
by Amazon

32251195R00169